Paul Ferroll

Paul Ferroll

Caroline Clive

MINT EDITIONS

Paul Ferroll was first published in 1855.

This edition published by Mint Editions 2021.

ISBN 9781513278407 | E-ISBN 9781513278865

Published by Mint Editions®

MINT
EDITIONS

minteditionbooks.com

Publishing Director: Jennifer Newens
Design & Production: Rachel Lopez Metzger
Project Manager: Micaela Clark
Typesetting: Westchester Publishing Services

Contents

I

Nothing looks more peaceful and secure than a country house seen at early morning. The broad daylight gives the look of safety and protection, and there is the tranquillity of night mixed with the brightness of day, for all is yet silent and at rest about the sleeping house. One glorious July morning saw this calm loveliness brood over the Tower of Mainwarey, a dwelling so called, because the chief part of the building consisted of a square tower many centuries old, about which some well-fitted additions of the more recent possessors had grouped themselves. It stood in the midst of a garden bright with summer flowers, which at this hour lifted their silver heads all splendid with dew and sunshine; and it looked down the valley to the village, which stood at a little distance, intersected and embowered with orchards, and crowned with the spire of the church. Early as it was, another half hour had not passed before the master of the house descended some steps which led from the window of his dressing-room, and walked through his blooming garden to the stable, where his horse was ready for him, as it had been every morning for the last few weeks; and whenever the day was beautiful as this was, he had passed the early hours in riding. As he got on horseback, he met a labourer belonging to the gardens coming to his work, and inquired what he was going to do. The man showed a basket of annuals which he was about to plant in the flower-garden, and being a simple fellow, inquired whether his master could tell if missus meant the blue anagallis or the white to be on the outside of the bed.

"Not I," said Mr. Ferroll; "whichever you will."

"Missus will be tremendgious if I'm wrong," said the man, scratching his head.

Mr. Ferroll frowned at this epithet applied to his young wife, and bidding the man go about his work, rode off.

"It's well enough for you who have the whip hand," said Richard Franks, looking after his master; "but if ever a lady provoked the poor wretches under her. . ." and here his murmurs sank into inarticulate rumbling—but Mr. Ferroll was out of hearing.

He rode gently. The morning was delicious, and he occasionally spoke to a peasant going to his work, or saluted a whole family busy on their garden before the man went to his hired employment. Several of the peasants whom he met while he was still in his own immediate neighbourhood, had a word to speak with him about a job of work they wanted, or repair for a cottage, which they begged his honour to grant. He gave attention and discussed their matters with all, so that he made rather slow progress till he was at some little distance from home, but then he touched his horse with the spurs, and the gallant animal willingly indulged him in the pleasure of a gallop, which he seemed to enjoy with eager relish. He had taken a circuit in his gallop, so that between loitering in his slow pace, and diverging in his quick, it was past six o'clock when he arrived at the village to which his course was directed.

"I'm very early, Mr. Aston," said he to the farmer at whose house he stopped; "but I knew I must find you at home at this hour."

"Not a bit too early for us, sir," said the farmer, "and I'm hugely obliged to you for taking the trouble. It's all over with me, I believe, sir; but if any can help me, it's you."

"When is the day for examining the accounts?" asked Mr. Ferroll.

"To-morrow week, sir, and I declare I'm as innocent as a babby; and yet there's a hundred of pounds as I cannot tell what's gone with him."

"Did not you keep your accounts like other overseers?" said Ferroll.

"Yes, I did just like the last two told me how; but there's a great difference now, I believe, sir, in the way the upper people add them up."

"Maybe so," said Ferroll; "and do you know there was a great man once in the same plight as you, and Bacon was his name?"

"Pickle, you might have said, sir. Bacon might well be in pickle," said farmer Aston, laughing heartily.

"Come, that's well said; I love a man who can laugh under his troubles. I've good hope of you. Let's see these books, these accounts; let me try to add them up the right way for you."

"Breakfast was just ready if you please, sir," said the farmer's wife; "won't you take a cup of tea and a bit of bread this morning, before you begin?"

"Thank you, I will with pleasure;" and he cut the loaf standing as he was, and ate with appetite the good bread, but rather made less of the tea without milk, seemed the produce of dried grass.

"I'm afraid you don't like our tea, sir," said the hostess, "though it's five-and-sixpence a pound at Dewson's shop."

"That's Dewson's new way of adding up," said Mr. Ferroll, smiling; "but, thank you, I'm more hungry than thirsty, and you see what a gap

I have made in your loaf. So now the books, Aston, and let us set to work."

The books kept by the overseer were indeed in a state of confusion, which the better order of things in the management of the poor might well find fault with. Farmer Aston, however, had not the least intent of cheating, but he had followed his predecessors' example in taking the arithmetic of the thing for granted, and forcing a suitable conclusion, when it did not come naturally. Widow Grant appeared at every close where a shilling or a pound could not be accounted for. The things for which the parish was creditor on one side, it was debtor for on another, and at the end of all, to make the expenditure agree with the receipts, appeared his concluding item—"Muddled away £9 4s. 6½d."*

Mr. Ferroll set to work to unravel as far as possible this confusion, and patiently listened to the recollection by which the farmer elucidated the written documents. The table was covered with little dirty bills, the summary of which Mr. Ferroll transferred to a fair sheet of paper, and among which he, with a clear head, was pursuing the almost hopeless clue, when the sound of a horse galloping furiously was heard, and a voice asking for God's sake whether Mr. Ferroll was there. He heard his name, and looked up startled, but finished the calculation he was that moment upon, before he followed the farmer's wife, who had rushed out of the room, and whom he found fallen on the bench before the door, while the messenger who had come for him stood trembling, and as white as a sheet before her.

"Oh, Lord! here he comes," cried the matron, as he ran out. "Oh! poor gentleman, don't tell him, Thomas."

"What's the matter?" said Mr. Ferroll, the colour mounting into his own face with expectation. "Speak out this instant."

"My mistress, sir," said the fellow, dropping his hands to his side, and the bridle fell loose at the same time, but the panting horse had no inclination to stir.

"Well, your mistress?"

"Dead!" said the man.

Mr. Ferroll's eyes fixed them on his face, his lips were squeezed together, he did not seem to take in the word.

"She is dead, sir," said the man; "oh! is worse than dead—they have killed her."

---

* So Mr. Earle told me, the Poor-law Commissioner.

"Killed your mistress!" he said; "you are mad yourself."

"How quiet he takes it," said the woman.

"He don't believe it," said the messenger. "Sir, she's been murdered in her bed."

Mr. Ferroll said not a word more; he asked not another question; but he walked like a drunken man to the stable, where his own horse was put up; and springing into the saddle, flew past the cottage almost like the speed of a bird, and vanished from their sight on the way home.

Home! and what a home! It was all peace and stillness when he left it. It was a scene of distraction, now—servants and villagers were about the door, and in the garden. Men were rushing for help, and only bringing more trembling spectators; the gate was wide open; the windows, some still barred, some thrown up; household employments all broken off—the household hurriedly one on another, terrified out of their senses.

They rushed to their master, when he arrived.

"What is the matter?" he said again, as if his apprehension refused all belief of what he had heard.

"It's all true, sir," said the constable, who had been secured among the rest. "Your lady has been murdered."

Mr. Ferroll was a man of powerful will and habitual reserve; he seemed to force himself to an action he abhorred—turned towards the room.

"You had better not go in," said the constable, holding his arm.

"*Seeing* it is not the worst part," said Mr. Ferroll, and went on.

The surgeon was in the room; he was still bending over the body, and his feet were dabbled with the blood, which was in a pool about the bed. The husband was deadly pale, but he forced himself on.

"Sir, were you here this morning?" said the surgeon.

"Yes, as late as half-past four. Is there no life?"

"Life has been extinct an hour or more," said the surgeon. "Was the window open when you went away, sir?"

"Yes, she bade me leave it open. Who? who? . . ." he repeated, gasping, and forcing out the word.

"There is no trace as yet—no suspicion. Did you see anyone, sir?"

"No one," said Mr. Ferroll.

"Well, it don't matter asking him now," said the surgeon, looking at him compassionately. "For God's sake, sir, come out of the room;" but he still gazed on, though a shudder ran at times through his strong frame.

"She was murdered in her sleep," said the surgeon; "it was some sharp, small instrument. The wound is not large, but deadly—just here," and he pointed with his finger below the ear.

"And no trace left?" asked the husband, looking over the floor.

"None whatever, except there," said the surgeon, pointing to a tub of water, which stood ready for bathing, and which was deeply coloured with blood—"the murderer washed off the traces there."

Mr. Ferroll shuddered: the scene was growing too much even for his strung up mind. The surgeon led him out of the room unresistingly; and through the crowd, before whom he summoned up his strength, and passed them with a firm foot; but once in a room, away from all these curious eyes, he sunk upon a chair and hid his face.

The constable had sent for the coroner, upon first hearing what had happened; and a jury was hastily assembled, who proceeded to investigate the mysterious affair. They visited the room, and the dead body, lying all unanointed in the deep dishonour of death; the intense stillness of the room contrasting with the confusion; the soiled bedclothes, the polluted floor, all so unlike the usual extreme neatness which accompanies the silence of death.

The chamber presented no appearance of having been robbed, until some one asked if there had been any watch in her possession. Mr. Ferroll said she was in the habit of putting hers under her pillow. They searched there but it was gone, and there was blood under the pillow as though the hand that had taken it thence was bloody: nothing else was missing, except a pocket handkerchief, which her maid said had been in the room when her mistress went to bed. They went into Mr. Ferroll's dressing-room next door, and here the things were lying about just as he had left them when he went out. His dressing-case was open on the table, and when one of the jury asked whether anything was missing from it, he said, as far as he recollected, it had contained a sharp-pointed knife, which was gone.

But it was in vain the weapon was sought for all over the dismal chamber. When the jury retired to deliberate, some curious evidence was brought before them. It appeared that Mrs. Ferroll had been a woman of violent temper, and unpopular among her servants. The footman was eager to tell that her own maid had complained of the trouble she gave, and that only the day before she had wished either herself or her mistress were dead.

Then the housemaid, sobbing and terrified, said, that the maid had got up that morning before five o'clock, being much out of temper, and had said, she was going to do something for her mistress, but it should be the last time. Here was suspicion, and the maid was examined; but she cleared herself, by saying, that her mistress had charged her to provide the whole milk of one cow for her morning bath. She had done it once before, and master had so laughed at her, the maid said, that she was afraid of his knowing it; and had made her promise not to tell what she was about. It was a troublesome order, and obliged her to get up at an unwonted hour, and she had resolved to leave her place in consequence. This story was confirmed by the dairymaid, to whom she had gone for the milk, and whose evidence, together with that of the housemaid, accounted for the suspected woman's employment from the time she left her bed to that when her loud cries at entering the room had announced the event to the household.

One of the jury, forgetting all the circumstances which showed the death to have been brought about by another hand, here conjectured, that since she was so violent, she might have committed suicide, supposing her to have been in a state of excitement. Had her husband and she had any quarrel? he asked; were they on bad terms?

"No, they never quarrelled; master was resolute not to quarrel."

An explanation of this was asked, and it seemed that one and another had heard very hasty expressions on her part, but that they were always silenced by Mr. Ferroll, who knew better than anybody how to manage her. They began to tell what she had said against him, but with this the jury had nothing to do, and stopped all such details.

A minute search was made in the house for the missing watch, and there was one woman also who had been in fits ever since the discovery of the murder, who showed the greatest reluctance to submit to the investigation. This was the wife of the labourer Franks, who lived in the house in quality of kitchen-maid. She refused to give up her keys, saying, she knew they would pretend to have found something which would hang her. The law had once found her son guilty of horse-stealing, though he never saw the horse in his life; and she saw they only wished to find her or her husband guilty of murder, to ruin them all one with the other. Upon mention of her husband, further inquiry was made about him, and he was brought before the jury for examination. He was nearly as much terrified as his wife, and kept his head averted from the room of death as they brought him into the house. He tried to prevent all questions, by conjuring them not to think he had done it. It was true his mistress had been very hard to him, but he would not have done such a thing for the world: his master, perhaps, thought much of what he said that morning, but, indeed, he meant no more than he said; and as to killing her, he did not like for his own part to kill his very pig.

On this mention of his master, Mr. Ferroll was questioned as to what he could tell of the man that morning. One of the jury remarked, that Mr. Ferroll said, he had seen no one when he went out. He answered, that he had indeed spoken to this man, but the idea of connecting so innocent and well-known a fellow with this horrible deed had not occurred to him.

"But where had he left him when he himself quitted the house?"

"In the stable-yard."

"What was he going to do?"

"To work in the flower-garden."

And it proved upon inquiry, that he had been there alone, that he had quitted it some time before the murder was discovered. One of the maids had seen him washing his hands, and, on being questioned, said, the colour of the water afterwards was as red as blood.

Mr. Ferroll remarked, that the soil of the garden was mixed with clay, and might give that appearance; but the jury was moved by the expression used by the maid. They closely questioned Mr. Ferroll as to what had passed between him and the labourer about the murdered lady, and he reluctantly related the expression used, for he saw the circumstances were making against the man, whom, from his previous knowledge of him, he could not but believe innocent. The distracted behaviour of the wife, and the terror of the accused added to the impression; and when they forcibly took their key, and went to search their box, everyone expected both the watch and the handkerchief would be found. They were not; but the suspicion was strong enough with regard to him, and absent enough from everybody else, to cause his committal to prison.

When this noisy and bustling scene was over, the silence of death settled in all its depth over the house. Then came the rites of the dead, and the body was composed as it best might, and the clean spotless linen laid over it. The chamber was set in order, the watchers took their place in the room adjoining, and between one day and another the house had passed from the peaceable domestic scene of life and employment, to the solemn, yet frightful inactivity of the death-place of its chief inhabitant.

Mr. Ferroll kept aloof from the eyes of his servants as much as possible. They could hear his restless step; and when night came, observed that he went out of doors, and paced hurriedly about the garden, as if unable to rest, but he did not come into the terrible room. It must have been very strong affection which could have brought any one to look upon that sight; and it was well known that although they had lived together with unbroken unity, both had soon ceased to love the other.

Mr. Ferroll was a man of profound passions, and powerful will. He had been disappointed in the affection he had fixed on a young girl; and the woman whom he afterwards married had been in some way mixed up with the story. The latter was young and handsome, and at one time passionately in love with her husband; and after the disappointment of his first attachment, he had hastily married her, but her character was one it was difficult to remain attached to; and when she found him far from returning the zeal of her adoration, and that her hold upon him grew less and less, she gave way to all her unamiability, and would have proved the bane of the life of any one less strong in character than her husband. But he resolutely avoided all quarrel, and maintained the decent and even friendly intercourse which became their position. A man more anxious about appearance would probably have constrained himself to visit the room where the body of his wife lay; but Mr. Ferroll was perfectly indifferent in this, and all other instances, as to what was said of him.

It was, therefore, with surprise, that the undertakers employed in making the last arrangements previously to closing the lid, saw him enter the room, and approach the coffin.

"My wife," he said, "has left directions, which I am about to obey;" and, with these words, he placed upon the body a small parcel which he had held in his hand. He then drew away the covering from the face, which he had not seen since the day of the murder. It was composed as decently as possible, but after so many days of death, and after a death so violent, looked indeed different from the fine face, the healthy glowing countenance of his young wife. He said not a word, moved not a muscle; but gazed at it, as deadly pale himself as the rigid corpse, and turned away at last with the effort of one struggling against a paralysis, but recollected himself before he had gone half across the room, and returning, said, "I must see the lid closed on that packet;" and taking hold of the back of a chair, stood resolvedly while the cloth was replaced, the sheet drawn together, and the lid put on and fastened upon the withered form within. Before it was done he had recovered his self-possession, and walked firmly from the room; and after that time, till the day of the funeral, more than once came into the chamber, and gazed for a few minutes on the coffin. He never wept, and never prayed beside it, nor pretended to do either; and the watchers, accustomed to see the mourners express their feelings in both ways, found fault in whispers with Mr. Ferroll for doing differently from other men; but it was plain that he was as careless of that as of all other blame or praise of his conduct.

It was not without hesitation that the magistrates before whom Franks was brought committed him to prison. The evidence against him was entirely presumptive. Even the bucket in which his hands had discoloured the water was in his favour rather than against him; for the murderer had plainly cleansed himself from the blood in the room itself where he committed the act; and had Franks been that person, it was most unlikely he should have left his hands still so deeply dyed, as to discolour water in the court-yard. Mr. Ferroll's conjecture, therefore, that it was the garden soil which he had washed off, seemed the most probable.

But one of the magistrates, Mr. Bartlett, the owner of the Hall, as Mr. Ferroll was of the Tower, upon whom the bucket had made a great but rather an obscure impression, remarked, that it was improbable water should he stained with blood, unless there was blood in the water; and observed, that Franks had washed his hands in the bucket, and therefore it was plain that his hands had been bloody. "And if you want my opinion," said he, "I say I can't think it's right to murder anybody, especially a lady; nor do I see the justice of letting a murderer go loose on the country to cut all our throats."

A light curl of contempt passed over Mr. Ferroll's lip. "Nor that of hanging an innocent man," said he, in a low tone; but the wife of Franks heard him, and flinging herself on her knees, blessed him for the word, and whispered to him, "Only save him from being hanged, and I will tell all, Mr. Ferroll."

"Tell all!" he exclaimed, starting back, and repeating her words aloud for all to hear. "Tell then."

The room was silent in a moment; only Mr. Bartlett rubbed his hands, and whispered, "I told you so."

But the woman, when she found what she had done, shrank back, denied she had anything to say, and declared that it was only a way she had; the neighbours knew she was not quite right at all times, and that her poor head was quite wandering ever since she had seen her dear lady in that dreadful room; and, in fact, when she thus strengthened the picture by putting it into words, she yielded to the impression, and fell into hysterics, which obliged them to carry her away.

But all this gave an impression unfavourable to the accused man, who stood trembling and pale as death, listening to one proof after another, almost as one might listen at a tragedy, not distinguishing the fiction from the truth. His dislike to his mistress was proved by many witnesses; that he knew she was alone that morning was proved by Mr. Ferroll's conversation with him. He was the only person, as it seemed, who had been in the garden to which her window opened, and he was known to have been there alone; no other door or window was opened in the house; he had some marks on his hands of scratches, which he said first, were given by a cat from whom he had taken its kittens; and then, being asked where the kittens had been put, produced a new story, and said, they were scratches from a bramble he was taking up from the garden.

All this confirmed suspicion, though Mr. Ferroll remarked that the man (who had been in his service for years) was noted for his confused manner if anything unusual happened, and for the excuses he would make and abandon the next moment.

Mr. Bartlett fidgetted and whispered to his neighbour, that if any one wished for his opinion, it was, that it little became a husband to make excuses for the man who had murdered his wife.

Mr. Ferroll heard something of this, and desired that it should be spoken aloud; and when the old magistrate was forced to repeat what he had said, the blood mounted in his face, and more moved than he had yet been, he said that the man whom he believed innocent, he would protect at any risk, in spite of any imputation, and then turning to Franks, he said, "I swear to you, Franks, you shall not be harmed—if you are innocent," he added, in a different tone of voice.

The man looked at him with a hopeful eye, but he drew back from the thanks he began to utter, as if he had done too much, and too publicly, and the magistrates, before whom all this was indeed somewhat irregular, proceeded, on their own belief, to commit him.

Mr. Ferroll was naturally anxious to get away from the scene of so much misery, but he had resolved to wait till the assizes should be over, and the fate of Franks decided. In the meantime he proceeded with the arrangements consequent on the death of his wife. She had brought him a considerable fortune, which by her settlement had been secured to him for his life, but he declined keeping any part of it. He instructed his lawyer to make it over entirely to her brother, who was her only surviving near relation, and even the ornaments which had belonged to her, he locked up without examination, in the case where they were usually kept, and delivered them the day after the funeral to the same person.

In all this there was more of sorrow at her fate, than of love for her person, for who parts willingly with every memorial of one they have pleasure in thinking of? But what shocked the feelings of the poor people, and of the common people, Mr. Bartlett at the head of the latter, was the tombstone he caused to be placed over her grave. Any one dead should be called according to them a good wife at least, but a murdered woman ought to be the best of wives; however, that she was not, nor did Mr. Ferroll's epitaph say she had been. It merely said,

"Anne, the daughter of Robert Gordon, and wife of Paul Ferroll, of the Tower—she died, murdered, the 4th day of July, 18—."

By whom, was not destined to be found out; or at the trial, Franks defended by Mr. Harrowby, a friend of Mr. Ferroll's, was, after the longest and most nicely balanced deliberation, acquitted. Still, people could not forget that he had been suspected. At his earnest request, Mr. Ferroll gave him and his wife the means of emigrating to Canada. Very great scandal was elicited by his protection of this man, but he was a person to whom public opinion was more indifferent than he could find words to express; and immediately after the trial he arranged his affairs for a long absence, and set off a widowed and a comparatively impoverished man, no one knew whither.

L ittle was heard of Mr. Ferroll for a good while after these events, for though through his agent it was known from time to time where he was, no information whatever was gained as to what he was doing.

A considerable time had elapsed after the murder of his first wife, when he wrote to say that his house must be got ready for his return, and that he was married. Not a word more did he add, and the simple-minded villagers were put out of heart by such repulsiveness of the sympathies which they would have gone before to offer. However, unassisted by any of the circumstances which usually attend a wedding, they did dimly perceive the propriety of a gala to receive the new lady, and were talking languidly of an arch across the road, with "Welcome," done in dahlias, when they were informed one morning that Mr. Ferroll and his new wife had arrived the evening before.

The pair walked out that day in the village, and to all the places which an old inhabitant introduces to a new one. It was a pastoral place, containing the Park and house of the Bartlett family, and the Tower; and besides these two great houses, there were the scattered village and the farms belonging either to the Park or the Tower. The former was much the greater estate, but Mr. Ferroll was perhaps the richer man, having fewer claims and more unencumbered means.

Mr. Bartlett, the old magistrate, whose sagacity had displayed itself on the inquest, had died since that time, and his widow, with a large family, inhabited the great house, and attended as well as she could to the interest of her eldest son's estate. She was an honest, simple-minded woman as ever lived, but she belonged to one of the principal families of the county, and had her own consequent notions of what was to be done, and left undone. She had said, and others had said to her, that it was very odd for Mr. Ferroll to go and marry somebody whom nobody knew in the neighbourhood, and never say a word about it till he was married; nay, as it seemed now, till he had been married some time, for a nurse and a little toddling child arrived with them—and his marriage must have been so soon after the horrible death of his first wife, poor thing! &c.

So that Lady Lucy Bartlett did not go directly, no, nor after the first Sunday, when she saw that Mrs. Ferroll was at church, to call at the Tower, as she naturally would have done. Mr. Ferroll observed it, and took his measures accordingly. He knew what conveniences would be gained, and what unpleasantnesses would be avoided by a natural state of things between his wife and Lady Lucy, and gave up an hour to obtaining them. With this view he took his hat before luncheon, and telling his wife Lady Lucy Bartlett was coming to call about three o'clock, went his way to the great house. Lady Lucy Bartlett was a little embarrassed, but he relieved her, by his friendly inquiries into the health of her children, and by giving her some advice concerning one of her son's tenants, who was worrying her and her steward. He then allowed some seconds' pause, and began on his own matters.

"You've got nobody to ask about my wife, Lady Lucy. Nobody hereabouts knows anything, so I'll tell you; and then there will be no need of picking it up by bits, which would not be true after all. My wife was Miss Shaledon."

"What, one of the Warwickshire Shaledons?" said Lady Lucy.

"Yes, that family."

"That's a very old family," said Lady Lucy.

"Oh, very; they were given as serfs or slaves by William the Conqueror to his Glovers, the Ganters; but that's so long ago, that their servitude is grown to be quite a credit to them. Well, Mrs. Ferroll is one of the daughters of Johnson Shaledon, the son of John, of Abororchards, who died soon after she was born."

"I know all about him," said Lady Lucy.

"I loved her very much before I married my first wife," said Mr. Ferroll: "but we were parted, and I did two things in consequence—I half broke her heart, and I married my first wife."

"Aye, indeed, poor thing—shocking! you must. . . ha! indeed. . ." murmured Lady Lucy.

"Yes, very true, shocking indeed! and there it is," said Mr. Ferroll, (imitating her manner, but so that she did not perceive it;) "and then, you know, she died, as you say, poor soul! and I went away. I met with Miss Shaledon—no, I went to look for her. She was ill; we had found out the inhuman stratagem that had parted us long ago, and we married. She is a woman whom I adore," he said, passionately, and went on directly; "that's her story, and she has not one shilling. Now you know all from the fountain head."

Lady Lucy did not know what to say; she did not feel quite sure that knowing all mended the matter entirely; but Mr. Ferroll did not want her comments.

"Are you going to walk this fine morning?" said he, rising from his chair.

"Yes," said she; "I'll show you the Green. . ."

"Then come and call on Mrs. Ferroll; I'll give you my arm."

Lady Lucy Bartlett went and got her bonnet, and never said a word to the contrary.

Here Mr. Ferroll was willing to have stopped, but his neighbour once set going, was sociably inclined. She was charmed by Mrs. Ferroll, who was a person to make an impression on any one; and her grace, her agreeableness, and the pretty pursuits with which she was surrounded, were not lost on Lady Lucy. She felt how invaluable such a neighbour would be, if the neighbour could be led into sociableness; and according to her skill, she dug round and cultivated her. Mr. Ferroll had been a frequent guest at her house in the year before the late disaster; and half afraid, half fond of him, she knew how clever he was, how able to talk to everybody, and how valuable at her table, and in her affairs. So first she sent a present of venison—for the Park had venison, and the Tower had not; and as soon as her visit had been returned, despatched an invitation to dinner. This was declined very civilly; but Lady Lucy thought the reason assigned, was rather one which had been sought for, than one which really existed. She was afraid that the refusal was in resentment at her own delay in calling. She wished with all her heart that she had been more eager to secure the advantages which had been within, and now were escaped from, her grasp.

At the dinner, where Mr. and Mrs. Ferroll were not, she talked very much about them, particularly about the last; and gave her cousins and neighbours, Lord and Lady Ewyas, a desire to know her. Next morning accordingly, they called from the Park—they and their hostess, and the children, and a man or two, all walking through the Park to the Tower. They entered through the garden; and as they came near the open window, they heard her sweet voice singing.

"How useful for one's dinner-parties in the country," said Lady Ewyas. Nearer, they saw her through the open windows, in a plain dress, made according to the best fashion of the day, her brown hair uncovered, her fair, pale face most lady-like.

"Oh, a woman to meet anybody," said Lord Ewyas.

They went in. She was alone, and received them beautifully—one woman against a host, she was enough for all; yet never too entertaining, never odd, never perplexed. She had drawings for them to see of a place which was mentioned; and the circle being broken, asked them to look at the garden, and give their opinion about an alteration, and found other ways of getting happily through the morning visit.

Mr. Ferroll came in before it was over; he was as well-mannered as his wife, in a stouter fashion, and had not to draw on his resources so largely, because he already knew all the party, more or less, and had subjects in common. Nothing could go smoother than he the host, and they the guests. But when a week after, before the call had been returned, Lord and Lady Ewyas sent to beg him and his wife to visit them for a few days, another excuse went forth from the Tower, again more civil than well-founded.

Lord and Lady Ewyas were vexed; for in the country it does not do to lose acquaintance who are better than common; and attributed the refusal to their own haste in dispensing with a return of their call, regretting that the game which was in their own hands they had thrown up by trying to secure it too soon.

Then what did they do if they would not visit their neighbours? Lived alone, in perfect contentment, and employed themselves at home.

A great deal of Mr. Ferroll's time was given up to literary employment; his name and fame as an author were some of the best parts of his existence, and made him necessary, as well as acceptable, in certain circles. He had written a few things which gave him fame, and from time to time there issued from the Tower a brilliant article, a few exquisite verses, or a fine fiction, which kept the attention of the reading public upon him. He was at the same time a man of that practical quality of mind which made him the most useful among those who carried on the business of life; and with these gifts, and the enjoyment of a well-ordered competency, he was in as good a position in life as it was possible to be. Lady Lucy soon found it would not do to send him presents with any view to keep up the relative position of the great and lesser house. She could only send him carnal gifts of pheasants and carp; but he, the second week in January, could make her a present of a bunch of roses from his hot-house, and had always the newest book to lend her when he and Mrs. Ferroll had read it. So much he did for her; but he never dined at the Hall, nor encouraged an extreme intimacy; and for his part, it might have gone on so to the end of time, but things happened at the Hall, which broke through his habit or plan of conduct.

The heir of Basall was a fine young lad, very much altered for the worse since his father's death; he was so headstrong, that the women were all afraid of him, and they could get no peace except by flattering and courting him. Accordingly, they were under the tyranny of caprices, such as should have been whipped away at school, and the boy himself was running to ruin by his own guidance. His poor mother was his guardian, and felt the helpless responsibility of her situation in the most painful manner. One day she sent in despair to Mr. Ferroll, to beg the favour of him to come to her immediately, and when he complied, he found her in agonies lest he should not arrive before the end of the half hour which had to elapse before her son should return from his walk.

The case was this:—Hugh Bartlett had been pleased to declare he should that day ride out upon a horse which was fit for anything rather than to carry a boy; he had declared his mother's objections to be bosh, and having so disposed of them, had ordered the horse.

Mr. Ferroll laughed when the case was stated to him. "You won't act for yourself, I know," said he, "but in your name I will at once desire that the horse be unprepared—the child must not break his neck," and he got up to ring the bell.

"Oh, no," said the mother, "he can't bear that—if you only would persuade him."

"Persuade is not the word for a boy," said Mr. Ferroll, ringing, and giving the necessary orders; "you have called me in, and I will act for you—what reproach would you have a right to make me if I were to fail in preventing the ride, and he were to be brought home with broken bones."

"Oh, me! oh, heaven!" cried the mother; "but you don't know how angry he will be."

"*He* angry—who ought to care for that?"

"It's very true," she answered, melting into tears; "but he is so changed since his poor father's death, and I have such trouble with him."

"You must send him to school," said Mr. Ferroll.

"I know it would be better," answered the mother, "but his dear father, the last thing almost, said I was never to do that; he took my hand and made me promise I would never send him to school."

"Oh, that's bosh, as your son says; how could Mr. Bartlett how what would be good for the boy, years to come?"

Lady Lucy was quite shocked.

"What! disregard my dear husband's last words?" she cried.

"Well, but let us see what sort of boy was he at that time."

"Oh, very different from what he is now, you know; he was very mild, almost timid; his dear father knew how to manage him, and I think he thought, perhaps, he had managed him almost too well, so when he felt was so ill, he said, 'Be kind to him, keep him at home—promise he shall never go to school.'"

"But you can't say he is timid now."

"No."

"Therefore this promise does not apply."

"That makes no difference as to the promise having been given."

"But it does as to keeping it."

"Oh, Mr. Ferroll, you to say so; such a learned man as you."

"What has my learning to do with it? but it does not matter reasoning; here is a fine lad ruining, and school is the only thing to make him find his level, to give him his place in the world. That is a positive fact—let the rest alone, and the only question in my mind is, the school where you will put him."

Mr. Ferroll kept to this point, passing over the conscientious and abstract part as if granted, and out of the way, and being once engaged in the certainty that it was desirable and useful, he now proceeded to carry it impetuously, treading down all barriers that opposed themselves. Lady Lucy was accustomed to yield obedience; and having nothing to answer, and her tears being disregarded, she came in a wonderfully short time to the point he had determined for her, and authorized him to write to an experienced friend on the subject. She was his only guardian, and all the time she felt internally that the thing would not be done after all; that it would be talked about, and threatened, and produce a good effect, and then, to be sure, if the threat should not produce a good effect, why it might really be done, still; but if she had these fors and againsts in her own mind, she little knew the man in whose hands she had placed herself.

What a change had taken place in the destinies of young Bartlett, by the time he was pleased to come in again, expecting his horse. Mr. Ferroll undertook to explain the matter to him, and that he must walk afoot, since his pony did not content him, and that he must go to school, since his mother could not manage him. He took the lad a walk, and like any other boy in the hands of a reasonable and a clever man, he was moulded like wax to the impression Mr. Ferroll chose to give. What sort of life he led his mother and the maids, I will not lift the veil to display; but certain it is, that one month afterwards saw him on his road to a private school of high repute, whence in a year and half he was to be removed to Eton.

This very important service was not the only one of which Lady Lucy Bartlett stood in need. She was misled by the ignorance, and cheated by the iniquity of the people about her, and she felt herself in a hopeless entanglement, out of which she had no power to lift herself. At last things came to a crisis, and the steward said he had a remedy to propose; he said the bills presented to his lady might be right, and might be wrong, but he could not answer for it if her ladyship continued determined to pay them herself. Things came to the confusion of which she complained, in consequence of her ladyship paying for herself; he, for his part, did all he could to keep them straight, but as long as he had not the power in his own hands, his hands were tied, and while his hands were tied, it was evident he could do nothing.

"Well, what was the remedy?" poor Lady Lucy asked.

"Why, it was this—let him have the power to draw her cheques in his own name, and then being always able to pay these bills alone, he should speedily bring her affairs into order. Her ladyship, he was sure, could be certain that a servant employed by her honoured husband, would be as careful of her money as if it were his own," &c.

Lady Lucy did as he wished. The steward loved power and credit, but did not mean to cheat her; nevertheless, he got into debt, and was tempted to set himself right by transferring a small sum from her account to his own, fully intending to repay it. That, however, soon became impossible, and it was at the moment that he found it impossible even to repay the small sum, that he began to help himself freely to large ones. When he was deeply her debtor, he suddenly doubled his debt in order to speculate on hops, which was to set all right; but the crop giving signs of failure, he gathered his money together, and went off to the United States, leaving a letter behind, in which he said he was sorry for the whole thing. Then it was Lady Lucy Bartlett appealed to Mr. Ferroll; and embarrassed, confused, and ignorant of business as she was, never did woman more need assistance. He gave it freely. Her world was out of joint, and he had to devote himself to her to set it right. Temporary retrenchment, a thorough reform of all her domestic staff; to cut off the cocks and hens from their barley, which came to a hundred a year; the neighbourhood to restrict of their ale, which they came from miles round to drink at Basall; to send away the gardener, who charged fifty pounds for seeds to crop the kitchen garden, yet begged the cook to be careful of parsley; these, and other reforms of greater and less extent, were the good work of Mr. Ferroll, in favour of his neighbour and her son. She felt saved, and as the crowning favour, besought him to share with her the office of guardian.

Mr. Ferroll was silent for a minute considering the matter. Then, although he must have perceived how much for the advantage of the boy it would be, he decidedly refused.

III

Since the beginning of our history several years had passed before things arrived at this point. The young heir of the Bartletts had been two years at school, and his mother's affairs had been directed nearly that time by the good offices of Mr. Ferroll. He and his wife were living in great and enjoyable retirement, and their child was running about, still the only new branch of the tree. As far as a young child can be lovely and charming, little Janet was so. She had the sweetest face and the sweetest temper possible, but she was less idolized than many a cross and many an ugly child. The whole tenderness of Mr. Ferroll's nature was centered in his wife; and anything that interfered with that passion he put aside. He would have her devote herself to him, not to her child; he would have no nursing, no teaching, no preference of a dawdle with Janet to the walk with him, or the long summer day's expedition. The nursery was Janet's place, a governess her teacher; she came to her mother when her mother was alone, and was happy with her; but she was happy everywhere, "singing, dancing, to herself," and it was rather her own resources than her mother's motherly devotion which made her happiness.

Lady Lucy, who had all the instincts of a good woman, and only one way of exercising them, could not believe Janet was happy; so little fondled, so little made of, as she was. Her own children were all important in her house, and when she knew Mr. and Mrs. Ferroll were out together in summer weather, and would not be at home till after Janet's bed-time, she would often walk to the Tower, and lead the little girl by the hand up to her own sociable and noisy garden or drawing-room. An extreme fondness naturally grew up between the little Ferroll and the rather larger Bartletts. Her father saw it with great indifference, not considering himself under obligations for services which he did not want. Only on one point did he suddenly and positively interfere—and that was when the young heir of the Hall, sharing in the fondness of his mother and sister for the merry and most good-natured Janet, declared her, according to the fashion of children, his wife. Mr. Ferroll's brow clouded far more than the occasion required: his severe countenance put an end to all the mirth of the moment, as a shadow passing over young chickens is said to inspire them with instinctive trembling, as if hawks were between them and the sun; and taking occasion to call Janet's frightened governess into the room, he desired such vulgar jests might never again be indulged in, upon the penalty of an abrupt separation from her pupil. Little Janet, therefore, was no longer the wife of Hugh Bartlett, and the governesses and nurses felt they had done very wrong in suggesting the union. Except upon this subject, he was kind and neighbourly to the Bartlett family; the helplessness and goodness of the widow laid hold on him, as a climbing plant upon the strong oak; and he found himself her support and necessary prop, before he was aware how far he was engaged.

Lord Ewyas was struck by the energy which Mr. Ferroll had displayed in her affairs—he himself was in need of aid, though of a different kind. He was Lord-Lieutenant of the County, and he found himself very ill-supported by the magistrates, who were an ordinary set of men, and who at this moment were wanted in circumstances somewhat out of the common order. The poor population had become exceedingly riotous, in consequence of reduced wages, and they had formed such strong combinations, and were guided by such efficient men, that a season of considerable danger seemed impending.

Threatening letters had been received by many persons in the county, and in several instances these threats had been put in execution by the destruction of property, barns and ricks, for instance, which had been set on fire. The last person to be thus persecuted should have been the quiet and alms-giving Lady Lucy Bartlett; but so it was, that a strange-looking epistle was one morning brought to her by her butler, a servant who had long lived in the family, and who lingered in the room evidently curious about the contents. She opened it, and found these ominous words—"In a day you don't look for it, fire will consume you." A shriek on her part, which was echoed by an exclamation on his, followed; and she failed to remark, in her terror, that the butler's alarm seemed to precede his knowledge of the fact, for he was wringing his hands and crying out they were all lost, before he had read the letter which contained the threat.

Mr. Ferroll was consulted, of course; he recommended caution, but supposed it was the work of some one intending to extort money, and would be followed by an appeal for relief. However, such was not the case; from week to week the ill-shaped letter continued to be delivered, and the words were still the same words—"In a day you don't look for it, fire will consume you." These were brought up by her trembling butler, Didley, with a face as white as a sheet, and still he lingered to hear the contents, which at last produced such an effect upon his nerves that he became unable to continue his services, and was reduced to the confinement of the lower regions of the house, whence the answer to his mistress's inquiries came every day "Very poorly indeed, my lady."

Under these public and private circumstances, a clear-headed and strong-willed man like Mr. Ferroll, was invaluable to all parties concerned in them; and Lord Ewyas, as well as his cousin, was very anxious personally to enlist his service.

"He's a magistrate, is not he, your Mr. Ferroll?" said he to Lady Lucy.

"Yes, a very useful one; he is constantly at the petty sessions, and the magistrates' meetings at Churchargent, and if by any chance he does not go, they stop all the business if they can."

"He gets an influence wherever he goes," said Lord Ewyas; "he is the very man I want to be able to send to upon occasion. I wish the fellow was not so perverse. What keeps him at home, do you think?"

"I don't know," said Lady Lucy; "unless, perhaps, it was that shocking thing about his first wife."

"Yet he's not a man to suffer from nerves and fine feelings—and the thing's so long past, now."

"But then they never found out who did it," said Lady Lucy.

"Ah, you think that would have eased his mind, do you. They suspected somebody, did not they?"

"Yes; though I don't think it would have eased his mind, for he got him off you know; paid counsel for his own wife's murderer. When one thinks of it, it's most extraordinary—it's carrying good nature quite too far."

"Indeed it is," said Lord Ewyas; "only I suppose Mr. Ferroll thought the man innocent."

"Oh dear no, he certainly did it—I saw him myself going about quite free after the trial—he making a hedge when I saw him."

"But I suppose he was not the murderer," said Lord Ewyas. "If not it would have been hard to hang him."

"But you know he certainly was; he was tried you know."

"And acquitted."

"Oh, that does not make any difference," said Lady Lucy.

"No, no, to be sure," answered Lord Ewyas, laughing; "but, however, Mr. Ferroll—let us talk of him—can you bring us together, do you think?"

"No, I don't think I can. Whenever I have anyone here, he keeps away; he only comes if I am alone—even Mr. Ewbury, who is so clever, he would not meet."

"He would not come to us, when I asked him," said Lord Ewyas; "but I want him, and will get at him. You shall invite him, as if you were alone, and I will be with you—I am sure you will be so kind?"

"Oh, certainly, only I'm afraid he will be angry—besides poor Didley can't wait, he's so nervous about those terrible letters, that sometimes in a morning he can scarcely stand."

"But you don't mean that your Mr. Ferroll is a man to care whether a butler waits or not."

"Oh dear no, it's the very last thing he would observe or care about. But it is meeting anyone, even you, that I'm afraid of."

"Even me! but nonsense, you must do it, will you, coz, for me?"

Lady Lucy hesitated; her cousin, however, persuaded her, and she despatched a letter of request to see Mr. and Mrs. Ferroll, as she did occasionally when needing their assistance. The pretence she took was the incendiary letter, and they complied with the summons, for Mr. Ferroll fancied he had traced them to their source, and was curious to ascertain it positively; for he thought he perceived more danger in them than Lady Lucy really believed, though less than she believed herself to believe.

Lady Lucy came forward in some trepidation to receive her neighbours when they were announced. "How d'ye do—it's so kind of you—are you quite well, Mrs. Ferroll? I hope you won't object to not finding me. . . that is to say, to being with. . . the thing is, Lord Ewyas came only half an hour ago, and I could not, could I?"

"Just in time to dress?" said Mr. Ferroll. "I was not aware I was to meet Lord Ewyas, but you were aware, my dear lady, that he was to meet me; and I am happy to be made by you the acquaintance of your friends." And so saying, he bowed frankly to Lord Ewyas, and accepted the intercourse thus pressed upon him.

"We were half afraid," said Lord Ewyas, addressing himself to Mrs. Ferroll, when after dinner conversation grew unrestrained, "that you would be angry with my cousin and me for obliging you to let some one beside herself share the advantage of her neighbourhood to you."

"Nay," answered Mrs. Ferroll, "don't have so bad an opinion of us as that. It is only too flattering that you should think it worth while to take the least pains to meet us."

"Any pains would be overpaid, if I could only, hear again the song which I heard some years ago—yes, really years. It was too good to be kept for one fortunate pair of ears."

"But, literally speaking, these ears of mine are not so fortunate," said Mr. Ferroll; "a brother author sometimes comes to consult, and a printer's devil very often haunts us, and by one means or other, I am very busy, my lord."

"Oh, but," interposed Lady Lucy, "you have only one man or so to see you. One Mr. M—was with you last week," she said, naming without knowing it, one of the most celebrated talkers of the day.

"Humph!" said Lord Ewyas, "you had him, and all to yourselves?"

"Yes, we had—he and I are old friends, and now fellow workers."

"What a charity it would be to invite your neighbours, who never hear or see such a big-wig."

"To meet one Mr. M—?" said Mr. Ferroll, smiling.

Lord Ewyas smiled too for half a moment. "True," he said.

"What's true?" asked Lady Lucy.

"Lady Lucy," said Mr. Ferroll, "is your butler better yet? I fear you will never have his services again."

"Oh, I can't think anything so shocking; but it's all the fault of the radicals. These fires have put him half out of his wits. They tell me he goes out two or three times in the night to see that the well has water in it, and that he calls the housekeeper up more nights than not, fancying he smells fire."

"He should consider," said Lord Ewyas, "that he is but a lodger; what is it to him if the house be burned?"

"Nay," cried Lady Lucy, "that's a remark I don't understand. Are not lodgers burned as well as the owners?"

"They say not," said her cousin; "but if he is of a different opinion, it's no wonder the letters you get frighten him."

"Oh, he's horribly frightened; the first time he brought me one, I knew something was the matter, by the shaking of the door in his hand."

"How did he know the contents?" asked Mr. Ferroll.

"By the shape, I suppose, and the look, and the writing," said Lady Lucy.

"Do you never have oddly shaped letters except from the incendiary?" asked Mr. Ferroll.

"Yes, the butcher, and begging letters, to be sure."

"But those never alarmed him?"

"I never remarked; but I wish you would not frighten me with those kind of questions that I don't know the meaning of," said the widow.

Mr. Ferroll laughed gaily; he caught his wife's eye, who said immediately, "I am sure Ferroll thinks some evil is going to happen. Danger puts him in high spirits always." He, perhaps, would have parried the charge, had not Lady Lucy said, "It frightened her to see people so fearless," and signed to her guests to move to the drawing-room.

"I think," said Mr. Ferroll, when he had shut the door, "that the butler himself writes the letters."

"Why so?" said Lord Ewyas, startled.

"It is borne in upon me," answered Mr. Ferroll, smiling. "More little circumstances than I can remember or detail, bring me to that conclusion."

"And do you think that he means any harm by it?"

"That I don't know; he either acts the alarm which he shows, in order to cover his design, or else he is going mad, and is haunted by the idea of mischief, and impelled to do it."

"He looks ill," said Lord Ewyas.

"Very; and much worse this evening than I have seen him at all. I am sure he must be watched tonight."

Lord Ewyas grew uneasy, but Mr. Ferroll turned the conversation, and exerted his great social powers to engage his companion's interest and attention. They both became eager in discourse, and Lord Ewyas was impatient, when the door was opened, and Didley, the butler, entered the room without a summons, and advanced towards the table, as if expecting to be spoken to. "Did you ring, my lord?" he asked.

"No, no, I did not ring," he said; "I thought the fellow was sick, and could disturb nobody," and then he continued the argument he was maintaining against Mr. Ferroll; but they had not long been engaged in the animated and interesting controversy, before Didley again interrupted them, and making some trifling alteration in the table, evidently waited for an opportunity of speaking.

"What is it you want?" said Lord Ewyas, impatiently.

"Why, my lord, if you'll give me leave to speak, I have a matter I very much wish advice upon."

"Can't you wait till to-morrow morning?"

"Really, my lord, I can't very well. It's about these letters to my lady, these threatening letters—so I hear they are at least."

"Which you write yourself," said Mr. Ferroll.

"Which I write!" said the butler, turning upon him eyes of the deepest perplexity. "Do I write them, do you think, sir?"

"I know you do."

"Who told you?" said Didley.

"Oh, one told me who cannot be mistaken."

"And did he tell you really that it was I?"

"Yes, positively."

"Well, that is what I never have been sure of myself, for when I see them, and take them up to my lady, they frighten me in a strange way for a man's own writing to do."

"Why do you write then?" asked Lord Ewyas.

"Why, my lord, it's partly all about that matter that I came to talk with you gentlemen. Do you know, that for months past there have been people coming into my room without any leave of mine. They used to be quiet enough, but of late they have grown troublesome."

"Who are they?" said Lord Ewyas.

"Why, there comes a good many. I know, and some I don't know; my late master, my lady's husband, is foremost. He will come and sit down close by me, and tell me to write to my lady, always these same words—'In a day you don't look for it, fire will consume you.' I have conjured him a hundred times to tell me if he comes from heaven or from hell, but he always shakes his head."

"That might give rise to unpleasant conjectures," said Mr. Ferroll. "Now you know who told me."

"Aye, sir, I thought so; though I wonder he came to you. I never saw him, nor any of them, when other living people were in the room, before to-day. Was it to-day, sir?"

Mr. Ferroll shook his head gravely; and, evading the question, inquired, "At what time was he with you?"

"It was when John, and Henry, and I were laying the cloth for dinner."

"Did they see him?"

"No; I asked them, and they said 'No.'"

"Nor hear him?"

"No; he would not speak, only beckoned me with him."

"But then he spoke?"

"Yes, yes; and I think I must do it."

"Well, I'm not clear that it is right."

"That's what I sometimes think myself; and I've kneeled by my bedside hours and hours, asking God, and praying till I have not known my head from my heels. But it's all dark there."

"Poor fellow!" said Lord Ewyas.

"Yet it's a great thing, my lord, to have the company of spirits; and the last hour or two, I must say, I've been easier than for a long time, and that I think is a sign that I've got leave to do it."

"It may be so; but you came like a wise man to consult us on the subject," said Mr. Ferroll. "From what he said to me, I think you're mistaken. Did he say precisely these same old words?"

"No, no; worse words—worse."

"Aye, indeed, I thought so. Sometimes I've known those spirits make very strange blunders; and with respect to what your old master orders, I advise. . ."

"I can't take it, if you advise against doing it," interrupted Didley.

"Why not?"

"Why, partly because it's already done."

"What's done?" cried Lord Ewyas.

"The house is on fire," said Didley.

"Good heavens!" cried Lord Ewyas, starting up.

But Didley, springing to the door before him, fastened it, and set his back against it. "Nobody shall hinder my work," he said. "I knew you would talk to me while my fires were burning; and if he had not gone and betrayed me to one of you. . ."

But before he could finish, Mr. Ferroll sprang upon him, and tried to force him from the door; but Didley was armed, and drew out suddenly a large knife, the sheath of which was just inside his coat. Mr. Ferroll just avoided a fatal thrust; and seizing his arm, said, "Is this the way you treat your master's friend?"

"Nobody's his friend that hinders me doing his commands," said the madman, his malady breaking out at this sudden excitement, and struggling with the violent strength of madness, to regain command of the weapon.

There was now a contest, which was plainly much to the disadvantage of Mr. Ferroll, his antagonist being armed, and his mind beyond all the usual motive of control. It was not only strength that was needed, but there was the necessity to avoid even a faint stroke of the sharp gleaming knife; Mr. Ferroll saw the disadvantage.

"Come," said he, "you're in the right. You must do as you will; loose me," and all the while half kept a powerful grasp of the maniac, "and I won't hinder you."

"Swear that," cried Didley.

"I swear."

"Again—again."

"Well, well, I *swear*; but it's all right, you see. Don't you smell the smoke yourself—you've done it."

In fact, the burning smell became perceptible.

"Ha! you say true, sir," said Didley, and turned his pale face towards the quarter whence it came, his iron grasp still held Mr. Ferroll; but Lord Ewyas perceived only the apparent relaxation in his purpose, and thinking the danger from him passed, rushed towards the door.

"You've sworn falsely," cried Didley, brandishing his knife, and straining again his vigorous hold; "my master shall be obeyed;" and again he sought to make a plunge.

"Good heavens! there he is," said Mr. Ferroll, suddenly relaxing all his resistance, and fixing his eyes on the door.

"Where?" cried Didley, thrown off his guard for a moment. That moment was enough. Mr. Ferroll closed upon him, and threw him down; Lord Ewyas sprang to help. They snatched away the knife, and now, notwithstanding his struggles, he was soon overpowered.

In another minute two of the servants who had heard the noise came rushing to their assistance. "So far, so good," cried Mr. Ferroll. "Come, my lord, there's the second act yet;" and they both ran to find the sources of the fire, whose smoke began to roll through the house.

"Go to the drawing-room, pray, my dear lord," said Ferroll. "Get Lady Lucy and the children out into the garden. There is no danger, I think, but they will shriek so hideously. Will you whisper Mrs. Ferroll to come to me for a moment? Thank you."

And without waiting for her, but sure that she find him, he gave directions what to do, and continued his search for any fresh spots in which the madman might have kindled the flame.

"Elinor," he said, "you see I'm quite safe, but I've a story to tell you. Not now, however, most certainly; about, dear Elinor, with your keen womanly intelligence, for that poor fool Didley, who I told you was ill, has been setting the house on fire. We have put out one fire already, but there may be many more. As for himself, he's out of the way; he's a perfect maniac, and they've secured him. Never mind that now; don't think of that just now, only keep close to me, and tell me if you perceive fire."

Luckily the discovery had followed so closely on the act, that although fired in several places, the house had not become dangerously inflamed; and under calm and prompt treatment, the peril subsided before long; and with the sacrifice of some silk curtains, and the destruction of some plaster ceilings, through which the water poured, safety was restored, so far as could be ascertained; but men were set to watch all night, lest any hidden danger should yet remain. The party got together again, when all was done that was possible, in the drawing-room, and then Mr. Ferroll talked seriously with his hostess, and gaily with his wife, of what had passed. His companion in peril shuddered still at the remembrance of their danger. He was full of natural pity for the maniac, whose ravings penetrated occasionally to the drawing-room from the room where he was confined and guarded. Mr. Ferroll tried his very best to look grave also, and to compose his sensations to a due harmony with the nerves of Lady Lucy, and the overpowered state of mind of Lord Ewyas; but he was like a man slightly intoxicated, who even while acting rationally, does so with a consciousness to himself, and evidence to others that he is doing it by an effort of self-command. The excitement had roused up every power of life; and his wit, his knowledge, his force of character, were all in activity. He enjoyed life, and no nervousness about himself, or sensibility to the sufferings of another, disturbed him.

"I should so much like to walk home, instead of the carriage," he said at last to his wife. "You don't mind it, do you?"

"Oh, I should enjoy it also very much," she answered, quite ready to go.

"What, after a shock like that?" cried their hostess; "all in the dark too!"

"Can my carriage be of any use?" said Lord Ewyas.

Mrs. Ferroll civilly declined; her husband said something like pshaw! but it would have passed had not Lady Lucy whispered "Hush," which was quite too late, as the thing was not going to be said again; "they have plenty of horses and carriages."

Lord Ewyas let it pass, and shaking hands with both, begged them to continue the acquaintance thus recommenced, and said to Mr. Ferroll, "We have been in danger of death together—an irresistible reason for trying to enjoy life in one another's company."

Mr. Ferroll smiled, and said, "The campaign had been a brilliant one;" and so they parted, without any promises made on the Ferroll side to cultivate the acquaintance; and Lady Lucy, as soon as they were gone, said, "He won't come and see you now; you have offended him about the carriage."

But her cousin answered, "Pooh, pooh! he has too much sense; he's too well bred for that."

IV

So it was, however, that the Ferrolls declined all invitations to Harold's Castle, and Lord Ewyas was offended. But this affected only himself; for Mr. Ferroll declined going, because he did not want to go, so that it just suited him that Lord Ewyas should leave off inviting him. He continued his active services as a magistrate; and the Lord-Lieutenant kept one sulky eye upon him, in case necessity should compel an application for his services, although he was in no hurry to seek them. But the distress which had occasioned the tumultuary spirit of the people, was leading to results which in some degree stopped the acts of aggression, and which involved the quiet and the turbulent alike in trouble. Disease broke out in the district, deaths were very frequent, and the fear and suffering became so general, that all the activity and reason of the acting part of the community were required in the emergency. There were very judicious measures taken, hospitals set up in several places, and means provided for supplying the infected with nurses and medicines at home, when the circumstances required it. There was some trouble, however, in finding superintending visitors, as the illness which had already affected many, deepened into the pestilence of the cholera, and alarmed people more than any familiar terror could have done.

Under these circumstances Mr. Ferroll was willing to do everything that was wanted, and what other people were afraid to do. But on the first intimation of danger, Lady Lucy went to him, as on all other occasions of distress, and was overcome at hearing that he did not intend to isolate house and family, as she herself was taking measures to do.

"I dare say you are very right, Lady Lucy," he said; "but I can't be right in the same way. I am wanted; and to tell the truth, I should have no pleasure in keeping safe at home."

"But it is not only for pleasure I do this," answered Lady Lucy. "You know it has killed a great many people, even of one's own acquaintance. Poor Mr. Waylett even died—a man I have known all my life—how very shocking!"

"Certainly you have known *me* a long time, and it might kill *me*," said Mr. Ferroll, reflectingly.

"Did you think of that before?" asked Lady Lucy.

"Well, I don't know if I did."

"And Mrs. Ferroll and little Janet?" said the lady, pursuing her discoveries.

"Yes, all run their chance indeed, as you say. As for Janet, her mother did talk of sending her somewhere or other."

"Oh, send her to me; I shall keep the park shut up, and nobody shall get in or out; only you must all three come, you must indeed; and come at once, to-morrow." Mr. Ferroll shook his head. "Then at least Mrs. Ferroll," said the good-hearted lady.

"Oh no. What, without me!"

"Why, you can't be so selfish as to wish to put her in danger, in order to keep you company?"

"Indeed I am, though; there would be no enjoyment of the thing without her."

"What thing? What are you talking about?"

"Oh, why—she and I must stay together; but it really is very good-natured of you, Lady Lucy, to offer to receive the little girl—she'll be so safe and so near, and off our hands. Upon my word, you lay me under great obligation."

"I only repay one out of ten thousand you have heaped on me," said Lady Lucy; "so you'll let her come?"

And thus it was settled. Mr. Ferroll announced it at home as a most convenient arrangement, and was surprised at himself for not having thought of it as a painful one, when he saw his wife's eyes fill with tears as she went with Janet to the carriage, which was to take her away.

"Good bye, Janet," he said, following hastily, and stopping her to kiss her; and then as the carriage drove away, he took his wife's arm in his, and walked out with her into the garden. "It is like the first days of our marriage," he said, "to be so completely alone."

Here the Author gives extracts from the Journal kept in common by Mr. Ferroll and Elinor:—

"The twelfth day of my superintendence. Cholera goes on increasing. I was in the town early this morning, and found the nurses frightened away from the close alleys. I went over every house to see what could be done. Money in such moderate doses as counties and committees can give, would not tempt them yet to brave the infection, though in a few weeks one shall get hired services as cheap as blackberries; but mothers nurse their children, servants their masters. There seems an instinct in common between mothers and servants. They can't help being faithful.

Ally Bean, No. 3, close alleys, was without shoes; she had sold them to buy what she called salamanca, which a neighbour said would cure her child. In the state it is in, no doubt salammoniac will kill it, but I did not tell her so. I said she had done very wisely, for the evil was beyond remedy, and she will think she should have saved it if anything could.

"Old Miss Felton, 5, Cheap Street, daughter of the Bishop Felton whom my grandfather bullied, is on the highway to death. She looks like a squeezed orange. She is the first in her street, and the neighbours have slunk away. The old water-carrier and his old donkey won't leave water at her door. There is a gray-haired man, her father's footman, living a mile out of the town, and I actually found him in her miserable room, making gruel for her over the fire. Neither of them seemed to think it anything out of the way that he should give his help thus gratuitously, only she lamented he was not a woman, and he seemed much vexed at himself for the fault. She will die.

"Family of Jones, at 42, first turn in the close alleys. Three of them ill; one just dead as I came in; nobody seemed to mind the dead boy—too miserable. The father who was nearly gone, fancied he should recover— he alone spoke of the dead. 'He'll be in heaven soon,' the father said, looking at him.—'When?' I asked. The father seemed puzzled. 'As soon as he's buried, sir, I suppose.'—'And the parish must bury him,' said the mother. They had in the house one dead rabbit, poached or stolen: no water, no plate, no salt, no fire. I gave money to a naked boy in the street to act as their page, and as he seemed not to know what cholera meant, I suppose he will. I must see them to-morrow.

"All day among the lanes and alleys—all day among the frightened and dying; the starving, fevered, tortured. It is a curious scene—a tragedy being acted all day long; and human nature naked and sincere as in the time of great passions. I, the well and strong man, have my stall at this opera, and see it all at my ease—the more at my ease because I have something to do in it. At seven o'clock I got away; mounted my horse, and galloped home. What pleasure there is in galloping home. The object is before one, at which to arrive quickly; the still air becomes a wind, marking the swiftness of one's pace—the fleet horse is his own master, yet my slave; the bodily employment leaves care, thought, and time behind; one feels the pleasure of danger, because there might be danger, and there is none. And I, when I get home, see the being than whom nobody in the world loves another as I love her. And after all that dirt, misery, and ugliness, I find her in her pure white muslin, the sleeves hanging about her fair arms, with gold chains under the muslin, her delicate hair so delicately dressed, her little feet in their silk shoes; her pure pale complexion, and the indescribable odour of beauty breathing in the room. She kissed me twenty times to-day, as if to make sure that if I had caught the cholera, she must catch it too. And if I had, I should like to give it her, and die; but I am well. I enjoy life—we both enjoy it. We dined, and sat down in the library for the blessed evening; and here I am finishing my journal, and then I will listen to her divine voice singing; and when we have had enough of that, read our book for an hour, and go to bed.

"Thirteenth day. I took a circuit of twenty miles before going to Wallcester. Cholera has inoculated the country, and the spots spread. I met High, the Ouston apothecary, as I rode along. He looked very blank indeed. 'It's getting very serious, sir,' he said; 'two medical men have died.'—'But none of the visiting committee, have they?' I asked.— 'Not yet, sir,' he answered, and went on in a very bad temper. Men don't seem so much to mind death as the pain of dying. Aymos, the old man of ninety, at Front Lane, who used to say he was afraid God Almighty had forgotten him, has left his cottage by help of a neighbour's cart, and gone to Wisley, because cholera broke out at a house a quarter of a mile off. As I passed through Wisley I called on him. 'They tell me, sir,' he said, 'that William died three hours after he was taken ill. It's awful sudden.'—'But you can't die suddenly, my good old Aymos,' I said; 'how many years have you been getting worse I wonder?'—'Aye, aye, sir, but they die all before they are aware, and folks are afraid to bury them.'

"I saw a case which would have frightened him. A young man, I don't know who he was, was sitting on some steps in King Street; he had that paleness in his face which looks like something that is not a man—a ghost, as people used to call it. I bade a man stay near him, and ran to the hospital for a stretcher. On this we laid him, helpless as a man of rag, and carried him to the cholera ward. Here, as we could not let him die like a more happy dog, the doctors began to torment him, and by wasting a good deal of flannel and brandy, succeeded in making him conscious of his agony. And I don't suppose the rack was ever worse. Those artificial spasms of the rack which jerk the joints in and out of their places, were here natural. There was one Anne, whom he constantly apostrophized; and he seemed to shrink from and put back imaginary kisses which Anne was giving him. No Anne was there—no human being who thought of him otherwise than as a cholera patient; yet the poor lad's distress arose from overkindness, and the danger to the life of this shadowy Anne. I said to him at last, 'she won't catch it,' and he unglazed his eyes to hear me; but pain was too strong for him, and I having no more time for this one among the hundreds, left him, and went my way. I believe he is in too much pain to die yet; for when the end is coming, these poor souls are quite at ease.

"I ran from lane to lane, for the work to do was enough for twenty men, and most of the committee were frightened, and passed a vote that everything would be best done by me. Amusement at their simple artifice, which deceived them, and made them quite happy, and the excitement of rushing about with a human spectacle everywhere, so kindled my spirits, that I stopped at the end of a by-way, and indulged in one quiet laugh. A window opposite was open, admitting the sound I fear, for a head came out—a pale head, with a black coat close up to the face, and a narrow white collar over it; a thin, white, large hand was laid on the window sill. 'Who laughs?' said the voice of the head.—I was rather ashamed; but I answered boldly, 'Mr. Ferroll.'—'Sinner,' said the pale head, making the sign of the cross over me; 'death will take you with the fool's scoff in your mouth.' I knew him then. It was the Roman Catholic priest from Allerby, and I was grieved to have shocked his sincere prejudices. I said, 'Let me come in, brother, and you will teach me better.' He answered, 'No; the living scoffer may not interrupt the last moments of the repentant dying.'—'But,' I said, 'will you reject me—will you fail to profit by your opportunity of converting the sinner?'—'The door is open,' said the priest, drawing in his head. He was easily gulled by my flattering words, so I pushed at it, and ran up stairs, resolved to see all that men were doing in this trying hour. He affected not to pay the least attention to my entrance, or rather he acted a part without confessing to himself that he was acting. His patient was dying—the most absorbing and interesting spectacle that we can see. The priest was engaged in the act, which to a man of his faith is the most important in the world—the act by which the soul is saved, and without which it is not saved. I was deeply interested in watching both—the poor mortal insensible, but labouring still with his heaving chest—the living man touching him with the mystical oil, which in his faithful persuasion was a communion with supreme spirits, a fiat made out by his own hand, that this dead man was to live with higher beings. Still even in those moments he was not proof against the pleasure of making or feeling himself valued by a man of better rank and education than his ordinary subjects. I could see he gloried in being a god before me; in having the command even of this obscure tragic garret—his gestures as much as said, 'See, I have no regard to you. Observe; I go on as if you were not here. I do not hasten or retard my speech for you. You must be quiet, and note in silence, and waiting upon me, all I do.' And so I did; touched more than he, by the ceremony which was comparatively new to me, but a matter of every-day occurrence to him.

"When it was over, he turned to me, and said a few words in dog-Latin, the meaning of which I did not catch—and then tried to pass. 'Are you going to more patients?' I said. 'You look very ill, brother; you should take rest yourself.'—'That's the advice,' he answered, 'which one of your archbishops gave to his own clergy; he said they had better not put themselves into danger by confessing their flocks, for the doctor, not the priest, was wanted.'—'According to his belief that's true," said I.—'Fatal belief, which sets the soul below the body,' he answered. 'Think, sir, which religion does that prove to be true?'—'Or does it prove,' I asked, very modestly, 'that he thinks the soul is not put into danger by omitting to confess?'—'But we know it is,' said the priest. I looked very much struck by this argument, and then I offered him some money for the use of the bodies of his people, or if he would keep it to pay himself for saying masses, he is very welcome. When we got to the subject of money he lost his dignity; and thanked me with the scrape of his foot, so unlike the character we had relatively borne to each other during the above scene, that I thought the tragedy wanted dignity at its close.

"When I came home this evening, Elinor looked pale. I thought instantly, 'Am I ill too?'—dying together, and now, would be such a pleasure; we are so happy, and at this moment so useful; and the inanimate body laid in its last rest, always looks to me an enviable thing, free as it is from every storm that can blow.

"Fifteenth day.—When I got to—to-day, I found a messenger waiting to call me, before I went anywhere else, to the committee. I found them round the table, taken up with a new man who had been brought over by Solly, who had an infallible remedy for the cholera. If the district was given entirely into his management, he undertook to cure them all. He had already done so in the district round Cape Matapan. Solly was wholly on the side of humanity he said, and of curing everybody. He said he longed for cholera in his own person, that he might show his reliance on his friend's remedy. I begged to hear what was the treatment. The empiric would not tell exactly, but said it was a particular application of cold water. Cholera he informed us was identical with hemorrhage; and then went off at length to show the absurdity of treating hemorrhage with stimulants. I gave a few reasons for doubting the first premise, but was not much listened to. Some of the committee thought it wrong in a body intrusted with the health of the district, to let the people die, when a remedy was at hand; and some said they had had bleeding at the nose, and had always used cold water successfully. I went to talk privately to the few rational, and found a party who could use their common sense, and having agreed to stand by each other, I got up and made my speech. I told them time was short; the East Indies was the native place of cholera, certain remedies were the authenticated remedies there; and that I, and those about me, should resign our superintendence if any other treatment were adopted. Solly said he would resign if another treatment were not adopted; but they did not believe him; and after a little blustering he gave in, and all things resumed their old course."

Journal continued by Mrs. Ferroll.—"Paul went away this morning at seven o'clock. We were so late last night singing, and then falling into talk, and talking till near two o'clock, that neither of us had a mind to get up. To be at the end of time would be a great pleasure, so that one might go on doing pleasant things as long as one liked, and find when done it was no later o'clock than at the beginning. I do not love growing older. We are young now; but there are not a great many years to pass before we shall be at the end of our youth, and I begin not to wish that a future day was come, whatever pleasure it is to bring. It is only when one is almost a child, that life seems long enough to wish one could skip over one of its weeks or months, in order to reach a given day. But then to be sure, in extreme youth one is not happy as one is (or can be) at our age. This time, which is dismal as far as the neighbourhood is concerned, is very, very happy to us. Paul enjoys life intensely; and when he comes home so do I. What a delightful companion he is—everything he has seen and done is reproduced for me, so that I and he become one as to the events and feelings of the day he has passed. All I have done, and am doing, is equally interesting to him. What I write, and what I read, what I sing, and whom I see; what I think, will all come before us two again this happy evening. It is like passing a hot summer noon in the shade on the Loire, as we did when we were first married—life flowing over with abundance, but as still as it was bright.

"I have been looking out the passages about great national plagues and sicknesses. The cholera is brooding in his head into an article, and those passages will contribute to it. Now I will read till I hear his step in the hall, then the thing longed for will be come. I shall want and wish nothing more; but whether silent or talking, reading, eating, sleeping, shall be happy from then till to-morrow morning."

Mr. Ferroll continues.—"I came home later than usual. Elinor had to pay for expecting me so confidently by two hours of doubt. 'Has anything happened; what can have happened; what can keep him so late?' I meantime, happy and easy, knew that nothing was the matter, that waiting for the doctor kept me; and while my pretty Elinor, my delicate, my fair, my dear, dear wife, was in the fever of vain fears, I was trotting home at the full pace of my horse, whistling and gazing from side to side on the eastern shadow and the western glow. But then came that clump, clump that she loves so well to hear in the hall, and that self-reproach it is so easy to make, when suspense is ended—'How foolish I was to fancy any harm.' After pain, to be at the end of pain, to be enjoying the hours instead of suffering the hours—that is the bliss of human nature, which the mind finds it hard to believe.

"Thus it is with me—me, who have suffered in this very house pain so inconceivable! I know well that I have really lived here, in this house, with that woman; fancied myself tied to her for my life; known what you, Elinor, were going through, and how I had had my fortune in my hand, and at the voice of a very devil thrown it away—all that is as true and real in my imagination as it once was in fact; and often it comes in the place of the blessed present time, making the exquisite *now* give way to the hated past. In my dreams I go back again into that horrible past; I become what I was, though the last waking thought has been the blessed thing I am. With you beside me, I dream you are not my wife; I dream you are divided from me for ever; the habitual misery of those two years resumes its presence in sleep. It never yet has come into my dreams how death delivered me from that woman, though it was a strange and tragical way that he took. Dame Partlett asked me one day (to ease her own doubts on the subject, I suppose), 'Ar'nt you very sorry for her?' . . . *I* sorry? No, I was *very*, VERY, VERY glad! . . . But I told *her* I was sorry. . . I dreamed nothing bad last night; I dreamed nothing at all, I think. Malthus speaks prettily of married life—'So much innocence, and so much happiness,' he says. That sentence worked in my head as I rode away from home, and seemed to keep a sort of chime to every variety of pace of my horse. Certainly the cholera increases; the more we do, the fiercer it rises. But the people who suffer most from it, being the inhabitants of miserable alleys, or of squalid huts, die at least better off through our attentions than ever they lived. When it attacks those who are a little more at ease in their circumstances, it is borne least patiently.

"I went on the accustomed round, and found all the houses I visited the first week had had, or had now got, a death in them. I came into James Bean's house just as the thread of his child's life was spun out. It is charming to see how poetical human nature is in its extremities. The expressions sometimes have a touch of ludicrousness; but the sentiment is that which a poet could best make use of. This girl of fourteen has always been sickly. Her mother weeping by her, the girl said feebly, for she was almost gone, 'Don't cry for me,' mother; I was always a poor body, and could not have bustled for myself in the world. I'm glad I'm going.' The pretty selfishness, too, pleased me. The dying are doing such an important thing, they are such foremost characters in the scene, that they feel a right to think of themselves, and to be thought of, first and foremost of all who bear a part in it."

Mrs. Ferroll.—"Paul set off in high spirits. He was delightful all breakfast time, reading passages here and there from the article he is writing, and bringing out his imagination and memory, one picture after another, ludicrous and pathetic, of what men do in the course of their great excitements. Nobody but me knows the perfection of his conversation; he must love as he loves me, to be so *one* with his hearer; to listen as he does, to talk all that is in his heart as he does, to be equally desirous of expressing his whole meaning and conception in words, as to work it out clearly in his own mind. This profoundly quiet life which I have led since I married him, is the perfection of society. His chosen friends, or rather I should say, his fellow workers come to us, with all their bright wits out of harness; quite at ease, yet in full exercise in our society, and excited by him. We have none of the trammels of neighbours, except good Lady Lucy, Dame Partlett, as he calls her, who is very useful, and very dependant upon us. Paul has avoided visiting all the others.

"While I wrote this the post came in. I saw Lady Lucy's hand, but waited to finish my sentence before I opened her letter; but it is far too interesting now I have read it. My pretty Janet is ill; they hope it is the measles; but they don't know yet what it is. The out-of-the-way place they are gone to can't furnish a good doctor. I wish I could go to her at once; but without bidding Paul good bye, I can't do that. I can't have him come home, and find me gone, without his saying go, to my going; and will you let me go, Paul? he always tells me that a nurse and a governess are better for a child than a mother, and perhaps it is so in general; but then she is ill, and they don't know what it is. Shall I go? I went up stairs, and rang for Preston to get ready for a journey, but I could do it. If I were away, at this time to-morrow I should be so wishing myself back. I never left him for pleasure in my life, because it was more pleasant to be with him than any other thing could be. This would not be for pleasure indeed, except the pleasure to myself of being with my poor little darling, and I could not be of *use* to her—yet I long to go. The miserable time when I thought it impossible ever to belong to him, when all hope was over, after I heard the fatal news of his marriage—that time often comes over me, and I don't like to lose a single day of his society. I feel afraid, lest there should be the same time again; a time when I shall not be with him; when I should think how mad I must have been to waste one day away that we might have passed together. I must wait till he comes home, before deciding about the journey."

Mr. Ferroll's hand-writing.—"Elinor is gone to little Janet. There was the prettiest strife about it in her mind; but when the post came this morning with no letter from Dame Partlett, her uneasiness got the better of her desire to remain, and here I am alone for the first time at home, for though I have left her sometimes, she never before left me. What am I without her? something, something like that horrible thing I was when I had lost her for mine. I have just returned from a most interesting day, and have no one to tell it to; no Elinor, I ought to say, for she is the companion to whom to think aloud. I can't enjoy anything without her to talk to about it.

"I went into Key's district to-day, because he is ill and gone away; how can he have the leisure to be sick, in such a stirring time?

"There is a cottage on the Moor, which the occupier had got by right of possession, and which had always kept him from applying to the parish. They are accustomed therefore to intense poverty. The name is Skenfrith. I went to it, and found all ill except the mother and one big boy. She said the neighbours had deserted her, and the doctor did not know of her. She knew the doctor must be paid if he came, and for her part she had no money to waste on doctors. The sick child lay by its father and was crying. I bade it be quiet, but it said it was hungry. The father was far worse, apparently sinking under the disease; he motioned me to come near him, at a moment when I had sent the mother to my horse, which I heard pawing outside. 'Sir,' he said, 'make her give this little one a potatoe, she has plenty there under the measure, but she keeps them for her and Jem, who are both stout and likely to live, she thinks it waste on us who must die; but the little one here breaks my heart to be so hungry.' This was a new trait in human nature to me—yet I remember the mother in the retreat from Moscow, who threw out her child repeatedly on the snow, saying, 'Let *me* be saved—*he* does not know what Paris is.' I went to the measure and lifted it, and true enough there was a store of provisions, which the parent with stern calculation kept for those whom it could profit. She came in at the moment, and suffered all the pain of detection—*doing* it had seemed right enough; but she knew how it would look to other people, and was ashamed. I did not reproach her. What right had *I*? I merely gave food to the child and money to the mother; but I told her I would have a nurse here, from whom I should ask account of what was sent for the sick; she was more womanly than her acts, for she began to cry. The big lubberly boy got on one side and grinned.

"At the next house I went to, John Parry's, the news, which they told me at once, and without any thought of John Parry's state, was, that Lord Ewyas had been attacked by cholera. 'They say my lord will die,' said Mrs. Parry; 'Lord a' mercy on us, to think of such a thing!' I asked why friend John was without medicine. Why, John's son was Boy's boy at the great house, and had been sent on the Boy's boy's pony to Whitchurch, to get mustard for my lord's plaster—the housekeeper being 'out of mustard.' All the family seemed so perfectly satisfied with these reasons, that I expressed my hearty concurrence in them also.

"I called at Harold's Castle, and found he really was ill. Lady Ewyas was frightened, and was kept in agitation by the apothecary, who was very happy in frightening the great lady. Lord Ewyas lay in bed, thinking he should die, and also, that it was the most serious calamity that could befall the whole country. How unobservant flattered men are! how came he not to know that the accession of the next Lord Ewyas would be the 'auspicious event' of the newspapers? I told him my sincere opinion, which was, that he would not die. He did not look like a squeezed orange; and the physician had left judicious directions. In the midst of his pain, Lord Ewyas kept in mind his desire to have me one of his private lieutenants—one of his *habitués*. He made a tolerably well-turned speech about the Rubicon and his threshold, and thought I should come here on a gaudy-day, a month hence—but I will not. They shall not say I have ever been their companion, any of them; they can't help being obliged to me, but I can help their saying I was intimate in their houses.

"Elinor's letter—dear, well-written, well-folded letter—so carefully directed, because she loves me best of all things, and keeps up all her superiority in my eyes now, as much, or more, than when she wrote me her first dear letter. Little Janet has nothing but measles; I want Elinor most. I will fall ill to get Elinor. Suppose I should catch this cholera, in the midst of which I live, and die before she could get back, how she would regret being away for that childish complaint. Thinking of dying, we always fancy we should live among the regrets for our death; should enjoy all the vain regrets; should be the object, enjoying being the object of their sympathy for our insensibility. We see the pomp of the dead; and when we are to play the first character in a funeral, feel as if we should be there as well as our body. Elinor tells me nothing about the pills or draughts they give poor Janet—how right she is. If Elinor had been like other mothers, bidding her child after dinner drink port wine to do it good, or telling the man-father about its stomach, I must have hated it. Children give me an unpleasant feeling naturally; they are slimy; the water is apt to run out of their months; their noses are out of order; one fancies the nurses pawing them all over to wash them. Without such a mother, and such conduct, Janet would have disgusted me, though she is a picture of beauty. In a frame there is nothing I should admire so much. She is far more lovely than her darling mother, and will be a beautiful woman. Then it will be her turn to be loved, to be adored by some young fellow now growing up behind some wall or mountain out of sight; or, indeed, no farther off than the park-gate perhaps; for that lad is in calf-love now; but that shall never, never be.

"This is four in the morning, and I am just come in, yet I can't go to bed—why should I, when that lace border is not there, that forehead fleshy-white under the muslin whiteness; that frail, pliant hand, which seems to squeeze altogether in mine. When I had written my Journal, I had nothing to do, for there was no Elinor. I got a fresh horse, and set out galloping quite away from home. I rode on till every cottage light was out. During that time I watched how the lower room ceased to hold the candle, and how it climbed to the upper chamber. I heard,

CAROLINE CLIVE

when I stopped my horse near one of those on the moor, a man's voice in the bedroom, which was but a little way above my head, repeating, during two minutes, a prayer. I could easily perceive the monotonous sound of repetition, then a steadfast 'Good night,' and the candle went out.

"The moor was in a white mist. On the little eminences I was above the mist, and the moon made it thinner and more full of light than can be expressed by words. Passing through the mist it was piercingly cold. It was a kind of cruelty of nature, careless of the human being who came out at an undue time, and in disregard of whom, nature went on doing as she was in the habit of doing. I rode straight into the Meer by mistake, for water and the misty land seemed all one; and once in, I took a great delight in swimming my horse across; he liked it, too, brave brute, tossing his crest, and ploughing along. I had great difficulty in getting out, for the bank broke away under his feet, and he grew impatient and alarmed. I was obliged to force him out at the first place he could hold at all, and he nearly fell backwards as he climbed the rock above the Trout's pool. You would never have seen me again, Elinor, if he had. Once out, we galloped wildly for half an hour up the scaurs and down the brakes, the frantic wind tearing past the other way. At last I came to the waterfall, the devil's milk-pail; and I put my horse's bridle round a young tree, so that he could eat the delicate short grass, pulled off my clothes, and went in to bathe. The water plunging heavily into the basin, and I had a strong, unceasing contest—it to push me out, and I to swim up against it. I came out, and dressed in the moonlight, and then ran with my horse's bridle over my arm down Stoney-pitch, and into the common-place high-road below. It was growing light, so I hastened home, made Rampage comfortable in his stall, got in at the window, and have lighted a blazing fire, by which I will now lie down and sleep for two or three hours, till it is time to go to the cholera again.

"Evening.—I could not sleep though the fire was excellent, and it came into my head that if I went to Bewdy post-office before the mail-cart left it, I could get Elinor's letter two hours before the time due here, so I got Fidget out of the stable, and let him take his own pace to the town. The postmaster believed I expected some important cholera communication from the Prime Minister, so sorted me out my letters—looked them over to the last, and there was none from Elinor. Now the time is a blank till next post. When I have read her words and got her hand-writing in my pocket, common things can get their due observance, but without it I care for nothing. And what can be the reason she does not write? While I galloped up to the post-office my bosom's lord sate lightly on his throne, and that always means evil. Yet the others, the Bartletts, would have written—she would have *made* them—evil, no! it's only some accursed pill or draught to be given to the child, and the letter was forgotten; so I did not put mine into the post for her, yet it was worth having, Elinor; a soul's adoration like that is preciously valuable. What, *forgot, delayed* to write to your husband, for thinking of a child? I'm a child though, half; I know that thou dost love me. Nevertheless, I turned back in a black temper, repassed my house, and went on to Cholera Town without stopping.

"The committee asked me to dine with them; but I could not eat, nor bear the thought of eating. If I had had a letter, food would have had its taste, wine its aroma, but not without. I went into Lad Lane, and did not leave a house without a visit; the atmosphere of horrible smells gave me pleasure. It was so like poison, that it took off my thoughts from the constant feeling of the want of a letter. I got people together, being so cross and peremptory to-day, who would not have come otherwise, and had drains opened, filth removed, patients changed from bed to bed. One dying girl had got a rose in a pot, and conjured me to give it water; her reason was half gone, half hovering still about her. I came home late—drank a river of tea—I shall go to bed.

"Eighteenth day.—I am a child and not a man—here axe two letters, yesterday's and to-day's, both sent in their due time; but one delayed by some d—d bag or postman. Now that the waiting is over, it seems as if it would be easy to wait. Oh, absurd prosperity, who givest lessons to those in trouble. Janet is round the corner of her complaint, and Elinor will be at home tomorrow evening. I am ill. I passed a miserable night. Horrid dreams—dreams that lasted when I was awake. I suppose the night ride, and the want of sleep, etc., did not agree with me; I'll set about getting well—go to bed and cure myself. They will all say it's the cholera; and I choose they should, rather than say I did too much for my strength."—End of Extract from Journal.

Mr. Ferroll went to bed accordingly, and began to care himself; but he was too ill to go on with his Journal; and though he was, in fact, better when his wife and Janet arrived, he could but just receive her at the door with his fond folding arms, and was obliged to go to bed again immediately. She was frightened, and watched him with alarmed anxiety; she saw it set before her, that her treasure was mortal, and every other feeling was absorbed in that one. He, on the contrary, was happy, was at rest, now that she was again in his presence; he was like a man after a hard day's toil reposing, and enjoying home; that man would as soon go out again into the cold and the heavy roads, as Ferroll let his wife go out of hearing and out of sight. It was her purpose and sole inclination to sit by him, to hold his hand, to pass the night at his bedside, and it did not enter his head to send her to rest, except such rest, as by every luxury attainable within his own room, she could enjoy. He had pillows and velvet coverings arranged for her easy chair; he had fruits of the very best prepared for her refreshment; he had her long hair twisted and cared for in his presence, and then he took her hand and fell asleep, as she sate by him to pass the watches of the night.

Little Janet meantime was hustled away to the nursery, nobody thinking much of her repeated questions as to how her father was. She had come home a little heroine, in all the honours of recent recovery; and her mother's maid had talked to her about how glad papa would be to see her safe and well. Janet was little enough in the habit of feeling herself of importance; but this time the attention paid her in her sickness, and her mother's journey on purpose to take care of her, had given some innocent sense of self-importance. She arrived at home, expecting to be carried upstairs perhaps by her father himself, and of coming down again to the almost unexampled pleasure of passing the evening in the drawing-room. But her hopes were entirely overthrown. She fell at once back into her unimportance, and felt she was the object of least consequence in all the house. Childhood takes for granted what is set before it. Janet was quite of the general opinion about herself; and all the unhappiness she felt was on her father's account; but the nurse was getting her own tea; the housemaid told Janet that there was nothing the matter, at the same time that she whispered to the nurse words more awful to the little girl from their mystery than anything plainly spoken could have been, and finally Janet was tucked up in bed, and bidden to be a good girl and go to sleep, rather before her usual time, because she had been ill, and because the maids wanted a gossip after their separation. Janet lay crying, and thinking her father must die; she could not get warm in bed, and she was asleep and awake all night long. By five o'clock in the morning she could bear it no longer; and getting softly up, put her feet into her slippers, wrapped her cloak round her shoulders, and set off on an expedition to the door of her father's room. Janet was very beautiful; there was not so pretty a picture in that shire, in a frame or out of it, as Janet in this dress, with the clouds of her fair hair in confusion over her head, descending the stairs in cautious silence. Mrs. Ferroll, who was watching still, heard the indistinct sound of some one passing in the passage—she perceived that the person whoever it was stopped beside the door, and there remained in perfect silence. Her husband was asleep, and she would not move, for fear of disturbing him. The little watcher staid so long, that her mother forgot the faint impression her indistinct approach had made; she was only recalled to it by a stifled sob, which Janet could not repress, for the silence, and the want of a comforter, made her think all mournful things—that her father was dead—that her mother was silent through misery, and might die too. Mrs. Ferroll heard the sob, and then understood that it must be Janet who was there; and very softly rising, undid the door, with her finger on her lip, and saw the little girl cowering outside. She got up at sight of her mother, colouring violently. "What are you doing here, darling?" said Mrs. Ferroll. "You'll catch cold and be ill again."

"I wanted to hear about papa," said Janet, beginning to cry in right earnest.

"Hush!" said Mrs. Ferroll, hastily. "He's better, my Jeannie—he is asleep, and will be well soon, I think. Don't be afraid of anything. If you'll he quite quiet you shall see him;" and she led the child into the room, and both stood at the foot of the bed, looking at the sleeping man. What profound admiration, love, veneration, there was in those two hearts for the man they were looking on. Kings on their thrones never get such worship as the husband and the father from the faithful, believing wife and daughter. The wife *feeling* there is no such man in the world; the daughter *believing* it. The helplessness of sleep was another charm upon them. The relaxed mouth, the closed eyes, the disarranged hair, the helpless attitude, gave a feeling of protection needed by him, not yielded. It was very rare, if not unexampled, to Janet to see her father asleep, and the filial adoration she felt blazed up higher than ever. It would have been a happy hour if she might have sate down silent by the bed-side and watched. But her mother, fearful of the cold for her, after her illness, before long kissed her softly, and sent her upstairs. The clock struck six as Janet came back to her room; and then full of the news about her father, began telling all she had heard and seen, undoubting about the interest she was to excite. But the nurse woke up in wrath, and seeing her charge proceeding to dress herself, at the same time that the clock on the table announced that there was yet time to turn again and slumber, she gave out her opinions upon the subject of filial anxiety. "You're a very naughty girl, Miss Ferroll, that you are, to be trapesing about the house at this time of night. It's only to make yourself disagreeable, you know, that you go papa-ing that way. Can't papa sleep or wake without you waking up all the house? Pull off your stockings, miss, and go to bed again; and you shall have no butter for breakfast, that you shan't."

Lady Lucy Bartlett returned after the cholera subsided; but not till the cold weather had begun, for the first frost she remarked was a great thing. She was very much disposed to be jolly, and to celebrate the general emancipation from fear, by feasting and merry-making. But though the simplest woman in the world, she was afraid that her character, as a disconsolate widow, would suffer by the renewal of gaiety in her house, and was wandering among common placeisms to find reasons to be merry. "It's a great sacrifice to me," she said, "to give up the seclusion I've lived in since my misfortune; but the young people are growing up, and young people will be young people, Mr. Ferroll."

"And you like to see them enjoy themselves," said he.

"Certainly, in a quiet way; there's nothing surprising in that."

"Nor in a noisy way either. Don't you think," said he, "poor Mr. Bartlett would have done the same if he had had the misfortune to survive you?"

"That's what I often say to myself. I am sure my dear Christopher would have exerted himself for the young people's sake."

"And have liked it himself too, Lady Lucy. You ought to like their amusements you know; Mr. Bartlett would have liked them."

"That's true, too, and so I sometimes think. If he had been alive, I say to myself, he would have conquered his own feelings for the sake of the children."

"Besides one is not to murmur, you know, at what happens to one."

"Oh dear no; I'm sure I'm the last person to say one should, and indeed people might think I was repining if they saw me always in solitude, without company; besides we are much better able to afford seeing company than we were at first after my misfortune."

"So you'll have a little society this Christmas?"

"Why—don't you think so?"

"I do, by all means."

"Nothing noisy you know; just a few neighbours."

"Or a ball; what do you think of giving a ball?"

"Well," said Lady Lucy.

"How your son would enjoy that, and so would Arabella and Mary; Janet tells me they have learned to dance this summer."

"Why, I thought they must learn sometime, though the sound of the violin in the house was very trying."

"And the Herberts' sons will be at home from college," said Mr. Ferroll. "Indeed everybody, when Christmas is come. . . and the saloon will do for the ball room and the Hall for supper."

"Oh no; the dining room for supper, and we can dine in the school room that day; and the Hall will be best for dancing, for it can hold a hundred people."

"That will be best," said Mr. Ferroll; "let us call Elinor, and you two can make out a list of guests."

From that time the ball was a fixed thing. The young Bartletts seized on the idea with ecstasy, and the mother was as happy as they in their pleasure and her own. She even thought it a duty she owed her children to leave off black, and order a lavender satin gown with a most delicate black fern-leaf upon it. She went alone into her dressing room one morning when the children's lessons were going on, and her maid was at dinner, and took out and looked over her diamonds which wanted a little cleaning, so she packed them up and sent them to London, with orders to have them back before the 17th of January.

When the day came she walked over to the Tower in the morning for a few words of consultation, and then, for the first time, plainly understood (for she had feared but would not clear up her doubts) that Mr. Ferroll himself did not mean to come to the dance. All the arguments she used were confuted; her next weapon was the assurance that her enjoyment would be spoiled if he did not come, and tears started to her eyes as she asked whether he would not do so much as that even, for a lonely widow like her. He told her that her enjoyment would be in seeing her children so happy; and that he had more right to ask whether she, with her neighbours and family all about her, would not do so much as leave the enjoyment of his own pursuits to a good neighbour like him. She was forced to smile; she saw, indeed, before her, the gay scene of the evening, and felt she had not told the truth in saying her enjoyment would be spoiled by his absence, but had said it would, had even *thought* it would, as a means to make him come. "Well, at least, I'm sure of Mrs. Ferroll and Janet," she said, rising to go away.

"Oh, there's no doubt of us," said Mrs. Ferroll, and good Dame Partlett withdrew.

Mrs. Ferroll was so much in the habit of thinking her husband would refuse all county invitations as a matter of course, that it did not occur to her that he might ever accept one; but while she was dressing, while she sat silent during the arrangement of her hair, her book dropped on her knee, and she began to consider whether on an extra occasion like this, it would not have been natural for him to break through his custom. "He loves everything loveable," she said, "loves pretty faces, pretty clothes, graceful music;—beauty and grace are better perceived by, are more perceptible to him than to most people, and he feels their merit more. The sound of the merry Bartletts' voices, and their large full hall would give him food for his appetite for pleasant impressions. Why does he so resolutely refuse ever to go from home?"

These meditations were broken off by the placing of the flowers in her hair, which demanded her own attention as well as that of her maid. Then came putting on the new gown, a gown most beautifully made by Mrs. Johnstone in Dover Street, and fresh from its deal box, and overlappings of silver paper. She was pleased with her own appearance, and went in search of Mr. Ferroll to show herself to him. He was in the library, and Janet was there too, well dressed in great simplicity, and standing by a table admiring some flowers, while her father sat reading near the fire. "Come and let me look at you, Elinor," he said, as his wife entered the room. "You are beautiful, you are embellished; you are all moonlight, and the breath of violets. How can there be such beautiful things made as women, as women like you. So that's the way you wear your lace frills. It's very pretty; it's new, yet looks like something everybody ought always to have done."

"And mamma," said Janet, drawing up to her, and pointing to the table, "there is your beautiful nosegay papa has made for you."

"Bring it, Jeannie."

And Jeannie brought it with the most scrupulous care, admiring with sincere eyes, and saying, "Papa cut it himself; he asked me for some silk to tie it up; papa tied it for you himself."

Mr. Ferroll looked at her as she stood by her mother's side, who was engaged in admiring what her husband had done, as was Janet also, and watching how her mother disposed of it. Mr. Ferroll took the scissors again from the table, went back into the green-house, and returned with a spray of euphorbia with its green leaves, which he held out to Janet. "A flower for you too, Janet," he said.

Janet looked as if she did not believe in her good fortune for an instant, then the brightest colour came into her face, and "Oh, thank you, papa," was said in the voice of childish delight, which receives something better than the child ever knew before.

"It's a beautiful flower, Jeannie," answered her mother, to her child's delighted eyes. "I'll fasten it for you with this little gold pin, it just suits your white frock; and mine I'll hold in my hand. What are you reading, Paul?"

"Oh, a stupid book, I think, my dearest." She looked at it, and saw it was a book which he usually appreciated as highly as it deserved; it was plain he wanted the power to enjoy reading.

"Come with us, my dear Paul," she said, putting her hand on his arm.

"Don't ask me, for fear I should," he said, speaking before her own words were finished.

The tone of his voice struck her to the heart; the warm exulting blood was suddenly chilled, and she repeated in quite an altered voice, "*Why* don't you come with us, my dearest Paul?"

"Shall I tell you?" he said, chasing away the seriousness of his face with a bright smile, but she could not forget the tone which had struck her, slight as it was, nor let him change the subject thus.

"Yes, tell me, let it be what it may, can there be a thought hidden between you and me?"

"What! would you stay from this ball and listen to me, supposing I would tell you?"

"Aye, all night," she said, beginning to slip off her gloves as she said so.

"Nay, it won't take so long," said Mr. Ferroll, laying his hand on her arm; "a word that will never be forgotten is soon said."

"Ah, for heaven's sake, tell me," she cried.

"Well then, Elinor, the reason why I don't go, is—listen, my dearest—because I don't like it."

"Oh, Paul—oh, husband, you laugh at me."

"No I don't, I could laugh at my saint much sooner; *with* you I will laugh—cry till you come back, and then laugh at all you have to tell me. Good bye, good night, Janet. I must work hard at my article, so farewell, my two."

Mrs. Ferroll was contented with the playful explanation she had received, and Janet adored her father for coupling her with mother in his farewell.

The Bartletts' hall looked admirably well in its gay dress, and all the family seemed so happy and pleased with what they had done, that it warmed their guests' hearts to see them. The eldest girl had got a new gown, made by a milliner, the first she had ever had of such an origin; the sign she was come out, too; her pleasure in it was intense; the admiration of her younger sisters unconcealed. "Janet," they said, "does not Emma's gown look beautiful? your mamma thought it too full, but it is not, do you think; is it?"

"And, Janet, is not the hall bright?" said the youngest. "Before any company came, I tried to thread my littlest needle quite at the end of the hall; and I could do it quite easily, as easily as daylight."

"Janet, you've got a very pretty flower," said another, "and Hugh has got a beauty for you."

It was quite true, but Hugh knew he could not dance yet with Janet, and he had put his flower in water, to have it ready for the time when he might so far indulge himself. Janet was the object of his boyish heart; though ever since Mr. Ferroll had so early forbidden the match, it had become rather a delicate point in the family, and had settled into a decision that Hugh loved Janet as much as if she had been one of his sisters. But young Bartlett at school soon began to judge for himself, and in his own mind it was quite clear that he should never marry anybody else. Janet had heard the matter talked about in the nursery, and how angry Mr. Ferroll had been, and had grown up in the faith that it would be both wrong and ridiculous to think about Hugh as her little husband; and this faith had gone on unquestioned as she became older, along with other childish principles, and as far as the subject ever occurred at all, acquired force with her years. Besides this, she was in a relative position to him, which diminished the influence of his greater age, and his situation upon Janet's mind, and increased her influence over him. Janet lived in an atmosphere of clever people, and subjects were familiar to her, which were kept for the sad school-room hours of most children. Feeling that she knew almost nothing at home, she came to know a great deal more than her contemporaries; and at the Hall it was a marvel to Hugh how Janet knew everything and his sisters nothing. She also got the quiet and good manner of a child living alone with highly-accomplished people; even her romps were better bred than the romps of the Bartletts. The outbreaks which were under least control, had the "sweet one of gracefulness," while the control over them came from the maids and a dull mother.

Hugh Bartlett therefore felt she was more of a woman than her years warranted; he was on the watch to please her; he must know and do something better than shoot sparrows to get Janet for his companion, so that at sixteen, and she twelve, he was really and seriously in love with her. "Janet," he came to her, and said, "promise to dance with me the fourth quadrille. I have done Lady Anne, and have got Bessey Price, and Joan Blunt, and Lady Peners to do, and then will you, Janet?" She willingly promised.

"Why, you've got a flower, Jeannie," he said; "who gave it you? don't you know my white camellia that I have been taking care of for you?"

"Have you really, Hugh?"

"Why, you know that as well as I do; why do you pretend you don't?"

"Oh, well; I'm very much obliged to you."

"Who gave you that red one? it does not become you."

"I'm sure it does, Hugh," said Janet, colouring violently.

"You mean you like the giver better than me?"

"So I do," said Janet, a little angry.

"Oh Jeannie!" cried Hugh, and very angry himself, he walked away.

"She's such a child," Janet heard her mother saying. "There's no need to introduce you. This is my little girl, Lord Ewyas."

He made Janet a low bow, such as she never before received; quite surprised, she made him a low curtsey. He told her his friend Mr. Standish would like to have the honour of dancing with her. Mrs. Ferroll said Janet would be very glad to dance, and the pair went away.

"Is not Ferroll here?" asked Lord Ewyas.

"No, not even here," said Mrs. Ferroll. "I tried to bring him, but it was all in vain."

"I shall try to get Mrs. Ferroll without him," said Lord Ewyas, smiling, "since I see she can leave him, and since he will have nothing to do with any of us."

"You are very kind. I am sincerely obliged to you; but without him it is impossible."

"Not impossible, for you are here."

"Oh, but that is to such a near neighbour; and for two hours."

"Two hours is the limit of your liberty?"

"No, no," said Mrs. Ferroll, colouring a little; "but it would be hard to leave him alone merely to amuse myself."

"Then it does amuse you?"

CAROLINE CLIVE

"To be sure."

"Then if I were Mr. Ferroll, I *think* I would come with you, to prevent the necessity of shortening your amusement. I *think* I would. I can't say positively what I should do, if I did not like going out myself, for man is a tyrannical and selfish animal."

"Are you?" said Mrs. Ferroll, smiling.

"Not I only. Men in general are so, though they often hide it; but Ferroll disdains to hide anything. He says openly, I have a wife whom everybody wishes to get into society, but she shall stay at home to make society for me."

"Well, and she is very glad he thinks it worth while to say so."

"But I am very sorry—we all are very sorry—we want you both. There is not so useful a man, so accomplished a man in the county, as your husband; but he refuses our intimacy, as if we were clods of the earth. Why does he, Mrs. Ferroll?"

"That I really can't tell you," she answered, thinking of the explanation her husband had given just before she left home.

"But tell me then, if it is impossible, why is it impossible, that *you*, who do like us a little, should not come to see Lady Ewyas; see the castle; it is what people come from Russia to see; and you hardly know it."

"You are very kind; I should like it extremely, but. . ."

"But *why* is it impossible?"

"To tell truth, I don't exactly know; I will think why it is—let me take your arm to go and look after Janet; the quadrille will be over in two minutes."

This was the third quadrille; and the fourth Janet was to dance with the master of the house. He was in high spirits; a good deal excited by being the master of the evening; by being necessary as the partner of the greater ladies; as being appealed to by the butler when lemonade was to be brought in, when supper should be ready, &c. But his excitement on other subjects did but make him the more eager about the dance with Janet. He ran for his beautiful camellia, and was not away half a minute, and holding it in his hand, came back to Janet flushed and triumphant. "Now, Janet, I'm ready. A quadrille, band," he said, looking back to the orchestra—"here's your camellia—it's pretty well, is not it?"

"Very pretty indeed," said Janet, taking it and admiring. "Thank you very much."

"But you must wear it, Jeannie."

"Yes, if mamma can pin it along with this one," she said, making a movement to go in quest of her mother.

"No, no, alone; you promised to wear my flower weeks ago, and you're not fair if you don't."

"I did not promise to wear it alone. I am fair."

"But who has a better right than I to give you a flower?" said Hugh, somewhat manlily.

"But I've a right to wear what I like," said Janet, somewhat childishly. "I do like yours, but. . ."

"But you like another's better," cried Hugh. "Tell me who, Janet?"

"I love papa better," said Janet, colouring deeply.

"You won't tell me, you trifle," said Hugh, and snatching at the euphorbia, he scattered the red blossoms and the green leaves on the floor.

"Papa gave it me," said Janet, bursting into tears, and stooping down to pick up the fragments.

"What, really," said Hugh, rather ashamed. Janet said nothing, but sobbed and picked up the flowers. Her mother hearing the childish sounds came up, and Janet's tears stopped; while Hugh also stooped and collected the fragments. "Look, I had this one for her," he said, when Mrs. Ferroll began to inquire; "and was it right of Janet to wear a red one, and not tell me who. . . not tell. . ."

"It's the best white camellia I've seen," said Mrs. Ferroll. "It will take the place of the red flower very well. Here, Janet, I'll put it on for you. I can fasten it, instead of the poor euphorbia, Hugh;" and while she did so, she said a word or two to Janet, which her training in obedience made perfectly effectual, both to dry her eyes, and to send her off at once to dance the quadrille with her hasty partner.

"Pray forgive me, Jeannie," said he, when they stood together—"I was so vexed."

"Yes," said Janet, meekly and decorously; but sadly she went through the duty of the dance with him. Directly after, her mother said it was already later than Janet should be out of bed, and with many sweet words on the success of the ball, she and her daughter left it, and returned home.

The first thing Mrs. Ferroll told her husband was Janet's adventure, and the tears she had shed over his flower. He laughed at the childishness of the catastrophe, and seemed to enjoy the discomfiture of young Bartlett. The next she told him was her conversation with Lord Ewyas.

"You've a mind to go to Harold's Castle," said Mr. Ferroll, thoughtfully.

"My dearest, tell me why not."

Mr. Ferroll smiled: "I told you last night my reason for not going to the ball."

"You did not like it?"

"Well, my wife, that's very true; and I was so miserable once, I suffered every day so much more than I could bear, that now I desire only to enjoy my intense felicity—my felicity which depends on only you—that is my selfish joy."

"Say that again, Paul; those are words that I remember hearing for the first time, and they are always a renewal of the good times."

He said the same honied words in varied phrase; then added, "Did not Lord Ewyas say I was selfish?"

"He said all men were selfish."

"That's true; but taking one thing with another, do not I, the selfish animal, who think of what pleases myself, who contrive how to have you always at home, though I go out busy with the business of the world—don't I make you happy? Think what you have changed for— think of those sad, sad days. . ."

"Oh, Paul, I don't want to think of them, when I thought I should never be here—never, never could be. And now, I *am* here. . ."

The dialogue broke off, and Mrs. Ferroll ceased to want to go to Harold's Castle.

Hugh Bartlett, notwithstanding the lateness of his ball, was up and about time enough to be at the Tower by Janet's mid-day walk. He knew that for once her governess was absent; for the governess at the Hall had secured the governess from the Tower, to assist in her share of preparation for the ball. The governesses had had their full share of dancing, and were still asleep in the same bed when Hugh came away. Janet was walking for exercise in the flowergarden, as she was bid to do; and she had a volume of Tasso in her hands, out of which she was learning her daily task.

"How d'ye do, Janet?"

"How d'ye do, Hugh?"

"Did you like the ball; did you think it did well?"

"Oh, very pretty, indeed. I'm sure it was a very nice ball."

"But did you like it? I don't care who else thought it nice."

"To be sure; I liked it very much."

"But really did you like it?"

"Yes, really."

"And you are not angry with me, Jeannie?"

"Oh dear no."

"I did not know it was Mr. Ferroll's flower. I thought somebody else had given you one, and I could not bear that."

"Why?" asked Janet.

"If you don't know, I'll tell you, my dear, dear Jeannie," said Hugh. "Some people might say I was too young to talk of such things, but they don't know me; they don't know what I have felt. I want you to be my wife, to say you will be my wife."

"Hugh, don't you remember papa said we were not to talk that nonsense?"

"What, years and years ago—child as you were then."

"So I am now; I am not twelve."

"But you have the sense, and the cleverness, and the beauty of girls twice your age; you know everything."

"I wish I did, then I should know my lesson," said Janet.

"Lesson, indeed; how they make you work; no, no, you shall teach me, Janet, all I don't know at present, and if I know anything about the ways people go on in the world, I will teach you, for I am older, and have seen and felt a great deal."

"You have not left school, Hugh?"

"Yes, yes, I have; I shan't go back to old Meagrim, I've made up my mind. I want nothing but to live on my own estate, and do good, and have you for my wife; perhaps not just yet; perhaps not for another year and a-half; but if you do but say it shall be, Jeannie, I will be more faithful to you than Jacob to Rachel, who had to wait, you know, ever so long."

"Indeed, Hugh, papa will be very angry with me," said Janet, looking frightened.

"And why angry? I'm not as clever as he, certainly; Lord Ewyas says few are; but I've got things to give you which may make you as happy as if I were. My house, my money, my place in the world; Lord Ewyas says with all those, and so on. . . but all I want is, to give everything to you, Jeannie; dear Jeannie, promise to love me?"

"I hear papa, I'm sure," cried Janet, snatching away her hand. "Pray, pray don't tell him what you've been saying." She stooped to pick up her book, and repeated in the lowest voice, "Don't tell him;" and Hugh was flattered, he hardly knew why, at there being a secret between him and Janet.

CAROLINE CLIVE

It was, in truth, Mr. Ferroll; he asked his daughter if her mother had passed that way; he was looking for her. Janet had not seen her. "Hugh," he said, "I hear your ball was excellent. Go on, and prosper. What it is to be growing towards a young man!" And he went on to look for Mrs. Ferroll, and was soon out of sight.

"Your father can't forget that he knew me when I was a little boy," said young Bartlett. "But he will be surprised one day when I go and ask him for his leave to marry you."

"No, no, pray don't say those things. You promised, you know, that you would not."

"Well, and I never will, till you let me, I give you my sacred word of honour."

"Then I am sure I never shall, for they would only scold me. And pray do let me learn my Tasso, for Signora Parodi will be back before I know it, and she will be very angry."

Mr. Ferroll had laughed at Janet's adventure with the flower he gave her, and had taken no thought about interrupting her *tête-à-tête* with Hugh; but, at the same time, he intended thoroughly that there should be no future love-making between them, and was ready to take advantage of any opportunities which might occur to impede it. "What have you been doing at the Hall, Janet?" he would say, after a visit she had paid there.

"We played at post-office, papa."

"And then?"

"We played one game of blind man's buff."

"One game, and then you. . . ?"

"I don't think we did anything then, except battledore."

"Do you like all that very much?"

Poor Janet did like it very much indeed; it did her good to be so merry, but she felt it not right to say so; she could only look down, and feel that the Hall was not a place of refined occupation.

"And did Signora Parodi make any new engagement for you there?"

"She said I might ride with Anna and Jane on Saturday to Troughley Common."

"Why on Saturday?"

"Because it is a holiday, papa."

"Oh, a day of real pleasure—a do-nothing day?"

Now it happened that Hugh was going that week to Harold's Castle; for Lord Ewyas was a good-natured man, and glad to be of any use to his young kinsman; and, therefore, as he was now growing up, frequently invited him to his house, and made him known in the county. But when Hugh heard of this riding arrangement, he resolved, far off as it was, to return home for the sole purpose of joining it, though it would cost him a gallop back again to the Castle to be in time for dinner. This he made known to Janet, who said she thought it was a very good plan, only would not he be tired with so much riding?

"Not I; I'm never tired if I have got anything agreeable to do."

"And I think this will be very agreeable," said Janet.

"I'm sure of it," said Sir Hugh; "so you will faithfully promise to be ready at twelve o'clock on Saturday?"

"Oh, yes; they have let me ride that day."

It was a little event for Janet to expect, and she was very anxious, but quite in secret, about the weather. There was no necessity, however, for the day was a pattern spring day, sunny and mild, and full of birds, and bees, and fresh vegetation. Janet was working in her own garden, when her father and mother passed by. They stopped to see her progress; they had come out of the way on purpose.

"You never once have ridden with us, Jeannie," said Mr. Ferroll. "To-day you shall come if you like; but I remember you have an engagement with the young Bartletts; do you prefer their refined society?"

"Oh, papa, I *should* like very much to ride with you," said Janet, to whom it was a totally new and unhoped-for pleasure.

"Well, you may put on your riding-dress then, for I have ordered our horses;" and without any more words they left her, Elinor to prepare also for riding, and Mr. Ferroll to write a letter. Janet, left alone, began to be uneasy. True, this was far the more unexampled, unhoped-for pleasure, and honour, too; but had she been old enough to be quite honest with herself, she would have acknowledged that she was very sorry to break her engagement. In great embarrassment she put on her habit, and her governess found her standing and looking out of the window, with tears in her eyes, which she could not conceal. "Ma, che c'è?" said the Signora Parodi; and Janet, in her best Italian, related that she was afraid Hugh would be very angry when he found she was not at home for him.

"What does it matter?" said the governess, who was in great dread of being supposed to encourage the intimacy of her pupil and Hugh. "Of course you prefer your papa's and mamma's society?"

"Oh, yes, I do," said Janet. "You know how often I have wished they would take me with them; only Hugh has been so very kind, coming back all the way to ride with us."

"Of course it was to ride with his sisters that he came back."

"Oh yes of course; only they were to call for me."

"Well, well, I'll tell them Mr. Ferroll took you out."

"Oh, thank you; will you be so kind, dearest little governess? And it's a very delicious day, do you know; suppose you would be so most good as to go to the Hall?"

"Oh, no, no; I'm busy; I've got the new music, and I only came to see that you put your collar right; but I'll go down to the door when they come, and tell them."

"You'll be sure to see them if you will look out of the window."

"There is no doubt of that; oh, I shall see or hear them in some way."

"But you don't think you shall miss them?"

"No, no; but run quickly. I hear the horses' feet, There!"

Such inroads on their good-fellowship as this were not very unfrequent; and they contributed to make Hugh feel himself of no consequence or importance in the eyes of Mr. Ferroll, and that Janet was entirely free from his influence. His passion, however, continued unabated; but he felt that it must conquer great difficulties thrown in his way if it ever succeeded; and that it would be contrary to all Mr. Ferroll's intentions and wishes if Janet became his wife.

It was some little time after this, that one fine spring morning Mr. Ferroll went in search of his wife, whom he found occupied in a flower-garden at a little distance from the house. He put her arm in his, and drew her away from the workmen, walking in silence for a little while, and enjoying the deliciousness of the weather, which shone and sounded round them.

"What's your letter, Paul?" asked Mrs. Ferroll, at last, looking at the open letter which he held in his hand.

"That's what I am going to tell you," he said, holding it up at the same time—"look."

"It's from Harold's Castle," said Mrs. Ferroll.

"And, moreover, I mean to go there."

"You do?"

"Yes, and leave you at home."

"With all my heart."

"False, faithless woman; naughty, cruel Elinor; with all your heart indeed!"

"Excellent!" she said, laughing, "when it was you who proposed to leave me."

"Oh, but I only think of myself; you must think of only me. I know you are very sorry that I am going away."

"I know I am."

"This is why I am going, dearest. You know there are the assizes going on at Bewdy."

"No, indeed, I don't."

"Oh, then, I forgot to tell you, because I did not mean to go; I'm so busy with this pamphlet for April; but it seems Lord Ewyas has heard there are to be disturbances about the prisoners who burned his works at Oak Park. And he has taken fright in a dignified sort of a way and wants to muster the forces of his own party to go with the sheriff and meet the judges."

"He thinks there is danger," said Elinor, "and therefore takes care of himself at your expense."

"Those are not the words he uses, I assure you," said Mr. Ferroll, holding out the letter and smiling.

"No, no; but it's the truth—there's danger, certainly, if you are wanted."

"How do I make it dangerous?" said Mr. Ferroll.

"They want you because there's danger there, and if you. . . if you. . ."

"If I get knocked on the head—yes?"

"Oh, no, no, no."

"Then I should die before you—die in prosperity. But what horrid nonsense to talk of dying; what are you seducing me to do? I am going to ride into Bewdy with half a dozen other men, and ride out again when the business is over. Nothing more heroic, darling; but, I may be kept over to-day because there will be such a dogged downfall of talk; so I came to tell you just how matters stand."

"Well, I'll come to the house with you and see you off; I thought you were to have ridden with me to-day."

Mr. Ferroll trotted away to Harold's Castle; it had once stood alone in its forests, with the small village of Y—sheltering at its feet, and in that state the ancestors of Lord Ewyas had inhabited it, poor and warlike proprietors who had taken great pleasure in appropriating the loose property of their neighbours. But minerals of enormous value had been found in later times beneath the soil of their acres; Y—had become an overgrown manufacturing town, and the possessors of Harold's Castle great iron masters, whose descendants had stepped upon their wealth into the peerage. They were become again, therefore, a separate race from Y—, with their own privileges to guard and be envied. At this moment there was great excitement among the working orders of the town in consequence of the distress of trade.

It was the rather antiquated custom of the capital town of this county to hold what is called the sheriff's breakfast, before setting out to escort the judge into the town. According to the standing of the sheriff in the county was generally the attendance of gentlemen upon this occasion; they flocked together by scores to pay their mark of respect to one of their established aristocracy; but at the shrievalty of a new man there generally appeared only the city member, garnished with two or three dawning fortunes. The sheriff on the present occasion was one of the newly rich, whom the iron of the soil had created; he had anxiously sought the post of sheriff, which men, whose gold burned and abounded less in their purses as anxiously avoid; but he knew that the sheriff is, for the time being, the first commoner in his county, and walked to dinner before Mr. Shirley and Mr. Beaumont. Nevertheless, he had sad misgivings about the success of his breakfast, feeling though not confessing to himself that there is sheriff and sheriff, and that his would be an empty show compared to Sir Amyas Rufford's last year. But the circumstance under which the present breakfast was held, collected an abundant company; and the delighted sheriff stood at the top of the great room at the Harold's Spear, and saw, one after another, all the dignities of the county come to eat his cold beef, and swell the train about to follow him.

"There's more," cried he, every minute, losing his self-command in his transport; "another—two more—more chairs coming in. Shall you have breakfast enough, waiter, for all my friends?"

"Never fear, sir—never fear," said the waiter.

"I hear Judge—expressed some alarm, Mr. Sheriff, at having to enter this disturbed town," said Lord Ewyas, "but with the escort you have provided for him I can't imagine he has much to fear."

"Thanks to your lordship, and all my friends," said Mr. Smith.

"A very full breakfast, indeed," said Lord Ewyas.

"And more coming in," said the sheriff.

"But I hear the crowd near the gaol is tremendous," said Lord Ewyas. "Is the police prepared to keep them in order?"

"Oh, I understand so," said Mr. Smith; "a hundred special constables (look at that fresh bench) sworn in to keep the peace."

"And should there be anything serious," said Lord Ewyas, "the troop from Stillvale would be here in half an hour."

"Or less, my lord," said Mr. Smith.

"And if that force is rightly used," continued Lord Ewyas, "it is enough, small as it is, to keep all right."

"If?" asked Mr. Ferroll.

"Why, yes, there is an *if*," said Lord Ewyas, in a low voice, "for the major is an obstinate man with an idea in his hand, and that is that the people must be reasoned with. If, with his small force, he undertakes to teach reason, he will be apt to get a lesson in brute force."

"However, we have all wit enough to play at that game," said Mr. Ferroll.

"Yes, I have had proof that it is well to be near you when either the wit or the arm is to be used," said Lord Ewyas. "Did you ever hear what became of that unfortunate fellow of my cousin Bartlett's?"

"We sent him to the lunatic asylum," said Mr. Ferroll. "I saw him there last time I visited it; he looked at me till he remembered my face, and then he shrank together like a tiger before Van Amburgh."

Desultory discourse followed, and amid the clang of voices, the public breakfast came to an end, and carriages and horses began to be called for to compose the procession which it was now time should go forward and meet the judge. The sheriff had his javelin men in very smart clothes, and a single trumpet blown with more good will than science was sounding, to call the javelins together. And though they prevented the necessity of its science by congregating so closely upon it that the trumpeter was hustled by them at every step, yet he still marched desperately forward summoning the men who already were an impediment in his way; and indeed he seemed to think trumpeting was the great object for which all this crowd was got together.

"Stop trumpet—stop trumpet," cried a dozen voices; "the sheriff is in; you will be left behind," and this adjuration had a pacifying effect, for the trumpet stopped and stared about him, and seeing his troop already beyond him, shook a little rivulet out of his weapon, and ran to get the place that belongs to those who blow upon wind instruments.

The sheriff was followed by his chaplain in full dress into his carriage, and his four new horses and two new postilions drove off. Lord Ewyas, Sir Amyas, Mr. Dixon, had carriages also; numbers followed on horseback, of which Mr. Ferroll was one. The crowd was great, but in this part friendly. As he got on horseback, a man from the crowd came up to him, and placing himself in his way said, "Mr. Ferroll, sir, I want to speak to you. I am James Skenfrith."

"You had the cholera at the cottage on Olly Common," said Mr. Ferroll, who seldom forgot any one. "I know your name but not your face, it's altered since those days."

"It was you, sir, helped the little one to the potatoe."

"I remember it," said Mr. Ferroll, smiling; "and what became of the little one?"

"He did not die, sir, nor I; but the property is entirely gone. I should have done very well only the mortgagee came in and seized everything."

"But I suppose you owed him everything," said Mr. Ferroll.

"It is a shame to turn a man out of his own; and I paid for all the writings for that there place," said James.

"I see nothing to be done except to give you half-a-crown," said Mr. Ferroll, taking one from his waistcoat pocket.

James accepted it with applause. "But that's not what I came to say, Mr. Ferroll; you've been a good friend to me, and I advise you by way of a returning of good, not to go along with those lords and their grooms."

"And why not?"

"We don't mean to let those men that you know of, be touched by those other men that you know of in their black robes and black caps."

"You have come to that resolution I suppose since the loss of your property."

"It is enough to aggravate a man," said James.

"Well, and Lord Ewyas is aggravated at the destruction of his mills; and so am I, and so are we all."

"The men wanted bread, and blood shall be shed before they are touched; but not yours, if you please, Mr. Ferroll."

"Thank you, James; but I won't promise as much about yours, or if any of you are simple enough to try violence, I'll be one of the first to do the very same by you—so farewell. How is your prudent wife—and how is the groom of the chambers I gave you—how's Lancelot Gobbo; what do you call him—Caleb Balderstone?"

James looked up doubtful and scowling. "Do you mean Thomas Jackson, the boy?"

"That's he, Thomas Jackson, the boy—I hope he's well."

"May be," said James, rather grumpily, and Mr. Ferroll rode on.

The procession had to go about two miles out of the town, and at that place the sheriff received the judges into his carriage, and turning about, his tail wheeled with him, and he set off like a comet behind, and a soda water bottle fresh opened before, to return into Bewdy. The conversation inside the carriage was of the most sober description—the judges very anxiously asked about the disposition of the crowd, and with less sincerity inquired into the health of Mrs. Smith, and the numbers of the young Smiths. The sheriff exultingly pointed out the dignity of his attendants; with great regret reported Mrs. Smith an invalid, and confessed with a blush that there were no little Smiths. The chaplain gave an account of the fiercelooking crowds which he had traversed to get to the inn, and the judge's attention seemed to wander from Mrs. Smith's lamented indisposition, and to fix itself upon the numbers of constables, and the question of their efficiency. But outside there were many gambols played by injudicious horses, obeying their riders' incitements to show their spirit, which ended by laying their riders low in the ditches. Little boys triumphed at the spectacle, and there was much laughter, shouting, and confusion of tongues.

As they approached the town, however, these sounds were mingled with occasional groans, and tones of disapprobation, and the progress of the procession became impeded by the crowds which gathered on its passage. It was with difficulty that the police kept a way clear for the carriages to pass along, and when they got into the town, the difficulties increased at every street. The judges' lodgings were on one side of an irregular space, which was occupied on the other sides by shops and dwellings, and into which several wide streets opened. The square was full of the mob, and as the sheriff's carriage and that of Lord Ewyas entered the square, a sudden and evidently concerted rush was made down the street, the entrance of which these carriage had just passed to get into the square, and they were effectually cut off from the train following them. Neither could they advance, for the crowd before barred their further progress, and there they were shut up in the mob. In less than half a minute, all the horses of these carriages were detached from them, and led without injury out of the place, the postilions following aghast, and instinctively conscious that their business was to go where their horses went. "Let us charge them," said Mr. Ferroll, after he and the rest had looked on for a minute at the vain efforts of the police to restore a passage; "let us get up to the carriages. I don't know what those unwashed are intending to do."

A dozen gentlemen agreed to his proposal—and putting their horses on their mettle, rushed against the crowd. But the charge of cavalry against infantry so serried and determined, could produce but little effect; the horsemen had nothing but their riding whips to strike with, and the strong men planting their feet firmly, seized the horses' bridles, and bore them back, and made them rear in the air. The gentleman who rode next to Mr. Ferroll was mounted on a pretty showy Arab, not much more than a pony, had it not been for its exact and fine proportions—a brawny fellow seized on its bit with both hands, and the horse, through pain and fear, darted upright on its hind legs, and losing its balance, fell over, its rider scarce slipping on one side as it came down to the ground, and falling himself, under the feet of men and horses. Mr. Ferroll sprang from his own horse, and by main force dragged his companion to his legs, and set him again in fighting order. "We'll get through yet," said he; and most of those who had been attempting a passage, abandoning their horses to any groom who might yet be behind, formed a mass, together with Mr. Ferroll and his companions, and wedging themselves into the mob, rushed through them, without offering any other violence, and forced their way up to the two carriages which were held in impotence among the crowd.

Lord Ewyas, and the friend who was in the carriage with him, jumped out and joined them. The appearance of the former were greeted with a loud yell from the populace, who pressed more and more upon the party of gentlemen. "I don't know what they would be at," said Lord Ewyas. "What are they waiting for?"

"Any impulse, I think," said Mr. Ferroll. "But the police are making what play they can outside the circle, and trying to force us a passage."

"And can't we get through?"

"Most of us could, but not old Delabre, scarcely Smith, I think," said Mr. Ferroll, pointing to the sheriff's carriage.

"My lord," said old Delabre, putting his head out, "what is the matter?"

A stone, a very small one, a mere fragment, was dexterously aimed at his head, from some little distance, and hit him sharply on the wig. Wig and head hastily retreated, and a great laugh ensued from the populace.

"It's rather a savage laugh, though," said Sir Amyas. "What is to be done?"

"I see nothing for it, except to stand by them till help comes. Outside there they are sure to have sent for help," said Mr. Ferroll. Saying this he got on the wheel of the carriage, and looked right and left down each street, to see what was doing. "Ferroll for ever!" said a voice in the crowd; and he saw his friend James with a red ribbon in his hat, waving his hand towards him. "Don't touch Ferroll, boys."

"If you touch one, you touch all," said Mr. Ferroll. "What is it you want?"

"There are men in those four walls that shall go free," said the spokesman.

"What do Englishmen want from Englishmen but a fair trial—trial by jury," said Mr. Ferroll.

"Fair trial were promised to the men at X—, yet they were hanged."

"The men at—were acquitted."

"We are not going to trust to that."

"You must. You can't force the law to do one thing or another. The law is not here—only the lawyers. The law is in London, in the North, in the South, everywhere. Though you should get rid of a lawyer, the law will do just as it would have done before, and take account for him into the bargain."

"We don't want to hurt them, if they will promise a few things. Lord Ewyas is to give up prosecuting those men in those four walls, and the judge is not to condemn them."

"Nonsense," cried Mr. Ferroll. "What business have you to talk for all these Englishmen, who know better than you what is good for the county? What are you come here for, gentlemen, I ask you all? for the purposes of justice; for the sake. . ."

What influence his words must have had on the crowd can never be known, for at that moment the sound of broken glass was heard from one side of the square, followed by a hurra from the spot where the sound came. Mr. Ferroll from his height had seen that one of the shopkeepers had been trying to steal up his shutters in presence of the mob; and in sudden anger at his precaution, those near him had in a moment smashed in his windows. The sound acted like contagion on the multitude; it was like the rush of galloping heard by a horse; all that were near houses seemed by the clatter that ensued to do as the first breaker had done. Shouts and huzzas followed, and all the multitude swayed to and fro with the impulse which ran through it.

"They'll murder us before they know what they're about," said Judge Delabre, again putting out his head. The old joke was repeated, but this time the stones were more and larger, and there was no laughing.

"You must get out of the carriage, my lord," said Mr. Ferroll, "and you, too, Mr. Sheriff; and we'll all form round you and Lord Ewyas, who are their objects, and rush for the judges' lodgings; the servants are there, they will open for us if we can get near."

The gentlemen consulted a few moments, then did as he advised; their movement was saluted with cries and groans; and as the first ranks of the body of gentlemen pushed a little forward, great efforts were made to separate them from each other, and to press upon and overwhelm them from behind. At this conjuncture, some shrill women's voices were heard crying out, "Soldiers! they're come—the soldiers!" And outside the mob, there was heard the trampling of horses' feet; and there was an increase of the noise of human voices, and of a human crowd. But it was for some time in vain that the struggling party looked for the relief they expected from this reinforcement; for some time no help appeared; but at the end of perhaps ten painful minutes, a shout and a cry were heard from the mob between there and the Town-hall; and on the steps of that building, apparently having entered it from behind, the soldiers appeared, few in number, but powerful by their weapons, and the fact of acting as one body.

"We are saved!" cried Judge Delabre, wiping his brows, which streamed with heat.

"Yes; now let him but shoot the leader dead," said Mr. Ferroll, "and all's right."

"If he attempt his fool's reasoning with them," cried Lord Ewyas, "we're lost. What's he doing? Ass! Quitting his men, walking down the steps?"

"Aye, aye, indeed; voies de douceur," said Mr. Ferroll.

And so it seemed; the major came down among the people, calling them my good fellows, offering them his snuff-box, saying he was sure they wished for nothing but justice. The party of gentlemen could not hear what he said, but saw his acts; and though they had pressed a little forward when the people were first occupied by the arrival of the soldiers, and were so much nearer their bourne, yet they felt the multitude bearing harder and harder upon them, and violent language began to be used as the mob saw the prospect of their prey escaping them.

"When we are all murdered, he'll fire at them," said one of the gentlemen.

"Push on, lads," cried James, who was leading on the mob close about the party. "The soldiers is come to prevent justice. Time's grown short, and we must make the most of it."

"Keep back!" said Mr. Ferroll, "you'd best," firmly planting himself against the burly antagonist, and again there were a few feet gained in advance.

"They must not go to do mischief," said James to his followers; "we've let 'em get too far already."

At this moment, the merciful major, finding his conciliation neglected, and himself in a precarious position, gave an order. There rattled a sharp volley over the Market-place of Bewdy, but it went high above the heads of the mob, and after an instant's stare, they felt themselves safe, and safer than ever. "That's unmerciful mercy," cried Mr. Ferroll. "Mistaken mercy—press forward, my lord, they're maddened!" He put his hand into the bosom of his coat as he spoke. The mob yelled; James Skenfrith, with imprecations, waved his hand, clenching a bludgeon, and pressing with all his might to get before Mr. Ferroll; that was his last effort. Mr. Ferroll drew a pistol from his breast, cocked it, and shot him dead. One man dead, and one man with fire-arms, staggered all that were near; another pistol was ready—they saw it; there were some seconds of wavering, and availing themselves of the occasion, the party of gentlemen, carrying and dragging the less active old man whom they had to protect, rushed to the house they were making for, and the door instantly admitting them, they were safe.

"They were terribly ill-advised," said Mr. Ferroll, as soon as they got in. "If they meant to kill you, why did they not do it at once? that game was in their own hands before we broke through."

"Oh, God! at what a price you have saved us!" said Lord Ewyas; "how he groaned!"

"So he did," said Mr. Ferroll. "The fact is, I suppose that they meant in the first place merely to extort a promise of favour for the prisoners from you and the judges, which they fancied would be binding, and by degrees they got warmed to a thirst for your blood. Did you hear how the fellow cursed?"

"Ferroll, I don't think I could have done it," said Mr. Wyars, "those words being warm in his mouth."

"It's lucky for you I could then."

"Nothing's truer than that," said Judge Delabre. "I don't believe the lives of some of us were worth two minutes' purchase. I, for my own part, acknowledge my deep obligation, Mr. Ferroll."

"I for another," said Lord Ewyas, shaking hands heartily with him.

"I am glad it's all right," said Mr. Ferroll, approaching the windows. "I suppose it is all right, but the seem in a devil of a fuss still. The best thing to do, will be to get out of the house the back way, and take these gentlemen to Harold's Castle—don't you think so, my lord—till the town's safe?"

Everybody agreed to this plan, the active officious servants ran off to get conveyances, and to find constables to make a guard. Things were quickly in train, and the gentlemen leaving the house quietly, soon found themselves in the carriage of Lord Ewyas, and ready to go off at best pace. "And you, too, Mr. Ferroll," said Lord Ewyas, stopping before he followed his guests into the carriage; "you are coming with us to-day, I'm sure?"

"No, indeed; I'm going home as soon as I find my horse; and I think I saw a groom of yours with him just now."

"Dine with us, at least? it's all on your road."

"Oh, thank you; I'd come for society if I came for anything. Dining is but the company of a knife and fork, yet it does come into our head whenever our friends are there. Many thanks, but I really must go home. Mrs. Ferroll don't expect me, and she will be glad; besides, a ride after all that heat will be so pleasant."

"In short, you won't come; well, then, I thank you again, and good bye."

"Good bye, you're most uncommonly welcome. There'll be a coroner's inquest, of course; and I shall be ready to answer for what I've done whenever they summon me."

"Is not it extraordinary the determination he has not to go into society?" said Lord Ewyas, as the carriage drove on.

"Perfectly extraordinary," answered Mr. Smith.

"He'll go nowhere, though I and all the gentlemen have asked him over and over again. Yet I don't think he's shy."

"Why, no; that does not appear to be his misfortune," said Lord Ewyas.

Mr. Ferroll meantime, happy in the past excitement, happy in the present exercise, pleased to get home, enjoyed the ride amazingly. He soon left behind him the smoky town, and the mean suburbs; he crossed at a good pace a wide turfy common, threaded some well-known bylanes, and at last from an open hill looked down on the scattered village of Churchargent, and a quarter of a mile from the village on his own Tower. The gray building looked out all calmly on the twilight; the church stood not far off, shaped in the form of a cross, each limb equal, and the spire rising from the centre. The churchyard sloped a little on three sides of it, a brook ran in the valley, and its murmur was heard on the hill. Mr. Ferroll stopped his horse, and contemplated all this innocent and happy-looking scene for some minutes. If he had been in the habit of talking over his secrets to himself, it is probable he might have said something very much to the purpose of this story. However, he was not; so what he thought remains unrevealed; what he did say, casts no light on the past or the future. A word or two he murmured, but they were merely the fragments or rough material of his thoughts. "An island of the blest," he said softly; "if there be a place of long repose, I'm sure. . . So very, very still." But this was all, and at long intervals; and when he had gazed his fill, he loosened again his rein, and quitting the hill, it was but a short time before he had left his horse in the stable-yard, and was at the door of his own drawing-room. Elinor had heard horses' feet, and alive to all sounds from without when her husband was absent, stood expecting a message or a note from him, in the attitude in which she had sprung up from her chair, when her ear first ascertained the approaching step. "You, Paul, you yourself!" she exclaimed, darting forward, and into his arms.

"Yes, indeed it's I myself, and I've got a great deal to tell you. Elinor, you remember James Skenfrith."

"I remember your Journal about him."

"I've killed him."

"Oh, husband! poor husband!"

"I have not thought of it yet in that light. Poor husband, indeed! all my pity has been for James."

"But such a horrible misfortune!"

"No, darling. It was on purpose; he had every intention, I believe, of committing violence, and I was first with him. Sit down—here, here—I'll tell you." He detailed the circumstances, and then feeling in his pocket, produced the pistol which had been the instrument of the deed. "I'm so glad I took it with me," he said, fixing his eyes on her, as he brought it out. She clung to his arm, shrinking back a little, and the colour mounting into her face.

"The very pistol," said he; "the very hand, moreover," laying his upon hers. She instantly clasped it in both her own, hiding her head upon it, and her tears burst out. "Suppose they were to make it out that I had committed a murder; suppose I were called a murderer—was a murderer, could you be faithful still, love me, no matter what I was; never change?"

"What do you mean, Paul? who are you talking of—murder?"

"Nay, it's really very likely the coroner's inquest may give this affair that name; but whether they do or not, would you stand that utmost test, my wife?"

"Why will you think of a thing like that, when what you have done has been in defence of others, no willing violence against a man?"

"Yes, it was willing violence. I could do it; I am not the best of men, as they say in epitaphs. I did do it, I tell you, Elinor; and suppose such a thing, only just to please me, suppose they were to hang me, could you love me if the law hanged me?"

"Oh, heavens! what are you talking of?" she cried, thoroughly frightened. "What has happened? have you got something I don't know to tell me?" and she looked out, half expecting to see her husband seized by impatient officers of justice.

He said nothing for a few seconds, only looked her steadily in the face. Her fears took form from his silence.

"Fly, fly!" she cried. "Come. . ."

"Come, aye, come," he answered, drawing her down again beside him.

"Then you'd have gone with me if there had been any necessity? but, indeed, I don't know of any such thing. I have no doubt, with regard to this James, that they will put me on my trial; but I was only going on from one supposition to another, for the sake of knowing what you thought."

Elinor heaved a deep sigh, like one relieved from utmost pain, but still agitated and nervous.

"Alas, don't try that experiment again," she said. "The matter is bad enough itself." And so she thought next morning, when a warrant arrived to arrest her husband upon the charge of the murder of James.

The coroner's inquest had sate, the jury was composed of townsmen, highly incensed at the death of their patriot, and had found a verdict of wilful murder against Paul Ferroll, and the coroner had accordingly issued a warrant for his apprehension.

"I told you so," said Mr. Ferroll to his wife, smiling as he showed her the warrant; but it would not do to ask for smiles from her. Frightened, dismayed, she was pale as death; and Janet, too, overpowered with fear, crept, or rather noiselessly flew into the room, and tears streaming from her eyes, caught hold of her mother's arm, and stood gazing on her father. Mr. Ferroll laughed. "It wants very little to make the scene heroic," he said. "The newspapers will get up a paragraph, I should think—'There stood the wretched man stained with the blood of a fellow-creature. . .'"

"Oh, my dear, dear Paul," cried Elinor, hiding her eyes, and burying her face on his shoulder, "why will you use such horrible words; they are too dreadful to be jested with."

"Can't you bear them said of me, Elinor?" asked her husband.

"Nobody can say them, so why ask?"

"Nay, but they will; you must expect whatever. . ."

"Oh, I shan't mind, I shan't hear what the mere mob says; nobody else can use those horrid words."

"One does not know that," said Mr. Ferroll. "Good bye, dearest, you shall hear all about it as soon as possible; here's a kiss for you, too, my little Janet. Look, Janet, that carriage at the door, that vehicle ready to tear the unhappy man from his home, that conveyance to the drear walls of a prison. After all, Jeannie, it is. . . it is. . . a fly—*au revoir*, Jeannie. Farewell dearest, prettiest Elinor."

Mr. Ferroll got into the carriage, and as soon as he was with strangers, resumed the cold manner and indifferent gravity which best suited him and them; but when the wheels grated loudly over new-laid stones, or over the paved way of a street, he murmured to himself the exulting notes of the last scene in an opera, or quoted lines out of the death of the Commander from Don Juan:—

> ". . . *Here we are,*
> *And there we go:—but* where? *five bits of lead,*
> *Or three, or two, or one send very far!*
> *And is this blood, then, form'd but to be shed?*
> *Can every element our elements mar?*
> *And air—earth—water—fire live—and we dead?*
> *We,* whose minds comprehend all things! *. . ."*

His companions did not hear him; when it was possible they should, he broke off short in the midst of his excitement. Near Bewdy, the carriage was stopped for a minute by a servant on horseback, with a letter for Mr. Ferroll from Lord Ewyas.

Dear Ferroll

I hope to be at Mr.——'s nearly as soon as you; but the scene of yesterday has been too much for me, though you, I dare say, would scarcely remember it to-day, if it were not for this vindictive inquest. Make use of me, I beseech you. They will bail you of course, and remember I am the first to offer myself as your security.

Yours gratefully,
Ewyas

Further on Sir Amyas Rufford put his head into the window, vehemently shaking hands with Mr. Ferroll. "There are a dozen fellows waiting for you," he said, "to show their proper feeling about you; but I thought I'd ride forward and meet you, and be the first to say, I'll be bail, or anything. Recollect I'm the first."

"Thank you, thank you; Lord Ewyas has just sent me the same offer. It would not have occurred to me to ask it, if you had not made it."

As Sir Amyas had said, a considerable knot of gentlemen were ready to receive Mr. Ferroll at the door of the magistrate. They were all eager to offer their services, and to support him by their presence-the feeling among them was as strong in his favour, as that of the towns-people against him. The magistrate was a citizen, and not inclined to look leniently on the act which savoured of arbitrary power, and of a separate class; but all he had to do was to take the brief examination which was necessary to show that Mr. Ferroll had fired the shot which killed the man, and that he had not done it in actual self-defence.

There could scarcely be any hesitation upon these points, and it was not without looks of silent complacency at the progress of the investigation, that the magistrate continued to extract from unwilling witnesses such testimony as tended throughout to a committal. He could even afford to deal rather hardly by the witnesses on the opposite side, and to exhibit a show of impartiality by the severity with which he examined the evidence of the mob party.

"These things being so," said the magistrate, taking off and wiping his spectacles, "it is clearly my duty, sir, to commit you upon the charge of the murder of this man. My lord seems angry, which I'm sorry for, but that don't make the smallest difference."

"No, no; certainly," said Mr. Ferroll.

"But you bail Mr. Ferroll of course," said Lord Ewyas.

"Is any one willing to bail?" asked the magistrate. "The offence is one of so serious a nature, that any question of bail becomes equally so."

"Yes I," "and I," "and I," answered a chorus of voices.

"Your rich friends are numerous, sir," said the magistrate; "but the bail for the death of even a poor man is not a trifle to be undertaken by anybody, I can't let the security be less than yourself in £5,000, and two gentlemen in £2,500 each."

Many pressed forward, but gave way to Lord Ewyas and Sir Amyas, the most considerable men there, who were prompt at once to make their zeal and friendship known. But when the matter had been brought to this point, and the attention of all the room was upon the offer, Mr. Ferroll said (and his clear, peculiar voice caught universal attention), "I am greatly obliged to you for these proofs of your approbation of what I have done, and your willingness to support me; but my obligation I think had best end here. As the assizes are going on, my affair can be discussed within the coarse of to-morrow or next day; and really the inconvenience of the gaol for that time is not of a degree worth shunning—at least I will not shun it; so I thank you, gentlemen, and decline your offer."

They remonstrated in vain; they pressed on him their services; but he was fixed in avoiding them; whether he gave them offence or not seemed indifferent to him, and he was more like a man in the position of hearing and refusing petitions, than of one upon whom in a situation of difficulty friends were accumulating offers and help. The commitment was therefore made out, and Mr. Ferroll being delivered to the care of the constables, was conveyed in the same carriage which had brought him to Bewdy, to the county gaol. Thither a number of his friends attended him, and at the door, as he got out of the carriage, pressed upon him once more to shake hands, to renew their offers, to wish him well, to prophesy a speedy acquittal from all but the credit of the action. The mob who had gathered round were thrown into the background by the crowd of wellwishing gentlemen; their expressions of hatred were lost in the sounds of good will, their demonstrations quite stopped by the nearer expressions of friendship from his own class—the doors unclosed for him in a species of triumph, and at the top of the steps he turned, took off his hat, in one last acknowledgment of their kindness; then entered the prison out of the crowd, and the door closed between him and a host of friends.

The court and its heavy buildings looked gloomier by contrast with the scene without—the barred windows, the massive doors, the complete solitude of the space, struck the imagination by the contrast. Constraint is always humiliating; and Ferroll's spirit chafed against the forms of receiving him as a prisoner, though the governor of the gaol used his utmost courtesy in going through them.—"You know best, sir," he said; "but I can't myself conceive why you preferred not accepting bail."

"It was not for want of offers of it," said Mr. Ferroll.

"Oh, sir, I'm quite aware of that; every gentleman in the county would have had a pleasure in furnishing it. I am aware of the pressing offers made you."

"You see I would have nothing to do with them," said Ferroll. "Some men, you know, will not be obliged; but pray go through your forms; I have inspected this place too often not to be aware of them all."

The Governor complied; his prisoner's name and the charge against him were entered in the book of crimes and their perpetrators, and a small room, the best at his command, was allotted to Mr. Ferroll. The room was of coarse a mere cell—a bare floor, a bed, and two chairs, the only furniture. The windows were barred, and the door when closed was also locked. Mr. Ferroll walked up and down the room chafing against himself. "This is disagreeable," he said abruptly; "coercion, under restraint, punishment—detestable words!" and murmuring the same over and over again without seeming to find they grew better, look at them as he would, he still walked from end to end of his narrow limits.

There are moments in the first changing of our fortunes for the worse, which seem to be a specimen of all the time to come, and which are intolerable. "She must see this," broke aloud from Mr. Ferroll's lips, and mechanically he turned to the table to take pen and ink, and write to Elinor, but nothing was there—he struck the ground impatiently with his foot; to be obliged to wait till some one should come, and that some one, find that he had been wanted, waited for, to furnish a common necessary of every day life! Again his soul chafed within him; but it was a short time only that he was left to solitude. Steps approached before long, the key turned in the lock, and there entered a gentleman, upon seeing whom, Mr. Ferroll's face brightened far more than was usual with him upon meeting an acquaintance, and hastily advancing to each other, their hands were friendlily clasped, and hearty greetings exchanged.

"But, Ferroll, why are you here?" said the new comer, in the same breath with his "how d'ye do?"

"Is not it ridiculous?" cried Mr. Ferroll, laughing. "I might be abroad of course, but only under obligation to some of these fellow-countrymen of mine, and weighing the advantage and disadvantage, I decided for gaol."

"And where's the advantage, except to give people an idea nobody chose to bail you?"

"People! what is it to me what people think!"

"It is a great deal, when a man is going to stand his trial for life and death."

"It don't matter. I will stand alone."

"You have the most pertinacious ideas, when once they are conceived, of any man I know."

"Never mind. But, Harrowby, I suppose by seeing you here, that you are engaged against me—are you?"

"I am; they were with me last night, and I took the fee."

"Of course."

"Or else I could not have seen you."

"That I know; and who is there left for me?"

"I came partly to talk to you about it. They have retained—and—."

"By Jove! all that are worth having."

"Yes, but your cause is very much the best. B—would make a good hand of it; I told him this moment it was most likely you'd employ him, and being young, he is anxious to be leader, and keeps himself out of the way of the other side. Who's your attorney?"

"Oh, I'll have Shadwell, I think."

"Well, send for him at once; don't lose time, Ferroll."

"Get me pen and ink then, for I've none."

"Anything else I can do?"

"Oh, yes, you must do several things. My servant is somewhere or other. At the Harold's Spear, I should think. Send him here, will you? he must go home with a message from me."

"That I'll do; anything else?"

"Bring me Life in the Fourth Century, from the bookseller, or send it."

"Yes."

"Nothing more, except to come again if you've time. Let us sup together, though it won't be like the round-room suppers. Elinor, and you, and I. I wish Mrs. Harrowby were here."

"You won't send for Mrs. Ferroll here?"

"Indeed I will, though. What am I without her?"

"But such a wretched place."

"It won't be so when she comes."

"But to her?"

"Oh, I must have her here. That's what I want to send home for; she must come, is coming. You are in a hurry, I suppose, so good bye, Harrowby; I'm so glad to see you."

"Good bye, Ferroll; and for heaven's sake do be quick with your attorney; I'll send you up writing things, and let your groom go to *him* first—will you?"

"Very well, very well."

Mr. Harrowby faithfully performed his commissions; materials for writing were presented as soon as he could ask for them, and they could follow his request, and by the time Mr. Ferroll had written notes to Elinor and his attorney, he heard the approach of feet, and rightly judged that the gaoler was conducting his groom to him.

As the door was unlocked he got up from the table, and turning his back to the entrance, approached the window, as though he needed its light to fold and wafer the two notes. Thus he could speak to the servant without looking at him, at least for a time. "Here's a note for Mr. Shadwell, which you must take directly, but merely leave it; don't wait for an answer, and then go home with this one for Mrs. Ferroll. Tell the coachman when you get in, that the carriage will be wanted directly. There."

The groom advanced to take them, looking awkward and puzzled. "Am I to come for orders, sir, in the morning?"

"What?" said Mr. Ferroll, putting his hands behind his back, and fully fronting the groom; "no, you need not come back, unless I write. And, George," calling him back, "Miss Ferroll's pony must be turned out every morning before she rides."

The man retired; the master whistled; but he had little time for that employment, so many friends came with offers of services; his attorney came so quickly, and had to receive directions, and offer advice about the course of defence to be pursued. Elinor at last came, closely veiled, and silent after her hand was in that of her husband's, till the door was shut again, and the sound of the turning key was over. Then she threw her arms round his neck and sobbed aloud. He drew her to a chair, and sitting down by her, tried to soothe her, but it was in vain for a time; the occasion, the place, the anxiety had overcome her.

"But if you suffer so from all this, which is but mere shadow," said Mr. Ferroll, "what would the reality be? To-morrow, you know, I must be tried for my life; I must stand accused of having done murder. Suppose they find me guilty?"

"That they can't do," she said; "because you are not."

"I killed a man; if the law says I did it unlawfully, I have done a murder."

Mr. Ferroll tried her too much; the words to which such loathing is attached thus fastened on her husband, overworked her nerves; her heart suddenly fluttered so, that she gasped for breath; and with a faint hysteric laugh and sob, she fell powerless, caught in the act of falling, by him. He shook his head, as if there were a grain of vexation felt by him in the midst of the fond and lavish care he spent to revive her.

"Could you not bear it, my Elinor; would it change me for you though I had even done that deed?"

"But you have *not*," she cried, clinging to him. "What is said of you can change nothing, while what you do, and have done, is best."

Mr. Ferroll sighed, but said no more. He arranged the easiest seat he could, and placed his wife upon it, sitting down beside her; her head was on his shoulder, her hands in his, and he felt round him in the prison the spirits of kindness and love, making a sunshine in that shady place.

The meeting that night between his friend and him was gay—was joyous. Elinor stayed only till their slight repast was placed on the table, and then went to the lodging provided for her, too nervous and fearful to be able to bear a part in conversation, and needing all her strength against to-morrow. The two gentlemen ate and drank; and then the flood-gates of their souls were opened, and they talked. They were companions in literary labours, and all the worlds of things and people that live in books, were the habitual subjects of their thoughts and talk. Released, too, from the presence of observances, no longer being obliged to think what other people would think of his situation, and his behaviour under it, Mr. Ferroll's spirits rose with the excitement of his position. "One can't come near the palaces of Death," he said, "without feeling. their majesty—without longing to look into the halls, which one sees like a traveller passing beneath a great sovereign's dwelling."

> "... When the mountains rear
> Their peaks beneath your human foot, and there
> You look down o'er the precipice, and drear
> The gulf of rock yawns, you can't gaze a minute
> Without an awful wish to plunge within it,"

said Harrowby; "but I suppose it's different if a man really and truly believes he is to enter the great gates. You know that you shall only pass near enough to have heard the great voice, felt the cold shadow—but imagine a condemned man, Ferroll, condemned for to-morrow?"

"Still there would be all to-night and part of to-morrow."

"Nay, but suppose to-morrow come—the minute come?"

"Even then it is not death, but the pain of an unnatural death; for the last minute comes to a man dying in his bed, and for the most part, he 'lays him down to rest, Calm as a slumbering infant.'"

"Yes, old Bidderley—do you remember him?—walked out in the morning strong and well, fell under a tree which was being cut down, and was crushed to death. He lay a little while on the grass before he died, and called his workmen and children round him to say his few last words, as contented as if he had been ill for months."

"Do you think perhaps that men dying, grow weak, have no mind to begin work afresh, however violently their fellow-creature's, sickness, or chance, burst the iron gates of life."

"That's fine," said Mr. Harrowby; "it would do for me to-morrow when I come to, the tragical part; for instance, see the rude hand bursting the iron gate of life of a fellow-creature."

"Pshaw! that's like breaking the park paling. Try again—the wanton aggressor, the violent man, surrounded by friends, by wealth, by honour, sees his fellow-man threaten for a moment, and ere the honest creature— his friend, gentlemen, mark me, his friend, though an humble one, can repent of his accidental movement, this man—this gentleman... Stop, I'm getting too low and scurrilous for the high flight of the iron gates."

Harrowby laughed. "Yes, but you began well; the wanton aggressor is good, so is the honest creature and the *friend* excellent.—Friends, yes, once friends as the high and low can be, mutual benefits bound them; for kind feelings are benefits as much as kind deeds, gentlemen; yet he forgot it all, rushed over the sacred bonds of man's right, with sacrilegious hand burst the iron gate of life."

"Very well, Harrowby; you grow in earnest; you cast such a fine glance upon me out of your eye—such real indignation. I can already see you sitting down to-morrow, wiping the sweat off your brow, and not yet quite enough out of your part, to look at me and laugh."

His friend laughed now; and both being in the highest spirits, they argued, talked nonsense, and travestied the world, till the gaoler came to say he was obliged to lock the doors, at which Mr. Ferroll frowned, and Mr. Harrowby laughed again, and went away.

It is to be supposed how crowded the court was next day, to see Mr. Ferroll brought in a prisoner, which was interesting alike to those who knew him a free man, and to those who never had seen him before. There is always humiliation in restraint; the person subject to it, is either an object of contempt, or of an unnatural demonstration of respect which shows that his companions are thinking of his degraded circumstances; and though Mr. Ferroll was surrounded by persons anxious to do him credit all the way from the prison to the court, yet still he was a prisoner and had to stand at the bar of justice, and bear the accusation of crime and the possibility of punishment.

The indictment was read. He was accused, that by a shot discharged from a pistol he had committed murder on the body of James Skenfrith at such an hour and such a day; and this was followed by the inquiry, "Art thou guilty of the murder whereof thou standest accused, or not guilty?"

To this formality Mr. Ferroll returned a hearty "not guilty," which was followed by as hearty a murmur of assent through the court, though it was unworded. But after this, the other forms were passed through with the ordinary respectful silence, and the jury being summoned and sworn, the clerk declared the crime of the prisoner, and the counsel for the indictment rose to deliver his speech. We have already in the prison seen something of what this was to be, and will not therefore follow it in its elaborated state. It was delivered with all that unction which a practised lawyer knows how to throw into his great forensic displays, and which, on this occasion, contained many of the expressions which the two friends had perfected between them the night before.

When Mr. Harrowby sat down, excited and exhausted, it so happened that he did hastily wipe the perspiration from his brow, as

Mr. Ferroll had pictured before them both, that he would do, and the moment he had done it, recollecting what had passed, he looked towards his friend hastily, and caught his eye fixed on him and a smile on his mouth, which quite banished the actor and brought back the self in Mr. Harrowby, who, suddenly losing his assumed character, had to snatch his handkerchief again from his desk, and crowd it over his face to hide the laughter which burst out. Mr. Ferroll also laughed—a little scornfully, and the court was somewhat scandalized by this unusual act of good fellowship between the accuser and the accused.

Except this variety, little occurred beyond the routine which every trial follows, in which the end appears very plainly in view. The witnesses for the accusation all tended to prove, that the weapon in the hand of James Skenfrith was such as could inflict no great bodily injury, and that his words and gestures were such as to show he had no intention of committing any; that Mr. Ferroll's conduct had been provoking and his actions hasty, and that the man who was undoubtedly slain was also murdered. On the other hand, the witnesses for the prisoner proved that the peril was imminent, the intentions of the man evidently fatal, Mr. Ferroll forbearing, and that he had acted only on extremity, and the latter evidence so much preponderated in weight and perspicacity that when the judge came to sum up, his charge was clearly and decidedly in favour of a perfect acquittal.

It now became the pain of the jury to decide upon the case they had heard. The weary clock in the gallery tolled out the half-hour after five. As they were beginning to consult together, the judge, sadly glancing at his watch, suggested that the court should adjourn, and appoint a time for hearing the verdict; but the foreman of the jury thought it was unnecessary, and requested a few minutes' patience. The verdict was indeed plain enough on the judge's summing up. With this prospect of release, the judge took patience and settled himself for the short time still to elapse before they could frame their verdict. Mr. Ferroll, sitting down, looked over a pocket book which he held in his hand, and in which he had been noting the traits of nature, and the remarkable words which had passed before him during the day. The counsel had all withdrawn after their speeches were made, except Mr. Harrowby, who had remained near his friend; the weary clerks of the court stood on their accustomed legs like hackney cabhorses, or slumbered sitting upright against the wall. Silence and suspense lasted minute after minute.

At last the foreman came forward and signed to the clerk of the court, who started into action, and said professionally, "Gentlemen of the jury, are you all agreed on your verdict?"

"We can't agree," said the foreman.

Surprise ran through the whole court, for the whole tenor of the day had been for a favourable verdict, but the habits of the court permitted no such expression.

"Then," said the judge, "you must return under the charge of an officer of the court, and the clerk of the court will wait till you return. The prisoner may be removed, and brought up again for sentence."

So saying, he rose from his seat, jerked his robes about him, quite too tired to think as much of dignity as he had done in the morning, and passed out of the court.

"The prisoner may be removed!" said Mr. Ferroll, to his friend Harrowby. "This is carrying the play into weariness—the joke grows tiresome—Harrowby, will you run on and tell Elinor to meet me in the gaol—poor dear, she has been keeping her fire bright for me too long already."

Mr. Harrowby, more dismayed than he cared to acknowledge, went out of the court on his errand. The friends who remained to this late hour, came round Mr. Ferroll, their faces blank in spite of their efforts to be gay, and to treat the delay as a mere temporary inconvenience. He himself was weary, and anxious to escape from the importunity of his situation, and to be free, to do, and look, and be as he pleased. But he preserved his self-command, unbroken, and passed away from the court with the same air of freedom that would have been his in his most prosperous day—he neither trifled with danger nor shrank before it. It was not his companion but his attendant.

"How pale you are, my dearest," he said, as soon as he and his wife were alone in the prison, "and you have been crying; all alone all day and grieving about me! Why did you grieve, Elinor?"

"It does not matter about me," she said, "it is you who suffer. Oh, Paul, when will all end?"

"It is vexatious," he said, "and the thing is so clear before them, that one does not know what they are hesitating about. The same tiresome fools who thought of murder at the coroner's inquest, I suppose, are meddling in the verdict. But there can be but one end to it." Elinor shuddered.

"What, do you think they'll hang me, Elinor?"

"For heaven's sake don't say those horrible words. You could look straight into a cannon's mouth, but I cannot."

"Nay, dearest; but I don't believe this time in the reality of danger. Keep that in view in your estimate of me. I know it is only passing by."

Meanwhile, more dreary than the prison, more weary than the prisoner, were the room and the men in which and by whom his fate was being decided. Without fire, in a cold March night, without any light, except a dim lamp in the top of the door, the room containing the twelve jurymen looked worse than any apartment in the gaol. The jury was composed of men unaccustomed to hardship. After the long confinement of the day, to return home and find an agreeable meal, an excellent fire, an arm-chair, and their own bed, was almost second nature—the miserableness of cold, and of the prolongation of fatigue, was an unnatural torment. To some it was much worse than others— the eager, hard man could bear it; but the man who (without blame to himself) cherished his body, had hardly power to stand against it. Eleven of the jurymen were agreed—one wiry man stood out for guilty—he had his own crotchet on the subject—his own persuasion that Mr. Ferroll killed James because he was a poor man—not because there was necessity to do it—and nothing that counsel, witnesses, or judge had said that day, had moved him for an instant from his persuasion.

"The summing up of the judge was as clear as any direction could be," said Mr. Ramhelme, for the twentieth time.

"The judge is not fit to try this case," said the wiry Mr. Holmes. "Ferroll saved his life, and of course he's prejudiced."

"You do admit then that the judge would have been murdered?"

"No, I don't—murdered? No; and besides that, there's no right to do evil to one man, in order to save him from doing it to another."

"Yes, there is. You'd defend yourself, I suppose, if I woke you at night, with a knife in my hand, touching your throat?"

"James had only a bludgeon—that's proved. Isaac Smith's evidence is, 'I saw James cut a stick out of the hedge; and he said this is enough for me.' Do try to remember the evidence."

"Enough for the judge too, enough for Lord Ewyas; a thick stick, alias a bludgeon, could knock their brains out."

"Could! yes, so could this poker knock out yours if it could move from its place."

"Pshaw! that's childish."

"However, I say Ferroll is guilty."

Another half hour passed, and things waxed worse and worse. The hours towards dawn came with their bitter cold—more than one of the jury shook with the cold, and their empty stomachs added a very positive pain to their other miseries. Their sense of the importance of their trust, kept away the expression of the peevish feelings which could not but arise, and what touch of the ludicrous there was in their situation, would have affected a bystander, but not themselves.

"How long can you bear this?" said Mr. Jones, to his neighbour. "It has ceased to be matter of argument, and become a contest of strength."

"To tell you the truth," said his neighbour, "Holmes I believe knew he should keep us at bay, and provided himself with lozenges to preserve his own strength."

"Well, a man's life must not be sacrificed for a lozenge," said Jones, trying to button his coat more warmly over his chest.

Mr. Montague was walking up and down the room with Holmes, trying to argue him into assent to the judgment of the eleven. Holmes himself was getting tired. Mr. Montague was a smooth-tongued man. "This Ferroll is a man of so much importance—not so much as to wealth and station, for his estate you know, Mr. Holmes, can't be two thousand a-year; but he is so useful, and he is of considerable consequence in the literary world; and then nobody knows better than you, Mr. Holmes, what exertions he made during the cholera, because you were on the committee, and I observed your name and his frequently together in the districts."

"Yes, yes, all very true; but we should look at facts."

"You have said that before; very truly too—but really we have gone through facts so often; and I do think, when we are not called on to give reason for our decision, when it is left to us to form our own opinion as to a man's motives, and so on, and that kind of thing, that our opinion may lawfully be moulded in some degree on our knowledge of a man's character."

"Yes, we are judges now."

"Very true; I, and each of us, you and I, are judges of this very remarkable man; eleven of us agree in a favourable judgment—so we have pretty well done with our office; but you have to convince us, or to allow us the weight of our united opinion—you are Ferroll's judge in fact. A judge should be merciful, Holmes."

"I have to speak to facts, Mr. Montague; otherwise I'm sure, if it depended on me, I should have no objection to mercy."

"You'd have him pardoned, even if guilty," said Mr. Montague, an idea suddenly rushing into his mind.

"Oh, by all means, if possible—*pardoned*—yes."

"Well, Holmes," said Mr. Montague, taking him by the button, and drawing him aside, "what do you think of this verdict, if the rest would agree? for indeed the *fact* of the death of James is certain—guilty, but strongly recommended to mercy."

"Guilty, but recommended to mercy—well, I don't want to appear obstinate—strongly recommended—humph!"

"Jones," said Mr. Montague, calling up that gentleman, "just come this way. Mr. Holmes has been arguing with me that the prisoner should be censured, that our opinion of the *fact* that he killed James, should be recorded, but that also our wish that he should be pardoned should also be mentioned, so we suggest the verdict—guilty, but strongly recommended to mercy."

The step gained, the hope opened of an end to their misery was a strong temptation. Mr. Jones hesitated, Mr. Montague called others, certain that if one of them could see that he should not stand alone in his agreement, he would agree—the hesitation was great at first; then, there came in three who had retired to a corner to argue this view of the question, and had agreed together; then another joined, and another. At last Mr. Talbot stood alone in opposition, becoming the new Holmes; and at last, ashamed of copying an example so odious at this moment in the eyes of all the men in the room, he too gave in, and they came to an unworthy but unanimous agreement that the verdict should be "Guilty, but strongly recommended to mercy."

Meantime the prisoner's night had been more peaceful. He was more tired with the wearisome day he had passed, than with any one of bodily or mental exertion which he remembered at home. "Indeed, dear Elinor," he said, "I will go into my narrow bed there, for my eyes refuse their office."

But Mrs. Ferroll's feverish excitement made the idea of repose impossible. "Could you really sleep? but every minute they may come to call you back to the court; surely it is quite impossible there should be any long deliberation. Don't sleep, Paul, speak to me."

"Are you frightened, my dearest wife?" he said, putting his arm round her, and pressing her trembling form against himself. "You tremble like a young hare caught under a boy's hat. Nay, never be afraid; the worst end of all would not be worth fear."

"No, no, I know it is only a little delay; perhaps this very minute they are agreeing to pronounce you free; they may be coming now into the court of this detestable place to call you?"

"I wish meantime I my weary eyes might close."

"But would you be found sleeping by them? Would you pretend such indifference?"

"That's true; they might think I feigned the indifference which I feel. Well, well, I won't go to bed; let us sit close together, and have a little rational discourse."

They sate down, hand in hand; but Mr. Ferroll's weariness overcame his intention of conversing, and gradually letting his face sink on the arm he had laid upon the little table, he fell into a profound sleep. Elinor sate by him, equally tired, but unable so much as to close her eyes, and her sense of hearing unnaturally excited to distinguish the slightest sound. When the morning light was thoroughly established, the sound she expected came. Feet approached, the lock of the door turned, and the Governor himself appeared to say that the jury had announced themselves ready, and that the Judge was proceeding to the court to hear the verdict, in presence of the prisoner.

Mr. Ferroll roused himself as the noise of the opening door awoke him. "I have been very comfortable, Elinor; have you been comfortable too? Stay here, my dearest pale Elinor; sit in my place till I come back. It will be but a very short process now; a quarter of an hour, or twenty minutes, will bring me back to you. Kiss me—God be with you;" for Mr. Ferroll often lengthened "good bye" into all its words.

When he reached the court in charge of the sheriffs' officers, the jury was already seated. The cold gray court with many an empty bench, looked forlorn in the misty March morning. A knot of Mr. Ferroll's friends met him as he came in, greeting and conducting him to the bar, where he took his place; and he was scarcely there, when the judge was ushered by his men to his chair under the canopy, and the clerk rising, inquired of the jury, "Gentlemen, are you all agreed on your verdict? Is the prisoner guilty, or not guilty?"

The foreman came forward; he paused a little, as if summoning his voice to speak before that eager assembly, and then when the silence was wound up to the last breathlessness of expectation, pronounced the words "Guilty, but strongly recommended to mercy."

There was a profound pause. Each one looked at his neighbour to see by his face whether he himself had heard rightly, then at the

CAROLINE CLIVE

prisoner; but his expression was that of a man who hears an odd piece of news, rather than any other feeling. The judge was discomposed, and with a heavy groan, as at the stupidity of his fellow-creatures, he rose to perform the duty about which there was no choice left him. In as biting terms as he could make consistent with his dignity and that of the office, he observed upon the conclusion which the intelligence of the jury had enabled them to draw from the premises before them, and which compelled him to pass the sentence of death upon the prisoner, and then proceeded to announce that he had more satisfaction in assuring the prisoner that the remainder of the verdict was such as he himself should gladly act upon, by forwarding to the proper quarter the recommendation to mercy of the jury, which he was perfectly convinced would be as promptly attended to. Ferroll made a dignified bend of his head to this address, and stood quiet while his friends came crowding round him.

"Take no notice of it, Ferroll," cried one; "it's the greatest blunder men ever made."

"The verdict is ridiculous," said another. "It will be reversed. The Crown and Parliament will take it up."

"I'll go to London myself, Mr. Ferroll," said Lord Ewyas; "whatever interest I have shall be employed for you."

"My dear lord, there's no hurry," said Mr. Ferroll. "I'm excessively obliged to you all; but really the merits of the case will stand my friends."

"Nay, but it's an honour to us to be of any use to you," cried Lord Ewyas.

"An honour to be the ally of a man who has committed murder?" said Mr. Ferroll, smiling.

"Oh, nonsense; it's the maddest verdict I ever heard."

"But it pronounced me guilty of the crime," said Mr. Ferroll.

"No matter," cried several, enthusiastically.

"No matter? Well, that's nobly said. And now, gentlemen, as the thing is over for the present I'll bid you farewell, with the best of my thanks; and under whatever circumstances we meet again, I shall always remember that you could hear me condemned for murder, yet remain my friends." So shaking hands, and bowing to others, he signed to the gaoler that he was ready to attend him, and resumed the way to the prison.

V

A Painful and anxious time passed for many persons after the scenes detailed in the last chapter. They were a call upon the patience of Mr. Ferroll, who longed to be again about his own employment in his own way; but to his wife they were a trial beyond what he had an idea of. The prolonged suspense—after suspense seemed just about to terminate—the horror of the sentence registered against her husband, even though it should be put aside, the fact, or rather the fancy, that there was not perfect impossibility that it should be confirmed, these things produced an effect upon her, undermining the very springs of life. It had been proposed to Mr. Ferroll to keep secret from her the fatal nature of the sentence, till the answer from London should arrive; but to that he would not agree. "To whom could I talk of the subject interesting to me?" said he. "How could I talk to her, if there were any secrets between her and me?" He told it to her himself, tenderly and carefully; and the excess of her outgushing love when she heard it, compensated to him for the suffering, and enabled her to wear the appearance of bearing it without any reference to her own part in the trial. She never thought of the ill-effect it was having on her, the inability to sleep, the distaste for food that came over her: the shuddering cold she felt, the floods of tears which, when she was away from her husband, and sometimes in his presence, burst forth—neither did he perceive that she was bearing more than he did; that she was involuntarily and unconsciously a martyr to her situation, while he carried off his martyrdom with all the boldness of his own spirit, all the assistance of admiration and hero-worship—and greatest of all, with the perfect conviction in his own mind, that in the end there would be nothing to bear. All he sought to avoid was obligation to neighbours. A petition was signed in his favour by all the best names in the county in the course of the day, and Lord Ewyas was ready to carry it to London, and to forward it with whatever interest he had; but Mr. Ferroll as soon as he came back to prison, sent for his friend Harrowby, and desired him to get himself employed by the judge to carry his message to the Home Secretary in London, and to undertake the other measures which would take the advance of anything that might be done elsewhere in his favour. He had support in men in power, who knew him chiefly for his literary character, and to whom he applied as asking a right rather than a favour.

"That kind of obligation suits me best, Harrowby," he said; "and I mean to pay you for the time which you will lose at the next assizes, and so be easy in my mind."

"But as your neighbours are so civil to you," said his friend, "would not it be better to tell them what you are going to do for yourself—work along with them at least, won't you?"

"No; I wish them to know that I can do without them."

"Do you dislike them so much?"

"I don't dislike them at all; some I like. Lord Ewyas is excellent good company."

"Then why are you so unsociable?"

"Humph!—Oh, I don't how."

"You don't know indeed!"

"Do you?" said Mr. Ferroll, looking up at him.

"No."

"That's said in the tone of yes. What is it then?"

"You know my feeling towards you, Ferroll. You know how I have regarded you these eighteen years?"

"Yes."

"Well then, supposing I have known a thing respecting you, it is plain that thing does not influence my regard. You are sure of that?"

"Yes—go on."

"It was something respecting your late wife."

Mr. Ferroll looked down straight on the floor. "And that was?" he asked. There was a pause which he could not bear. After a minute had passed—"What about her?" he said.

"Ferroll," cried his friend, "your blood boils, your face. . ."

"It does not matter about my blood," said Ferroll, speaking slowly. "You know partly what a time of agony her life was to me."

"Yes; you were as nearly mad as a man of your rocky intellect could be. Let it be what it will that you did at that time, it was not you did it."

"It *was* I. You don't mean what you say. You don't think I ever fell under the command of my impulses."

"No I don't; I believe you never did anything you had not fully purposed to do. You would never have beaten the woman—you would not have killed her, but I don't think you were quite yourself to do this thing."

"And what thing is it?" said Mr. Ferroll, looking up again.

"What they say, Ferroll, is, that you shouldn't have kept her fortune, having no children, and you and she. . ."

"Oh, and they say the county avoided me on that account?"

"No; they say *you* avoided the county—not being pleased with yourself."

"Well, Harrowby, I did *not* do that thing. One single penny of that woman's money did not stay with me, nor near me. I can prove it to you or anybody; and if I were at home I *would* prove it to *you*. I have the brother's receipt and declaration that I gave over everything to him, and did not keep the value of one penny. He knew I hated her."

"Is it possible? How can the story have got about?"

"I don't really think it has got far about. Have you ever inquired into it from people in this part of the world?"

"No; I never talked of it at all except to those who told me."

"Who were those?"

"Your own set in London; it's a common story among them."

"Why did not you talk to me?"

"Nay; why should I? I did not care about it."

"You did not care whether I had committed an action which. . ."

"The like of which you never repeated; anything more unlike your usual character it was impossible to conceive."

"So you would not give me up, if—or rather although—I had done a thing which would fix a mark upon my name—make the public loathe me."

"Oh, that's too strong an expression; the public would care very little, after the first talk was over, where your money came from, so that you had it."

"Well, but suppose they had, or thought they had reason to loathe me?"

"Oh nonsense; but it would make no difference to me."

"Though some to me," said Mr. Ferroll, smiling; "suppose they hang me now, what shall you say to having been the friend of a murderer so many years?"

"I should be quite a lion, almost as much a lion as yourself."

"Should you like it?"

"Like it? pshaw! There is not chance enough to make me see my way in that question, so talk no more nonsense, but give me my errand, and let me be off to London."

Mr. Ferroll slightly shrugged his shoulders, and then went on talking to his friend about the persons to go to, and the means to be used. That very evening, while the officious High Sheriff and the zealous Lord-Lieutenant were driving from place to place, adding name upon name to the respectable list of petitioners for Mr. Ferroll's release, Mr. Harrowby was in London, already engaged with the men upon whom the success of the request depended; and the next day, when Lord Ewyas was travelling up with the petition to be presented, he was travelling down with the pardon granted. He kept a vigilant look-out for the carriage of Lord Ewyas; and finding horses had been ordered along the road for him, waited at one of the towns, to arrive at which Lord Ewyas's appointed hour was come, in order to meet him so far on his journey. He had been walking about the entrance to the inn for a quarter of an hour, and his own post-chaise stood all ready for his start in the street, when the clatter of four horses, and of a travelling carriage at post-boy's speed, was heard rapidly drawing near. Up drove Lord Ewyas, and jumped from the carriage while the fresh four horses were suddenly taking the place of the tired ones; he was stamping for a few moments up and down the pavement, when the sight of Mr. Harrowby caught his eyes.

"Ha! are you going to London, too," he said, shaking hands, "and upon the same errand?"

"Indeed, my lord," said Mr. Harrowby, somewhat embarrassed, "I am coming down upon it."

"Why, I thought I saw you in Bewdy yesterday morning?"

"That's very true; but Ferroll sent for me the moment the trial was over—indeed, I went with him back to the prison—and would hear of nothing but despatching me at once to Mr.——, and Lord—, and Mrs.—, and the—of—, to state the case to them, and get their interference."

"On what ground?" said Lord Ewyas, rather drily.

"Oh, as a literary man, he knows them all well: they take a prodigious interest in the case."

"So do I, I assure you; and shall be happy to add the mite of my influence to such powerful protectors."

"Your lordship is really and truly kind and generous to him," said Mr. Harrowby, "and, therefore, you will have pleasure in hearing that I have been successful—that I have his pardon in my hand."

"You have got it?"

"Indeed, I have, the case seemed so very clear;" and he showed the document.

"I'm sorry in that case. . ." Lord Ewyas began, but stopped.

"So am I truly, my lord; I endeavoured to prevent your lordship, and his other friends, from taking such kind trouble until it was known whether it should be necessary; but Ferroll. . ."

"Oh, not at all; I have some business of my own in London," said Lord Ewyas, "and I should have been happy to have added Mr. Ferroll's to it: but as it is, I'm glad, Mr. Harrowby, that you have taken that trouble off my hands. Good morning, Mr. Harrowby. What a state this turnpike road is in—remember me to Mr. Ferroll, and convey my congratulations."

The two gentlemen shook hands; the one got into his carriage with a slower and statelier step than he got out of it, the other into his post-chaise doubly quick, and glad to have done with an interview which he had rather dreaded.

The health of Mrs. Ferroll had undergone a shock from which she could not rally. Her husband saw the reflection of her sufferings during his imprisonment, in her present trembling state. He had been the first actor there, and he had forgotten the lesser actors in the scene; now she was the first, very unwillingly so, but she could not overcome the nervousness into which she had fallen, and which made her weep bitterly if a door were banged, and be on the brink of hysterics if in the course of reading aloud, or conversation, there were mention of situations identical with the one her husband had been in. Mr. Ferroll's whole soul was moved by her situation; his attention was drawn to her, and fixed on her; and all that human tenderness could do to soothe human suffering, he did for her. To enter on new scenes was the evident remedy to be adopted; and though her reluctance to the expedient was great, his unceasing patience in combating the natural impression that she was to die, and would fain die at home, and his gentle firmness in removing all the objections to travel, which her unwillingness discovered, attained his object, and they were to leave the Tower. Where to go? to brighter skies certainly—to places unseen before; somewhere where they should meet with all the convenience of life; where there would be an attractive natural scenery, and the possibility, at all events, of associating with human beings.

They were acquainted with all the principal objects and places of Europe. Sometimes it occurred to him to cross the Atlantic, sometimes to go to Cairo, and float upon the Nile, to see the first outposts of tropical vegetation, and to lose the sense of personal feelings in the ruins of dead empires.

While these plans were in discussion, it happened one morning when

CAROLINE CLIVE

the letters were brought in, that Ferroll received among others one upon which his attention seemed greatly fixed for the minute that he spent in perusing it. His wife perceived without much observing this; she expected him to put it into her hand when he had read it, but he crushed all together that he had received and soon after went out of the room. In the course of the day she went into his sitting room to ask him a question, but he was not there, and on the table she saw lying the letter in question. She was in the habit of reading his letters, and he hers indifferently; she took up this one, and half opened it; then something struck her that it contained what he meant should be secret between them; she did not like the unusual feeling, but she laid by the letter. A minute after, she saw her husband walking along the terrace towards the open window.

"Paul," she said, as he came in, "I have not read your letter. I fancied I was not to read it."

"Nay," he said, "it's a curiosity in its way—look at it, Nelly," and he unfolded and read it aloud—

MOST RESPECTFUL MR. FERROLL

I fear you'd have thought us long in impressing our gratitude for your kind compliance with our necessities fifteen years since; but though silent we have always had pleasure in reflecting on the money then sent. Poor Richard don't feel so much of that sentiment as me, but without much blame to him, for he is dead, and now safe under ground. Your honour think I am going to troubling him for more names; but I feel a pleashure in saying I am nearly above benevolence, having got a sum of munny out of poor Richard's sudden death, who had the assurance to lay by a good few dollars in the place where they assure one of sudden death, and indeed any death. These things being, honoured sir, this come hopping for your honour's pemission and advice to come back to England, where I think poor Richard's sudden death will make me safe and comfortable. Please write me your consent, and direct America with speed, for I ought to have had a letter once from my sister Ann, and for want of a proper direction it got into death's post office, and never came out as I was since informed.

I am, your honoured servant,
MARTHA FRANKS

"Is that all?" said Mrs. Ferroll, laughing at the letter; "and I fancied you did not want me to see it."

"Did you," said her husband, folding the letter and putting it in his pocket.

"Who is she," continued Mrs. Ferroll, "and what was your benevolence to her fifteen years ago; why that was soon after we married?"

"Oh, she was a poor woman in the village, whom with her husband I helped to leave this country and get over to America."

"What did you say her name was?"

"Her name? oh Martha—but never mind that. It will do very well to-day to take your sketchbook to the waterfall, and I'll come with you. I must answer this letter, and two or three others, and then I shall be ready."

Mrs. Ferroll would rather have liked to read the letter herself; but infinitely as her husband loved her, did not venture to ask more—there was something about him which she felt was secret even from her, and she never got nearer to understanding it, than she did on the night of Lady Bartlett's ball, to knowing why he avoided going into society. Soon after, he said he had given up the idea of any remote journey, and he thought they would go to the south of France. Somehow or other she connected the relinquishment of the project with the odd letter which he had read to her, but not put into her hand.

When Lady Lucy Bartlett heard the project of an absence from home she very much disapproved of it. "It would look," she said, "as if he felt himself rather guilty and got out of the way to avoid reproach."

"I never thought of that before," said Mr. Ferroll, "but you don't think me rather guilty, do you?"

"Oh, I? what a question, almost a foolish question. I have known you for eighteen years now; and of course you could not do anything so out of the way; but other people have not known you so long."

"Yet you know, Lady Lucy, I did do it."

"Do what?" cried she.

"I did kill that man."

"Oh not at all, Mr. Ferroll. I'm sure. . . oh nobody can think. . ."

"But I did, indeed, it is a plain matter of fact. Nobody ever denied it, everybody saw it; they heard the pistol, saw him fall, he died by my hand."

"Pray don't—oh dear no; the judge and all the court said not."

"Pardon me, they said I did—a few friends suggested that I killed him only, but the majority, agreeing to his being killed, said also he was murdered."

"Then why did. . ."

"They not hang me? that was the royal fancy."

"Oh, dear, I did not mean that."

"Yes, indeed, dear Lady Lucy, you did; and they might have done it, you know. Now pray what should you do by Elinor if she were here all in black and white mourning for me, the hanged? She would have done no harm, you know."

"Oh my poor, dear Mrs. Ferroll! how wrong of you to talk of such things."

"Nobody can realize," said Mr. Ferroll, moodily.

"Mrs. Ferroll and Janet want nobody's merits but their own, do they?" said Hugh, cheerily.

Mr. Ferroll looked up at him suddenly. "Nay, family merits are not to be lightly dispensed with," he said. "Equals should mate with equals, distinguished names with distinguished names, parks with parks," and as his speech went on, it took a lighter, even a sarcastic tone.

Hugh's countenance fell; he looked angry, took up a book, and presently went out of the room. "What does ail Ferroll about me?" he said to himself; "he never misses an opportunity of implying that he does not want me to marry Janet. I cannot think what it is. Perhaps he thinks I hunt too much; I did talk to him about Preston, the other day; he always contrives to make me talk of hunting. And then it comes out in Janet's hearing that he himself has been writing a book all the time I have been hunting. I've a good mind to take a first class." Hugh walked on thinking over the things that troubled him, but when he reflected that Janet was going away for a year, perhaps two years, certainly that thought was the worst of all. He went towards the Tower, and as he came near, he saw Janet in the garden, watering her own bed of flowers, among which were some verbenas which he had given her. "Janet," he said, "is it true you are going to leave me?"

"We are going away, I believe," said Janet. "Mamma has been, and is so unwell, and can't get better, that they think it is right to change the scene for her."

"Are you glad?"

"I'm glad if it does her good; and I shall be glad to see other countries. Should not you like it, Hugh?"

"Why, at the vacations, perhaps, I could come and join you; that is if Mr. Ferroll would like it."

It occurred so strongly to Janet that her father would *not* like it, that the colour mounted in her face, and she was silent. Hugh saw it, and coloured also; neither spoke. "Ah," he thought to himself, "if I believed *Janet* would like it, I should not much mind who did *not*."

"And why do you think he would not?" said he, after a pause.

"Would not what? who would not like it?"

"Nay, you know what I mean; what reason does he give for hating me?"

"Hating you! oh, indeed, indeed, you are quite entirely wrong."

"Well, perhaps so about quite hating; but you know he does not like. . . you know he objects. . . you know, Janet. . ."

"No, I don't know."

"Does not he abuse me to you? does not he say I am an ignorant country squire; a horse master; a horse myself?"

"No, upon my word, he does not: you are quite wrong; he never says anything, not so much as he says to you."

The young squire still felt dissatisfied. "I'm not that, Janet. I could have got the prize for verses this year, my tutor said, if I had tried; and as for field sports, why, you would not have a man sit at home and work Arabs on horseback, like my sisters?"

"No, indeed, I would not."

"Well, Janet, don't forget us all; don't fancy other people better than your own people, and fine places better than these places, though they are not, I know very well, as fine as some are."

"Oh, but papa only said that because children, he says, come to fancy what they know first are the best things in the world. I do think, Hugh, that the Court, with all those fine woods, and the hill behind, is as pretty as it is possible any place can be."

"It is a nice place, is not it, my dear, dearest little Jeannie?"

Here the Misses Bartlett were seen from a distance, coming to take their share in Janet's farewells, and so the dialogue broke off.

In another week they embarked in London for Bordeaux, Mr. Ferroll never having again given one thought to the impression Lady Lucy feared his absence at this moment would make. It was summer time, and the weather so calm that the Bay of Biscay lay all trembling and murmuring beneath the vessel. They did not land at any of the places where she touched. Sight-seeing just now was more exertion than suited Mrs. Ferroll. Profound and perfect quiet, the deep rest of the spirit, exhausted by emotion, was what did her good; and in this calm sea voyage she enjoyed it to perfection. Separated from the land and all its cares, the two objects whom in different degrees she loved with all her love, close to her; the idle progress over the sea, to which no self-exertion of any kind contributed, all soothed, and parted her from trouble, and made every day and hour a healing medicine. They arrived in the Gironde soon enough to leave this impression in its perfection, and before they were tired of being so happy; and quitting Bordeaux with deliberate haste, set off on a journey still more south, avoiding all the roughnesses of travelling and enjoying the sun, the profusion of life, the progress which was the natural occupation of the day, the halt, and the rest, which there was no reason to abbreviate or to avoid. Mrs. Ferroll got better and better; her husband watched her daily improvement with heightened spirits; his plan for her quite succeeded, and he enjoyed the pleasure of success. He loved her the more vividly for being so susceptible to his good influences. Janet, too, was happy; she was very useful, very handy; very strong in health, and active. When her mother rested on a sofa at the hotel they stopped at in the evening, Janet watched her father's face, to see if he would take her with him on his walk; but she was accustomed to be left behind, and did not complain even to herself, though the evening sun glowed into the room, and she longed to see the new world of a foreign country. Tenderly as Mrs. Ferroll loved her, she received Janet's sacrifices as matters of course, and felt her rewarded enough by thanks and kisses. Janet felt so too.

The country below Bordeaux presents but an uninteresting aspect to the traveller. Nevertheless along the coast, with the sea on one side, and the strange aspects of sands, and bright masses of cultivation on the other, there is enough to please eyes which have already enjoyed the essential glories of the world. They came one morning to the small village of Pontaube, a fishing village without any great trade, and which was a favourite retirement for men who had collected a little money in the province. There were several small, prettyish houses in the street, with figs, and vine trees growing over them; and the inn was a new building of considerable pretension to be comfortable, built round a small court, where, on a bench beside one of the walls, sate the landlady knitting stockings, and basking in the sun. Mrs. Ferroll and Janet went for breakfast upstairs; but Mr. Ferroll did not like the heat and the narrowness of the room, and going down thought he would drink his coffee in the common room. But the common room did not seem to be open to all; for when he went in, and would have sate down towards the top of the table, the waitress, a nice little *fille*, remonstrated, observing, "But, sir, the gentlemen will be here soon."

Mr. Ferroll submitted willingly, and went lower; but when sitting down, he asked for some coffee, and appropriated a small loaf of white bread which lay at his hand. The little waitress again interposed, "That roll is for the gentlemen, sir, but I'll get you another. Sit here, sir," she added, dusting and putting a chair still lower down to entice him into it. Mr. Ferroll complied again; and the girl, who seemed to have doubted of his tractability, was pleased, and grew very tame herself, and willing to express her surprise at the sight of an Englishman, and at what he could do. He spoke French remarkably well, but a few tones had betrayed that he was not a Frenchman, and before she went for his coffee, the little waitress satisfied her curiosity by asking a few questions. "You know France, do you, sir?" said she.

"Yes, I've often been in France; but you have found out, have you, that I am an Englishman?"

"Yes, sir, and besides your servant told me, and besides I heard you speaking English to him. Speaking English is very clever; we poor people could not do that."

Mr. Ferroll looked up and laughed; he had a sheet of paper before him, on which he was writing some memorandum, and it caught her eye. "Do you write in English, too, sir?" said she.

"Yes, I do."

"Is that possible?" said the girl, lifting and letting fall her chin with a slight sigh, and going off to get the coffee. When she had brought it in, and while she stood looking for some further opening to conversation, a noise was heard in the outer room; and starting away, she cried, "The gentlemen," and ran to open the door. In they came, three in number; and it seemed that they were habitual visitors, whose arrival was the great event of the day, and for whom all other guests were to be thrown into the background. Mr. Ferroll observed and listened, and by force of observation, and questions to the maiden when she was unoccupied, found they were the great men of Pontaube, who every day breakfasted at ten, and dined at six, at the sign of the Père Pierrot, for the sum of four francs, wine included. One was the inspector of weights and measures; another Jacqueline called the Lawyer; and the third was the doctor. They sat down as to a pleasant occasion, each man drew out his napkin from its ring, and prepared himself for the breakfast of the morning. This day it consisted first of a dish of cow-heel, and they ate all that; then they had stewed mutton, and they ate all that. Then came in the glout morceau, a roasted chicken; and upon the appearance of this dish, the mistress of the inn herself entered, and sat down to cut it up. She took her place, and her share in conversation, as if the woman must be the first person in the society of men, though when she had dissected the chicken, she ate only bread and butter herself, while they proceeded in their more substantial breakfast.

"You'll believe me another time, Mr. Beuthe," she said to the lawyer; "Dreux is really appointed agent at Bordeaux, is he not?"

"Well, but I don't know even now that he is," said Beuthe.

"Madame Filejean is perfectly right, as she always is," said Lahrotte, the doctor. "I myself believe Dreux is agent at Bordeaux."

"He did not know it last night," said the unbeliever.

"Perhaps not; but this morning," said the lady.

"Ha! you have it from himself!" said Beuthe, spreading his arms, and bowing.

"Perhaps I have."

"Well, that will console him for the barrel," said the inspector. "It was spilled, every drop."

"No, they caught it just falling," said the lawyer.

"Who caught it—who could catch a barrel full of wine?"

"Why Louis himself. He was behind the cart, and saw the board cracking."

"Please to forgive me, gentlemen," said the little waitress, whose back bent backwards, and whose arm stretched over dirty plates which she was carrying out. "I was passing, I saw it: the great beast of a horse saw Madame Lère's new bucket at the door, and he snorted so, and sprang so, all on one side; and the cart jumped over the large stone in the road; there, you know it, gentlemen; and so the poor barrel fell with all its weight upon the board of the cart, and broke the board, with such a crack! and down it came—down!"

"Take care what you are about, Jacqueline," cried Madame Filejean— "the plates, child!"

"Brava, Jacqueline! well told," said the doctor. "Get along, my little girl." And the girl laughed softly, and went on her errands.

Mr. Ferroll was amused with this little scene out of the life of Pontaube; and when "the gentlemen" had finished their meal, rose also; and attaching himself to the doctor, resolved on making acquaintance.

"Is it possible, sir," said the doctor, "that you and your lady should be travelling for curiosity in the Landes. There's not much to see."

"We are travelling for health more than anything else," said Mr. Ferroll. "My wife has gone through great excitement; and a quiet alteration of scene, where there is something new, and no trouble, seems to be the best thing for her."

"This is the very place for her then," said the doctor. "I felt it myself in 1813. I had really been too much interested."

"What, you were really one of the fortunate men who came safe?"

"Not I only, but my horse too. He went through the whole campaign, and died in his stable years after," said the doctor. "Oh, after all, matters look worse in a book than in reality. Here I am, as young as I was then nearly, some good pickings in the bank yonder; and I have built that houselet there, which I shall have great pleasure in showing to you, sir."

Mr. Ferroll bowed too; and after he had admired all that was to be seen in the doctor's house, went on to walk with him about the little town. The doctor was a widower, he had a son at college, who came home but seldom. One oldish man composed his whole household, cherished his carnations, fed his horse, made his bed, mended his stockings, played at *écarté* with him on a Sunday morning, and kept his floors bright and slippery, by skating about them with brushes under his shoes. The doctor was the busy spirit of the town. He had nearly ceased to practise his profession; but he was very active in promoting everything that he thought good for the community; and for the most part the things were good which he judged to be so.

Pontaube is a fishing village, with a bad harbour, rendered better by a long breakwater, used as a pier, up to the level of which, and often over it, comes the rude water of Biscay, while at low tide it leaves the vessels stranded at its side. The construction of this breakwater was due to the exertions of M. Lahrotte, and he took Mr. Ferroll with pride and pleasure to see it. It took an angle about the middle of its length, the better to shelter the port, and in that point some steep steps went down five-and-twenty or thirty feet to the sea. Workmen were doing some repairs there at the time—they were putting a very low edge to the wall, to prevent the falling over of goods laid upon the pier; but it was necessarily low on account of the violence of the sea, which would have torn away anything it could have laid hold of. M. Lahrotte paused here to show his guest the skill of the arrangement, and to hold a little argument with the workmen; and while he did so, Mr. Ferroll's attention was caught by the scene which this spot commanded, and which was beautiful, though the means to make it beautiful were so small. The tide was swelling in, the hot sun glancing deep into the water, and filling it with light. A few boats floated, a few boats were stranded on the shore; the buildings of the town grouped themselves round the spire of the church; red dresses here and there gave their spot of bright colour; there was a fig-tree in deepest green against a grey wall; among the sand were long yellow, mixed with green, rushes. The air stirred a little from the west, and breathed a few moments' coolness from across the water. M. Lahrotte took off his hat, and wiped his head.

"Ha, this is a delicious place," said he.

"You've a deep sense of the good of life," said Mr. Ferroll; "and I congratulate you on it."

He returned to the inn, pleased as with a Dutch picture; and when the evening cooled, took Elinor and Janet to look at the things which had given him pleasure; but when the sun had set, the charm was gone. It was a lorn and pale scene, and Mrs. Ferroll, though willing to see its merit, could find no epithet except "very melancholy."

"Do you think so?" said Mr. Ferroll; "then we won't stay here. We'll order horses for to-morrow morning—and so let's go back to the inn, for it is getting late."

He accompanied them on their return, and took a book to read to his wife; but his attention was not fixed as usual; he laid it down now and then, and talked of things foreign to the subject of the book—he was thinking of the barrel of wine that burst, and of the servant of M. Lahrotte; then the great Atlantic rose before him, and his mind's eye went across to the continent which was now opposite to him, with nothing interposing. He asked his wife if she would like to go to Halifax. She asked him what made his thoughts so restless. He did not know; he said it seemed to him as if there were a tempest approaching across the vast ocean—or else there was a moral tempest somewhere—presages of real storms, or their ghosts, were passing about; and he laughed at himself for the impression; and when she prepared to go to rest, said he would walk out into the night air, and try to get rid of the feelings. He did so, and went out to the little pier, which now lay in solitude, jetting out into the advancing tide. The waves rushed against it, and dashing up in a sudden influx of water, were broken with loud murmur, and then seething back, grated over the shingles, and left a dry space again. The moon was hanging just on the edge of the horizon, with a brassy dim light, which was reflected over the water, but which grew dimmer and dimmer as the disc of the moon sank, and left the heavens and the earth by degrees in the shadow of a summer's night.

Mr. Ferroll walked on musing; his thoughts were full of past scenes, and of scenes which might yet come to pass. Spectres of pain and part pleasure passed before him—of things to lose, and of the time when they should be lost. He came to the part of the pier where it made an angle, and where the rude steps went down to the beach—but he had forgotten all; his foot struck against the low parapet which the workmen had been labouring at. He made a forward step to recover his balance, and fell sheer down the wall upon the stones below. His consciousness was not gone; he had not fainted; he was not stunned. He struggled up, but fell again instantly; his legs bore no weight whatever. What, were they numbed? Yes, numbed surely—try again. No; no weight whatever, and the horrible pain. Are they broken? Never, never—yes, that is the horrible truth—broken—helpless.

"Am I what I was one minute ago?" he thought. "What pain; it grows to agony—help, help, I say! and the water coming on to suck me in, to come and go, come and go over me till I die. I won't die so—poor Elinor!"

He tried to move; those free limbs a minute ago were now useless and agonising logs, tied to the living will; but the strong will moved them, he grasped the stone and earth with his hands, and dragged himself to the steps, which were just to be seen in the darkness. On the lowest he sate, and gnawed his lip for pain. The water was half way to his knees, and the swell of the next wave rose as high as his breast. He set his hands firmly on the step, and raised himself one more. The crushed limbs were dragged after him by the torn flesh and ligament. One knee was useful still, and setting that and his hands to work, he found out how to climb the dreadful steps, and neither daring nor desiring to pause, mounted to the very top by one well-sustained effort of his will. He had six-and-twenty steps from top to bottom to surmount. He could hardly have climbed much quicker with his free limbs, than he did in this ecstasy of agony; but once there, and once having paused, nature refused to make another effort. The nerves had sunk from their tension, and what they had just accomplished seemed incredible.

But while he lay thus, and he had lain probably a quarter of an hour, a sound struck his ear of human voices, and he recognised the plashing of a boat approaching the pier; then hope gave him life again, and he called loudly. The instant stillness showed that his voice had alarmed those who were approaching, he thought to hear them in another moment push off from the pier, and leave him to his fate. He called again, "I'm an Englishman badly wounded. I'll give you twenty livres at the Père Pierrot, to carry me there;" for, thought he, they are likely enough to make an end of me, if they think I have money about me, or if I offer too much. He repeated the offer eagerly, as the silence lasted, and as none answered him. Again and again he repeated it; but there was a perfect silence; and strung up as his ear was to every faintest sound, he heard nothing—no departing, no moving, no stirring of the boat—and yet he was plainly alone again.

"Can this last till morning?" he thought, and made an effort to move again; but it was, or seemed to have become impossible. He saw the lights of the town, at a distance which seemed to him beyond hope. He was growing cold and faint, still he stretched and held alive his faculties, and did not lose them, because he would not.* He had lain there he knew not how long, when he thought he heard, and soon was certain, that he heard a girlish voice sobbing. He lay still, and it approached. He feared to frighten it away; as it came nearer he ventured to speak. "My little friend, come here."

Instantly the voice was quite still.

"I am hurt; I beg you to come and help me."

"Papa," said the trembling voice; "pray don't be angry."

"Janet!" he exclaimed; and Janet was at his side.

"What's the matter? Why do you lie there. Are you hurt? Oh, what's the matter?"

"Are you alone?" he asked.

"Yes; I got softly away, for the landlord said there were dangerous places; but mamma did not think you would like to be looked for; but I could not stay then. Papa, papa, what *is* the matter?"

"I have broken my bones, and am likely enough to die, Jeannie, unless you have saved my life indeed, by coming to look for me. Good Jeannie, now mind what I say. Don't cry—run back and call up Capel, without letting your mother know anything about it. Send him here instantly, and tell him to bring M. Lahrotte, the surgeon. Then go to your mother, and say I have broken my leg, neither more nor less, just those words, and that Capel told you, and you know nothing more about it. Make no fuss in

---

* Scott's Journal.

the hotel. Tell Capel to say nothing till he is out of the house, and then to call and send as many people as he pleases. Janet, kiss me. I love your mother—run, but take care."

She obeyed him implicitly; and again he was alone, helpless, defenceless, he who that very night had been independent, and aloof from the world. "I have often thought to die, but never of this," he said; and the nervous feelings of the weak assailed, if they did not conquer, him. A shudder came over him at the idea of the boat he had heard approaching, and which he had never heard go away. He more than once fancied footsteps stealing near him, and which the wind partly concealed. He imagined the blow of the assailant with horror, though an hour ago he would have thought of it with scorn.

In an incredibly short time (and Mr. Ferroll was just, and knew how short it was, though it seemed so long), his servant arrived with help, and he was lifted upon a stretcher and conveyed towards the town. M. Lahrotte met him on the way, his breeches knees unbuttoned, his dressing-gown floating far on the air behind. He asked no questions, just felt the pulse, and ordered the bearer to his own house, which was near at hand. Mr. Ferroll said nothing and was laid upon the floor in the surgeon's room, and the apparatus of the severely healing art quickly prepared.

"I must write first," he said, raising himself on his elbow; "or rather you may begin while I write. Capel, pen and paper;" and Capel obeyed his master, though the surgeon imperiously forbade him.

"My Elinor," he wrote, "I am hurt, but in good hands. Come to me, dearest, when I am settled for the night: and don't come till I send. You see my hand does not shake, so believe that I am neither too much hurt, nor in too much pain.

Your husband,
Paul Ferroll

And, in fact, he controlled his hand to form the letters as usual, though the convulsions of pain involuntarily wrung his frame at intervals.

"At last; have you done?" cried Lahrotte, very angry at the delay. "Thank you—now for it."

The fractures were terrible; one knee crushed, the bone of the other leg sticking through the skin.

"Can you save the leg?" said Mr. Ferroll.

"Yes, yes." said Lahrotte.

"Well, don't cut it off without giving me the choice," said Mr. Ferroll.

The skilful surgeon performed his part with dexterity. The quivering machine was pieced again, the broken frame put together like some frail fine china, and as far as the surgeon was concerned, all independently of the agony which the living subject went through. He was placed in bed, and sent for Elinor; when she came, all the apparatus of pain had been removed; and though he told her the whole truth, he told it with her hand so tenderly held in his, and it was his own living voice that spoke in such fond and soothing accents, that she went through the shock without succumbing to it, without the frail frame he had been so anxiously nursing, losing all the strength it had so recently gained.

The first few days were days of extreme distress. The surgeon could not tell whether the limb most injured must be amputated or not, and Mr. Ferroll knew as well as he what were his doubts. His frame had received so great a shock, that his strong nerves still vibrated, like bells in the gale of a tempest. The ideas within his mind got shape and sound like the vibrations hidden in the bell. "I have thought to die often," he repeated to himself, half aloud, "but never, never thought of this."

This was the thought that haunted him awake; when he slept, or approached to sleeping, the impressions of the dreadful minutes when he lay helpless on the pier, were uppermost. The boat that had approached, and whose retreat he had never heard, was a spectre to him; the impression of foes coming from that mysterious boat to kill him, defenceless, brooded over him. Janet was the person who had interfered between the darkness and him, whose living real voice he had heard; and she it was whom he now involuntarily associated with relief.

"Janet," he would say sometimes, rousing from his troubled sleep, and if she were there to answer him, his thoughts and feelings resumed more easily their natural channel, so that she found her presence was really useful, and no exertion on her part was so much as thought of in comparison with that pleasure, night and day she was by his bedside; he was so important an object in the eyes of all, that her interest quite vanished from their sight, and she was allowed to tax her strength to the utmost. Mrs. Ferroll, who had but so lately revived from excessive exertion of her nerves, resisted in vain this new attack. She had no strength to use, and she sank under her own efforts to put some forth. The doubt, the fear, how so violent a shock might work upon her husband's life, the consciousness that any hour might develop an unfavourable change, overpowered her. When near him, it was impossible for her to prevent the big tears from following one another down her cheek; and she had no voice to answer the tender anxious words which she knew might be the very last she should ever hear. Janet would have comforted her, but had nothing but caresses to offer, and of these she was prodigal; coming at the intervals when she was dismissed from her father's room, to comfort her mother, and as active and diligent in rendering her such service as might make the outside of life easy, as in soothing and sharing the sorrow within.

This helpfulness of Janet's greatly took the fancy of the doctor. He rejoiced in seeing her always at hand, always able to do any service, however disagreeable; always neat, always pretty. The doctor was seldom without a project; and it came into his head that he might make a match between his son and his patient's daughter, much to the advantage of the former.

"Mademoiselle," said he to Capel, Mr. Ferroll's servant, "is a very serviceable young lady; I dare say she has money also?"

But Capel was an English, not a French servant, and far from confidential. "Yes, sir."

"How many brothers has she, pray?" asked M. Lahrotte.

"None, sir."

"An only daughter?"

Capel did not answer at all, only went on rubbing the table bright.

"By your laws," said Lahrotte musingly, "does the daughter or the proprietor's brother succeed to the fortune?"

"Can't tell, indeed, sir."

"Mr. Ferroll has brothers?"

"No, sir."

"And plainly he is rich? You send to Bordeaux, Mr. Capel, regardless of expense, whenever your master takes the smallest fancy, or whenever I so much as suggest something that may be useful."

"Yes, sir."

"Where is Mr. Ferroll's home pray, when he is at home?"

"The Tower, sir."

"The Tower? oh, yes, I know where the Tower is. Your master is guardian of the Tower is he, where you keep traitors, and cut off their heads?"

Capel resorted to silence, not understanding the flight M. Lahrotte's imagination had taken.

"Has Mr. Ferroll anything to do in their trials then?" asked Lahrotte.

CAROLINE CLIVE

"No, sir."

"But he takes pleasure, perhaps, in seeing that kind of spectacle?"

"No, sir."

"Does mademoiselle see them also?"

"No, sir."

"Do *you* see them pray, Mr. Capel?"

"What, sir?"

"The heads cut off?"

"No, sir."

"And pray what brought a guardian of your famous Tower to this remote part—an English whim?"

"No, sir, the packet-boat."

"Ha, ha," quietly laughed Lahrotte to himself, "how thick he is. But I mean, was the money spent a little too fast in England, and so was it useful, perhaps, to come where money goes a great way, where lodging is two francs instead of two English pounds?"

"I don't know the charges, sir."

"But Mr. Ferroll does."

"Don't know, sir."

M. Lahrotte shrugged his shoulders, and could not understand him; but he felt certain the Ferrolls were rich—rich at least for the Landes, and yet, perhaps, embarrassed a little, and not unwilling to leave their handy little English girl in a house which would become her own, when he, an old man, should die. He wrote, therefore, to his son to leave his college for the next three months, and to take up his residence for the time under the paternal roof—a summons young César Lahrotte was willing enough to comply with. He was very little like his Roman namesake; to hear them call César, and to see this long-haired quiet lad approach, one could not but think at first of the fate the same sound may go through in the world. To have belonged to the man at whom the world grew pale, and now to belong to the lad who grew pale at everybody in the world. And yet young Lahrotte was merely simple, not a fool. In book-learning he was very much advanced; and having been extremely well taught at school, he was in a fair way to be ready for any mode of earning his bread which his father should fix upon.

M. Lahrotte introduced him to the sick bed of Mr. Ferroll, and was anxious to show him off to the greatest advantage both before the father and daughter. But the young man sat with his hands crossed on his knee, his head on one side, and his mouth a little open, answering all that Janet tried to say to him before she had finished, and before he could have understood her, with an "Oh, yes, mademoiselle," which thoroughly disheartened her in her attempts. Mr. Ferroll was rather amused than otherwise by the embarrassment both of his daughter and his guest; and he perceived that the young man felt relieved whenever he himself addressed some question to him on the subject of his education; and it occurred to him to turn César to account, by making him a reader of such books as Janet could not undertake. Before the end of his first visit, therefore, he had put a Latin author into his hand, and before the end of the reading was pleased with him, for he read with understanding, and gave the hearer the satisfaction of going along both with the author and the reader.

"Come again, will you," he said, "to-morrow? I can't manage that book comfortably in my present position, and your reading is very useful to me." So young César was sent by his father every morning, whether he wanted to go angling in the river, or catching crabs on the shore, and sometimes wished he need not have gone to read; but it did not occur to Mr. Ferroll to inquire whether it suited César or not. The father and son came to an understanding on the matter. "Persevere, my dear," said M. Lahrotte; "Mr. Ferroll is very rich, and very proud; he will not like to be under obligation to anybody, and he will make you a present, or he will advance you to some good place."

"Yes, father."

"Does the reading go much against you, César?"

"No, I am sometimes interested in it; but this morning I was just in the midst of a shoal of little fish, when the tide was leaving."

"That is rather childish for a boy of your age," said the father, frowning. "You are of an age to think of better things; you might even keep house yourself if you had a wife." César laughed.

"Why not, César? I have sometimes thought that the little Ferroll might be a match for you; she has money, and she has certainly beauty."

César looked at his father, doubting if such could really be his meaning; and when he saw no symptoms of the contrary, the idea fell upon him, as if some one had proposed that he should have been king of France, or bishop of the diocese.

"Miss Ferroll, father! yes, she is rich, and she's beautiful, that's very certain. Why, of course, she is to marry an English milord, not me—me who am at school, me whom she sees come in and out like the little dog."

"In what way do you mean?"

"Oh, I *am* a little dog to her."

"Don't be too sure of that, my boy—rich as these people seem, there's no doubt they must be embarrassed for money, or they would not be here. Mr. Ferroll's appointments in the Tower of London are, I doubt not, great, but possibly the chief part may die with him, and then, though I firmly believe he leaves considerable sums behind him—for he has never felt any anxiety about his wife, and daughter, while in his present danger—then I say, a husband ready provided for the pretty young girl may not be without attraction for the prudent father. And you, César, don't think too little of yourself; you are your father's only child, and your father has not spent his long life in vain. This little property of ours, this jewel of a house, and three fields, let us say they are worth twelve thousands francs; in the bourse at Paris let us say there are six thousand more—my pension, you know, is two thousand; enough to live upon certainly, so that much of what is besides, multiplies and accumulates, and when I die, César, all this is yours—you hear me, my son."

César heard with all the enjoyment which the sudden possession of a new sense could give. To see himself in the light of a rich man, of a good match, as a man to be somewhat esteemed on account of his expectations, was as delightful, as it had been hitherto by the prudent reserve of his father a secret to him. He had been taught that he must depend upon his own exertions, and that his hard work at school was essential to the future support of his life; and, indeed, nothing but the necessity of raising his self-esteem to the point of aspiring to Janet could have induced his father to reveal, and even exaggerate, those possessions which would one day descend from his own hands to those of the young Lahrotte.

But it was with less confidence that he approached the subject with Mr. Ferroll; for however plausible the scheme seemed when he had it all his own way in his own head, it lost some of its appearance of ease, when it came to be submitted to a less prejudiced eye. Lahrotte was sitting by the bed-side of his patient, and to-day he had not taken any pains to present the case in its most favourable point of view; not that he said anything to give alarm, but he insensibly, nay unconsciously to himself, let the conversation take rather a sad tone, feeling that the project he had to propose was rather a remedy in case of evil than a positive good. "In my old age," he said, "I am quite contented indeed to be at rest. I would not be young again, sir, I would not be what I was, when I expected to die field-marshal, nay, king if you will, even if all those expectations might be fulfilled."

"You are like a man in sight of the inn for the night, and glad of it, though it be not quite the grand resting place you expected."

"Exactly, sir; I have seen too much of the discontentment that goes with the attainment of the highest wishes—men who get what they have always wanted, want more—it is best to get some good thing one did not want, though it be less than the good one first proposed to get."

"Let me see," said Mr. Ferroll, smiling; "if you had been made field-marshal you would have been discontented, you would have wished to become the emperor; but you are pleased at being the first gentleman in Pontaube, because to be so, never entered your head."

"And at having a son of whom I may be justly proud."

"Aye; your son—domestic affections take the place of ambition."

"Yet ambition is not extinct since it has an object in my son; I don't say I look for any wonderful elevation for him—he is my only treasure, I am old, and wish to see him settled near me. My means are, and will be, his means; and to see him marry a lady whom his heart and my reason should approve, would be the summit, I confess, of my desires."

"Marry! oh, you take that line for him? what, has he fallen in love? no, no; I understand now, you have cast your eyes on Jeannie for him."

M. Lahrotte coughed and took a pinch of snuff—the unveiling of his project was rather abrupt. Mr. Ferroll was silent, and he was obliged to say something. "Miss Ferroll, sir, is a lady. . ."

"A child rather," said her father, "about whom no doubt her mother has formed many ambitious designs; but not I. Your idea is not a bad one; it is new to me, that is all; but it strikes me, as having advantages."

"If you knew my son as I do. . ." said Lahrotte.

"Of course—of course."

"If you knew the state of my affairs. . ."

"Yes; and if you knew mine." Lahrotte looked a little anxious.

"As for money," said Mr. Ferroll, after a moment or two, "there would be plenty; in this cheap country they would be lords."

"Then you would not consider it indispensable that she should marry in England?"

"By no means whatever."

"And without great wealth, an honest competence might, without presumption, be offered her?"

"Oh yes, an honest competence would do very well, considering what besides her own would be."

"And to my son, sir, you see no objection?"

"Not I; but it is not I who shall marry him."

"So young a lady. . ."

"Oh, but young ladies have their own wills in England; I don't answer anything for Jeannie; myself only I can speak about; and as far as I know, on so sudden a view of the matter, there are advantages in it."

Lahrotte was surprised as much as he was pleased by this reception of his hint; indeed, the hint had been converted into a positive proposal, a thing which he had not anticipated, but at which he was much delighted. He told his son what had passed, and César was less surprised than he was; for ever since the conversation in which his father had revealed his undreamed of expectations, his thoughts had been running more upon his own unexpected importance than on the merits of anybody else.

When he saw Janet again, he meant to wear the air of a prosperous lover, but in her total unconsciousness of his pretensions, she treated him with such quiet superiority, and seemed so entirely uninterested in what became of him, that his success was bounded by his own meditations; and he sometimes pursued these triumphantly with an imaginary Janet, while the real Janet by his side was the last person to whom he would have dared address anything aloud beyond the ordinary forms of conversation. It startled him occasionally from the most agreeable day-dreams to have her find something to say to him; and the habitual "Oh, yes, mademoiselle," with which he answered her, was quickly said and quickly forgotten, to pursue his own dream, of a parlour belonging to himself in the paternal house, with a rich wife sitting opposite to him sewing.

Lahrotte thought it would promote courtship to send Miss Ferroll out walking with César, and to do her good, as he explained it to her mother, he prescribed an early walk every morning by the sea-side, and César was then to protect her from the dogs or boys of the town. Mrs. Ferroll had no objection, César being in her eyes, very much on a level with the dogs and boys; and Mr. Ferroll laughed and asked Janet if it was not good-natured in the young man to be found regularly, thus early at her service. Janet sometimes walked and sometimes stayed at home; and gave herself a good deal of trouble, to find subjects on which César could say anything. "Are you obliged to be up very early at your pension, Mr. César?"

"Very early," said César.

"At what o'clock?"

"Five, or half-past, mademoiselle."

"Do you like being up so early, Mr. César?"

"I don't mind it, mademoiselle."

"Do all the scholars get up equally early?"

"All, mademoiselle."

Early rising was pretty well exhausted, and they walked on in silence. "The steamboat is come in I suppose," said Janet, observing a few people advancing from the pier, bearing parcels, or a hamper, and one man walking along with an umbrella in his hand.

"Yes," said César; "the tide is high at seven this morning; they could come alongside the pier early."

"Yes, so they could," said Janet. At that moment she stopped walking altogether, and César got ahead of her without observing it; then turned round to see what had become of her, and Janet ran by him, and up to the man walking with an umbrella, saying eagerly, "Oh, Hugh, what is it you really? How are you? how are you?"

"How d'ye do, Janet?" said young Bartlett, for it was himself. "I heard all about Mr. Ferroll, so I came over to see him. How is he?"

"Oh, papa is so much better; and it is very good-natured of you indeed. I am very glad to see you."

"Is *he*?"

"Is he what?"

"Glad?"

"Oh, he will be of course, when he knows you are come. Are you tired, Hugh? When did you set out?"

"Not tired, certainly; but very dusty you see. Can I have a room somewhere, do you think, Janet?"

"Oh, yes; there's an inn close by us. We are at Monsieur Lahrotte's. . . Oh, dear. . . That is Mr. César Lahrotte—Mr. Bartlett," introducing them. "We are at Mr. César Lahrotte's father's, who has been extremely clever, and most kind about poor papa."

"Perhaps all this will make you come back sooner—won't it?" said Hugh, walking slowly away by Janet's side, and both of them quite forgetting César, who stood looking at them a little while, and then went to search for crabs in the ebb of the tide.

"Perhaps; papa can't travel you know, so we might as well, and better, come back and be quiet at the Tower."

"You'd be sorry not to go into Spain and Italy?"

"No, indeed; I don't think I like travelling very much. I thought I should have liked it better."

"Indeed; indeed, Janet? Why don't you like it?"

"I can't tell hardly. I often think of the Tower, and how cool it must be, and how the flowers are coming out, with nobody to look at them."

"That they don't exactly, for there's hardly a day but what I find myself in your garden."

"Well, but even you are away now."

"You'd be glad if the flowers could come to you?"

"Not so glad as to see you," said Janet. "I'm very glad to see you."

So she was—so was Mrs. Ferroll. A familiar face in the monotonous place, a friendly action performed in their favour, a friend come from so far on account of the interest he felt in them, was very acceptable to these female hearts. Less impression seemed to be made on Mr. Ferroll. When he heard of Hugh Bartlett's arrival, he said, "Pshaw! what unnecessary trouble;" and though he received him courteously, there was something in his manner which threw back any self-confidence or hope to please, which there might be in the young man's feelings. "You are going to see the world, are you?" said he. "Do you propose crossing the Pyrenees, or going by sea?"

"I have not exactly thought," said Hugh, embarrassed, for he had no object in the world except to see Janet, and Janet's father.

"You had better go over the mountains then, and get to the east coast of Spain. There is very fine country to be seen."

"I hope you will be better soon," said Hugh.

"I? oh, yes, in time. *We* shall go back home when I can move."

"I should be glad if I could be of any use to you."

"Oh, thank you, thank you; don't you trouble yourself about us. We shall all do very well."

"Without me?" said Hugh; "yes, I know you will—but *I* can't. . ."

"And then," said Mr. Ferroll, interrupting him, "I advise you to go on into the East. It will be a good thing for you to travel a little, as you don't intend to stay any longer at Oxford."

"I have no thought of travelling," said the young man, doggedly.

"Well, I would if I were you; but even to do as much as you are doing is good. You must go into the Pyrenees at all events; and before you go, I will look over some books I have, for an excellent guide to the

Mountains. I am afraid I can't do it to-day, but perhaps you are not in such haste as that."

Hugh answered nothing at all. It made his heart go backward to hear the plans of Mr. Ferroll for his departure from among them, and for a totally separate interest, which he and Janet were to pursue. He and Janet! who he thought ought to have but one path in life. "And why not?" he repeated to himself. "If I could gain her love, where am I so greatly deficient? I have done no great wrong in the world. I am young; but I shall mend of that. I have got an estate, which is not anything very wonderful to be sure—I don't mean it is; but it would make my Janet comfortable. I wish I knew more history, and Greek, and chronology; but then she never seems to care whether I do or not; but I suppose that must be what Mr. Ferroll means. I do wish I had read more," continued he, and he took up a book which lay on the table—a history of Rodriguez, King of Spain. He read a page and a-half, asked himself whether the Moors were still in Spain—forgot to answer—thought of Janet's light activity in climbing the rocks, and walked out to the pier, where he meditated while he made ducks and drakes in the water.

"That young fellow," said Mr. Ferroll, to his wife, as she sate by his bedside, "has got some fancy about Janet into his head—ridiculous!"

"Poor boy—ridiculous!" said Mrs. Ferroll; for such was the accepted mode of treating the subject.

"When does he go away?" said Mr. Ferroll. "You must hasten him—will you?"

"How can I, Paul? He does no more harm here than at the Tower, does he?"

"Harm—oh, no; only Janet is such a child, that she might be flattered by anybody in the world who thought himself in love with her; and it is just as well to avoid scenes."

"Oh, she is as you say, such a child; besides she knows. . ."

"What does she know, Elinor?"

"Why; she knows Hugh is not the kind of person. . . indeed she has never thought at all."

"I like the way parents dispose of their children here. They still settle the marriage, and then show the children to each other; and being the first thing of the kind that has occurred to either, they of course agree."

"It is not the way *we* married."

"No, indeed; there are exceptions of course, and our way would not do for the rule, let me tell you that."

"Except that I never for a moment ceased to love you through all that bitter trial."

"Nor I you, Elinor."

"You only married another woman," said Elinor, smiling, and caressing his hand.

"Yes, what a madman; how desperate, how frantic of me, and of that poor woman! Elinor, there are some things one has done, which as one grows older, one feels could not be done again; no, not even for the blessedness of being your husband."

"It was not a good plan with a view to that, to marry another," said Elinor, again smiling.

Mr. Ferroll looked at her inquiringly, and then smiled also. "I should not be sorry," he said, "to see Janet marry César."

"César! Janet—César Lahrotte! the doctor's son. Who do you mean?"

"I thought we were talking just now about Janet marrying; it is not necessary to marry in England. I even think for a woman, France is a better country. In the first place, she would be very rich here, instead of moderately so in England. If married young, she would be safe from all speculators upon her fortune. César is a good lad, a dutiful son."

"But such a young cub, such a child; why, Ferroll, if you want her married young, and rich, and to a dutiful son, what's your objection to Hugh?"

"Hugh," said Mr. Ferroll, the colour passing over his face; "oh, that's quite out of the question."

"Well, perhaps, but César is more so; oh, inexpressibly more."

"My dearest, then let César be; I am sure I don't care for him."

"Hugh has more sense if he has less reading; has good connections; he loves Janet I do believe as far as such a young lad can."

"Aye, as you say; they are both mere children. Oh, it's not to be thought of." With that he begged his wife to read to him, and the conversation ceased.

With Janet also he had a word to say against Hugh Bartlett. The young squire had not profited much by the teachings he had received; and when he was forced into display of his proficiency, the exhibition was not in his favour. Thus the few words of French which necessity wrung from him in company with the Lahrottes, generally contained three-fourths of mistake. Mr. Ferroll did not spare his colloquial deficiencies in talking of him to his daughter. "César reads with a good intonation enough," said he; "he read the passage I wanted, in Les Horaces, so that I could enjoy it."

"I am glad of that, papa."

"That's what Hugh says, poor dear Hugh. 'Je suis très heureux de cela;' he says to Lahrotte—'très heureux de cela!' poor dear Hugh." Janet answered nothing; but her thoughts were unlike what her father supposed. "It is bad French, to be sure; but César could not speak to *him* even in *bad* English."

Things went on in an uninterrupted course notwithstanding these conversations. Mr. Ferroll's will was so strong, that it habitually carried all before it, and being certain of attaining its end, he neglected the intermediate steps. Whether Janet married César or not, he did not care, but that she should not marry his young neighbour was a fixed point with him. He did not trouble himself about what happened in the time between; whether they saw much or little of each other he did not care; they did not disobey even his wishes in doing so, nor did he offer any other kind of obstacle to their meeting, except an habitual attack upon the young man's intellectual acquirements, with which he amused himself, and never met with so much as contradiction from Janet. But Janet was happy in walking and talking with her old companion; they were both so young, and they were so intimate, and they had their homes and their interests to converse about; and they climbed difficult places with strength of limb and lightness of heart, and were never tired with long walks, or with rides upon queer obstinate horses. Hugh was very seriously in love; but he could never approach the subject with Mr. Ferroll, though the time for his departure came near, and he felt that he could not prolong it. He had fixed it himself when he came, at what seemed to him then a considerable distance, and one which would certainly see Janet his affianced bride; but now it seemed coming very quickly, and nothing had been followed up by love avowals, for she still looked on the subject as one which it was *naughty* to talk about; one forbidden in the nursery, and nothing had released her from the obligation of avoiding it, more than when he called her once his little wife, and both had incurred such serious displeasure. Marrying was far from her thoughts—to change her maiden state, and her home, had never been the subject of her talk; she loved Hugh kindly, and so she did his sisters. Hugh himself had more knowledge of the world, and perhaps the unaccountable difficulties of his present pursuit added to his inclination for it. It perplexed him to find out why Mr. Ferroll so objected to him. "Your father advises me to go to the Pyrenees; to travel down the Mediterranean, and across somewhere into Africa. I don't mean to do it, Janet."

"I would, I think, if I were a man."

"And I would go where you go, Janet. If you travel I will travel, but I'll go home when you do."

"If you do, I shall be very glad."

"Shall you, dear Janet; what really?"

"Oh, yes, really."

"When's your birthday?"

"The 19th of October."

"And mine—my coming-of-age birthday, I mean—is the year after next, 15th of December. You'll be at home then."

"Oh, no doubt, I think."

"And I shall have learned a great deal before I am of age; I am no boy now, and older men than he treat me as a man, and look upon me as one. Does Mr. Ferroll like people to be in Parliament?"

"Yes, though he never would be a member himself; but I remember hearing him say to Lord Ewyas, that he ought to put his son into Parliament as soon as he came of age."

"Did he? Well, I always thought of getting in myself—that is, if I could. I will; I'll talk about it with Rodenham when I get home. Your father will hear of my first speech in Parliament."

"What will it be about?"

"Oh, Janet, I don't know, but perhaps, then, when he sees I can speak to an audience like that, he will have a higher opinion of me than he has now."

"I am sure, I think, he has a high opinion now."

"You are sure, you think, Janet? Ah! I wish he had, then you would have."

"I am sure I have," said Janet, frankly.

"And something more, my dear, dear Janet; something answering to all the love there is here for you?"

Janet looked round frightened; then answered as it had been instilled into her to answer, "I love you, of course, Hugh, quite as much as I do any of your sisters."

"That has been taught you," cried Hugh; "it is not the natural answer of such a girl as you. Do they say then you are never to marry?"

"Nobody says anything about that," said Janet.

"What, do they never say, 'When Janet marries,' or 'when you are married,' or things of that sort?"

"Oh, yes, they may say that perhaps."

"Only it must not be me," said Hugh, in a low voice, as if commenting to himself; "their nearest neighbour, their most intimate acquaintance, the most natural person in the world to marry their daughter, if they did but like me—what can it be? Janet," he said abruptly, "did you ever hear your father say what he thought it most necessary for a man to know who wants to get into Parliament?"

"I have heard him say that a good knowledge of the History of England was indispensable, and of the constitutional history."

"Did he? I'll read it again then; Hume and Mrs. Macauley, and a great many more; you know, they are all on the right hand of the halldoor into the library."

These, and similar resolutions, had an ultimate object, of course; they referred to his secret suit with Janet, which was so unaccountably checked even in the bud by Mr. Ferroll's distaste to it. But Hugh, unable as he was to perceive any valid reason for the opposition, ever looked to the future as certain to produce a better result, and aimed at this or that effort, hopeful that it would be the one that would bring him into favour; but one morning he had taken a walk with César, and was standing looking at the young man eagerly employed in setting a brick trap for little birds, the produce of the traps lying by, in the person of six sparrows, which César said would make an excellent ragout.

"How childish he is," thought Hugh; and as he thought so, César said, "I wonder if Mademoiselle Jeannette knows how to cook them; she must learn from Mère Marguerite."

"Why so?" asked Hugh, not seeing the concatenation.

"On pense à nous marier; vous le savez bien sans doute," said Cé.

Hugh's ideas, both English and French, were overthrown, and driven to utter incomprehensibility and confusion, and he found no other word in which to express them than this one—"Quoi?" César looked up from his trap, and coloured; but he again asserted the fact, giving it to be understood that the two fathers had come to the arrangement.

"Et Janet?" said Hugh, struggling for some French. "Sait Mademoiselle Janet, qu'elle doit vous marier?"

"M'épouser?" said César: "mais, je ne vous dirais pas."

"Et pour quoi ne direz vous moi pas?" cried Hugh, vehemently.

César shrugged his shoulders, "Mais parceque je ne sais pas," said he.

The young Englishman felt like a man knocked down, and unable to recover his dizzy senses. César was again busy with the trap, and Hugh walked away, hardly knowing that he did so. "What does the fellow mean?" thought he. "He says he *won't* tell me, and *but* because he does not know. What does he pretend to mean, marry? épouser, as he calls it—épouser, indeed—épouser César Lahrotte; yet he is too great a fool to invent it all." The superior advantage of a match with himself, except so far as for some reason or other he was hateful to Mr. Ferroll, could not, and did not escape his common sense; why did Mr. Ferroll so dislike him? That evening was the last but two that he was to spend at Pontaube. He begged Janet to walk with him when Mr. and Mrs. Ferroll were engaged together, she in reading to him, he very little desirous of the presence of any other person. Therefore, he heard Hugh's request, and Janet's acquiescence, with indifference, nodding at once his approbation to his daughter's inquiring look, before she agreed to the walk. It was a still, fine evening; the sea broke quietly along the beach, the set sun still coloured the waves, the gentle air came with delicious coolness after the heat of the day. They walked quietly on, and Hugh was less full of talk than usual. "To-day seemed a long way off when I came first," he said at last, "but here it is, and the day after to-morrow close at hand, and I cannot prevent it; I did not think it would have been such a day as this."

"It is come very soon," said Janet; "I wish we were going back too."

"And perhaps you will never come back."

"Never come back—why so?"

"Do you really know nothing that should keep you here for ever—that should part us entirely—that would make us no longer friends?"

"What do you mean, Hugh?"

"Nothing about César Lahrotte?"

"Poor little César; no, he can have nothing to do with anybody, I should think."

"Janet, I tell you the truth; it is too true, your father, Mr. Ferroll, means you to marry him." Janet stood still, and fixed her eyes full on Hugh's face for a few seconds; that was before she realized the truth of what he said to her—then a blush began to spread over her face, the first Hugh had ever caused, and suddenly she hid it with her hands, and turned away from him speechless.

"Will you marry him, Jeannie?"

"Oh, what can my father mean?" she cried; "to marry anybody has been the very last thing he let me think of."

"Yet he means you for that young idiot; he means to leave you behind with those base people in a foreign land; in a state of life of which you have no idea; you, Janet, whom. . ." Hugh took her hand, and Janet clung to his like one who wants protection.

"I can't do that, Hugh; I cannot stay here. I care for nothing here; yet, if he has resolved, I shall do it. Oh, I hope he has not resolved."

"Janet, you know that I love you better than anything in the world. I will defend you even against Mr. Ferroll, if you do but say you want defence."

"Only, Hugh, I cannot stay here."

"And will you not go with me, dear, dearest Janet? It is not a time to be children any longer. I have a right to ask you, and you have a right to listen to me, and this time I do solemnly, earnestly entreat you, my Janet, say whether you can love me." Janet was silent, too full and hasty a crowd of feeling was breaking through the barrier of her thoughts. "We've been friends always," said he, "dear friends; you know me and all my faults, and you must know also how dearly, deeply, how long I have loved you—be content to love me in return; to confess that you love me; I think, I hope, I almost believe you can one day say so." And truly Janet's eyes were unbandaged, and she began to know it in her secret soul. The idea "why should not I?" had crept in; the unanswerable question which as yet Mr. Ferroll had kept unasked.

"Yes, it is true," cried Hugh, pressing her in his arms; "without words you have answered me—you will be, you are my own Janet. Now I can go boldly to your father, and I will; I have a right to go."

But Janet withheld him. She felt her father's eye upon her, and heard him ask if it were really true that she loved this young man; and she knew perfectly well she should say no. "Don't go; I shall never see you again if you do; I can't disobey him. I have never thought of it," said Janet. And Hugh in vain besought, remonstrated, grew angry, grew miserable. Janet wept, Janet trembled, but he felt that the idea of belonging to him was as yet too new and unfixed to give her courage to assert it. The nearer be brought it, the more she shrank from it; and at the last he was forced to confess to himself that the miserable expedient of having recourse to time, was the best that could suggest itself, though time to a young man seems the very dullest comforter that exists in the world.

CAROLINE CLIVE

Hugh went away. Mr. Ferroll saw the parting between him and his daughter, and understood how matters stood between them. They, however, thought their affair unknown to anybody. That day Mr. Ferroll talked about him kindly and justly; Janet's feelings which were alive enough, were not injured by anything he said; by the end of the day they were soothed, and at the same time further than ever from opposing themselves to her father's will. He had talked confidentially to her, and joined her in conversation with her mother, telling both, particulars of his affairs, letting Janet know something of the fortune she was to expect from him, and discussing with both, the project he had for an essay, of which the materials were before him, and in displaying which, his fine imagination and strong power caught the mind of his hearers. He said nothing directly about forbidding any intercourse between her and Hugh; he did not see her receive the letter from him which came a few days after, but he saw her blush when he purposely made a wrong guess as to whither the young man was gone. He said, "Has not Hugh written to you, Janet?" and she felt so terribly, desperately, grateful to him for not asking to see his letter, that the only one she wrote to her young lover, was to beseech him not to write again.

The post which that morning brought several letters to Mr. Ferroll, seemed to have a malign influence over him. He opened them in the presence of Mrs. Ferroll, and one after the other gave them to her, except a few which were bills or receipts, and which he put by on the other side. Janet, who watched him unobserved with the most assiduous care, saw him, as he read one of these, colour for an instant with a sudden flush, and gnaw his lip, though the betrayal of his feelings was but momentary. That letter went aside with the uninteresting ones; Mrs. Ferroll did not know it was there; but before long, he contrived a pretence for being alone, and then he took the letter out again from its concealment, and read it deliberately, and sadly through.

When M. Lahrotte came to him that day, he told him that it was very possible there might be an absolute necessity for him to go to England.

"Which is quite impossible," said the surgeon.

"No; at least it is not impossible that I should try. It may be more impossible to stay; but I tell you, in order that you may do anything you think necessary in preparation."

"But what kind of business could that be which should oblige you to kill yourself?" asked Lahrotte.

"To tell you the truth, a person's life may depend on my journey. My personal testimony may be essential respecting a circumstance which occurred when I was a young man; and if it be so, I will go at every kind of risk—my life, and anything else. But for my part, I don't believe the journey need kill me? Do you think it would?"

"Kill—no, perhaps not; but all hopes of a cure would be at an end. You must be lame for life."

"Well, life may not be very long," said Mr. Ferroll "But I *will* go, if necessary."

"It would be grievous for mademoiselle." said Lahrotte, after a pause, "if any evil should happen to you."

"Very, very," said Mr. Ferroll.

"And if you could resolve upon the scheme I have suggested."

"Well, I'll tell you frankly, that if I must go to England, it would be a remarkable relief to me to leave her behind, a married woman, with a house where she could receive whomsoever she liked—her mother, or any one. If things were managed as easily with us as with you, it should be done; but our girls learn traditionally to choose for themselves, and father and mother have in fact nothing but a veto, and not always that."

"At all events your veto is not upon my son?" said the surgeon.

"Oh, dear, no."

Nothing more was said at this time on the subject. M. Lahrotte was very anxious to keep his patient quiet, and would not have said so much about his personal danger, had not his mind been very much upon securing the handy and moneyed young Englishwoman. He found Mr. Ferroll's pulse was higher than it had been since the first days of the accident, and he hastened to close the conversation, and hoped to repair what ill might have been done by offering to send César to read to him. But Mr. Ferroll refused, and said he would be alone for a little while. When they returned to him, his mind seemed to have regained its perfect equilibrium, that indeed had hardly been disturbed for an instant; but the effect of hurried and eager thoughts on his body at this moment was like the too hasty swelling of a flame within a ball of glass. It set in motion causes which the frame was not powerful enough to resist; the impetuous blood flowed too unrestrainedly through the weak vessels; fever came on, sudden though slight twitchings ran through his frame, and he himself knew the danger that was arising of some strong convulsion in the disorganised nerves, ending all in a few moments. He called Lahrotte to him, and pointed out the symptoms, or rather told that he himself had observed them, and asked him how far the danger was imminent. The surgeon instinctively replied there was none. Mr. Ferroll shook his head impatiently. "Nay," he said, "don't treat me like a child. I see and know myself what my state is; but I can't judge so accurately as you, and I really should be glad to have your opinion whether I shall die or not."

Thus adjured, Lahrotte resolved on a finer artifice than the base denial of all danger. He considered what it would be best to say, taking into account the kind of patient he had to deal with, and arranged his ideas accordingly. "I think," he said, "that something agitates your mind, and causes this temporary alteration for the worse. Is not it so?"

"Not at all. A letter that I got made my thoughts surge for a short time; but the subject is one very habitually before me. It does not agitate me the least in the world now."

"No; but it has done so, and your frame does not recover its equilibrium after any disturbance in its present state."

"That's it, I dare say. And you think it never may, I suppose?"

"I don't deny the possibility."

"But do you think I shall die? or don't you think so?" said Ferroll, very impatiently.

"I think," said Lahrotte, "I believe if you will have my sincere opinion. . ."

"That I *shall*," said Mr. Ferroll, in a voice so suddenly calm, that it was like that of a person relieved from pain.

"This eccentric Saxon wishes to die," said the surgeon to himself. "Certainly, sir, it may be so," he said aloud in a melancholy voice, and his quick gray eye watched his patient covertly.

Mr. Ferroll heaved a sigh—a sigh of relief rather than any other expression, as M. Lahrotte thought. "Call my little Jeannie, will you?" said he, in a quieter voice than he had yet spoken. "I've something to say to her alone; and then come back if you please." M. Lahrotte did all he was desired, first conveying a few dark drops into a glass of water, and administering them to his patient without making any observation.

"Janet," said Mr. Ferroll, "I'm not so well to-day as I have been; and I've some idea I may die. Why, Janet, of course you've thought of that as possible. Now listen—your mother, some little time ago, would have been firm enough to hear this; but she has suffered, and cannot yet bear to suffer again. She must suffer, alas! but she won't bear up at first. You will have to do all—therefore remember, if I die, to write directly to Mr. Harrowby. You know his direction, don't you?"

"Yes," said the trembling girl.

"He knows what to do; he has all my papers; there are directions at home to apply to him, which Elinor would have found if we had been there; but as we are here, I tell you, which will do as well. I'm very weak. I feel like a man going to rest, Janet."

"Papa, my dear, dear father," said Janet, sinking on her knees beside him.

"Don't you know this?" he said: "a deep sleep after a long day of toil, is what men covet most." Then he added, "When I am dead, marry the one you love best, Janet. Freely, truly, I consent; and now tell Lahrotte I am very easy—he may come or not."

Lahrotte came, felt his pulse, said nothing, but moved softly, and drew the curtains before the window. Janet waited for him outside the door. Words she had not; but her terrified eyes interrogated him. The old man took her hand. "I really think he is so composed by the idea of dying, that he will not die. He seems to have got his will, and getting it, will, I trust, lose it for him again. I suppose he's so afraid of being infirm for life, that death seems to him preferable."

"That must be his thought," said Janet; "but he will—oh, he will live, dear M. Lahrotte?"

"Well, I think so."

Mr. Ferroll after this fell into a deep sleep—partly that he was weak and exhausted—partly that his mind was very much at rest; the dark drops probably contributed. He opened his eyes again upon a world, where his part in the drama seemed to have tired him; and whatever he thought on the subject of his late danger, he expressed no regret or pleasure at escaping it. He received his surgeon's congratulations, and his daughter's joy, with the merest commonplace phrases. One thing which Janet had scarcely noticed at the time, rose to the surface when her memory began quietly to recall the scene gone by. "Marry whom you will," were the words she had heard. She longed to approach that subject, but dared not. Lahrotte was bolder. "Has not the young Englishman been away long enough?" he asked one day; for he had expressed his hope that when Hugh should be gone, Janet would be more favourable to César.

"Nay, César should know that best," said Mr. Ferroll.

"César knows nothing, nor mademoiselle either, I think," said Lahrotte; "children as they are, why not determine for them?"

"That's impossible in my case," said Mr. Ferroll. "There is one thing only I can determine, and that is, that she never—never, I being alive to forbid it, shall marry the young Englishman."

"Well—well, sir, don't agitate yourself about that or anything else."

"Not I; I can carry out my purposes without agitation, I promise you."

"Nevertheless, the other day you suffered from your letter."

"Yes—this ricketty house might have fallen, being at this time so frail; but that would have been a splendid solution to all perplexities. I *was* in perplexity; but I have taken good measures; and they will probably answer."

"I am sorry to hear it—sorry I mean for your embarrassments, and if my advice or even assistance could be of service in any. . . I don't mean in any pecuniary view, I am poor, and I know you are a. . ."

"Oh, I am rich, don't fear it. Janet will make César rich if she marry him, never fear."

But what Hugh had told Janet had frightened her so effectually that if the marriage depended on her loving young César, there were very little hope indeed. She no longer would adventure herself to walk by his side thinking of something to say; she would no longer, when he was sitting in her father's room, seek to keep up a conversation about the manner of laying fishing lines, or trapping mice. She let him shift for himself—he was not now in her eyes a gaunt schoolboy, but a strong enemy, who laid himself open to every sort of passive resistance. César would sit openmouthed as usual, and uncomfortably silent, but Janet would work resolutely at her embroidery and let him feel how dull he was. César would come in the morning and wait an hour for Janet to accompany him as heretofore, while Janet, when forced to walk by her mother's desire to do so, would get up at daylight and be out of the way before he came upon his post. Her father was amused by observing all this, and with no pity to Janet, made this note in his pocket-book:—"Janet went out at four o'clock this morning; I heard her door open. When she came to me afterwards I asked, Did you see César? deep blushes and the alarm of a young fawn. 'I thought he was to walk with you on account of the dogs,' I said. 'I can't think where he was papa—I walked where he generally comes to take care of the dogs and he was not there.' Womanly dissembler! how was he to know you meant to walk at four o'clock in the morning?"

Things went on in this way through the summer, during which Mr. Ferroll recovered, more rapidly than at one time seemed possible, and was able to begin again resuming plans for the disposal of their winter. Hugh had obeyed the injunction not to write Janet, but instead of doing so himself he had made his sisters keep up a close correspondence with her, and by this means gave Janet notice of what he himself was doing, and tried to regulate his movements upon hers; but here again he was baffled. Mr. Ferroll would entertain his family with projects which he was sure would reach Hugh through Janet's correspondence, and the autumn following their arrival at Pontaube, he had talked so much of a visit to Egypt, and seemed so intent upon passing the cold months there that he had heard, and smiled to hear how Hugh had taken a fancy to see the pyramids, and had actually taken measures to leave home for the purpose. "Perhaps we shall meet him," said Mr. Ferroll, and the project went on till Hugh had actually left England; then by some means it died away, Sicily was nearer, and presented many advantages as a winter residence; and at times Athens seemed the more desirable place, and was one which Mrs. Ferroll had never yet seen. Janet had never allowed to herself how glad she should be to see Hugh in case they had met in Egypt, and did not therefore allow that she was very much disappointed not to do so. In fact her strongest wish was for the time when they should all renew their old habits of intercourse at home, and in the course of next summer she was sure both the families would be in their right places just as they used to be, so that she was willing to like every project in a certain degree, and always in reference to the health of one or other parent.

By this time it was the middle of October, it wanted but ten days to that on which Janet would be seventeen; she had grown up insensibly among the closer and more prominent interests of her family, into as lovely a girl as ever eyes beheld—her beauty and herself, however, were quite secondary objects among them—familiarity made them little conscious of the first, and their habits kept the daughter of the house in the background; so that she was like some exquisite specimen of the wild animals of the forest, using those beautiful limbs, exposing that angelic face, as though they were but the commonest clay that can be fashioned, and unconscious what an impression of loveliness they left on the spectator. She was proud of being of use to her father; habituated to do everything for her mother. Praise was rare and valuable, her customary feeling was their superiority, and her own humbler pretensions as less clever, less learned, less accomplished than either of them. It was a suitable healthy feeling for a young girl, and contributed no doubt to her peaceableness and content.

"Jeannie," said Mr. Ferroll, one day when she was alone with him, "I think we shall go home. I shall give up Egypt, and all other travels."

CAROLINE CLIVE

Janet looked up, and coloured deeply; the surprise brought colour into her face. "And mamma?" she said, after a few seconds' pause, during which many thoughts passed through her mind.

"Mamma? what do you mean?" asked her father.

"Would it be good for her, especially at this time of year? I don't think she is very well."

"Where do *you* want to go?" said Mr. Ferroll.

"Where would be best for mamma," said Janet, looking up at her father.

"I do believe it, little daughter," said he; "and come here, and tell me why going home would not be best for her."

"She is not so well as she used to be; she thinks so much of you, of your fall, she is always afraid of something happening."

"Do you think so? Since that stupid accident I have always believed her to be better—nay, well."

"She wishes to seem so; and you have not seen her so much."

"Not observed so much, you mean; you have been observing, it seems. I have been selfish, Jeannie."

"Oh, no, no, my dear papa; you are so patient, so firm."

"Oh, yes, yes, my dear daughter, patience has nothing to do with observation; and you may be right, the Tower may not be exactly the place to amuse and interest her enough; after all, Egypt or Athens may be best."

Janet said no more; but a feeling of great satisfaction came over her that her opinion should be taken, and should have any weight with her father; she enjoyed it all day long, and fancied she was present to her father's mind, and of some use in his councils, until next morning, she heard him in conversation with M. Lahrotte, say, as if nothing had ever passed between him and her, "I have made up my mind to go to England the week after next." In fact, it never occurred to him, however he might listen to another person, to act on any one's opinion but his own. Poor Lahrotte had his own disappointment at this announcement; he still clung to the project about his son, though Mr. Ferroll had long since put it by, among objects upon which he did not care to exercise his will. It was become a mere amusement to him; and when the worthy doctor, on hearing of the proposed departure, made one more forlorn petition for the interests of his son, Mr. Ferroll rather encouraged him than otherwise, to come boldly to the point, and lay his pretensions fully before Janet. "César has never made the proposal; he does not know what effect his silent suit has had on his mistress; perhaps if he were to speak out, he might find that silence alone has been in his way."

"I doubt it," said the doctor: "don't you perceive that she may be said rather to shun than seek his society?"

"I have made some observation of the kind," answered Mr. Ferroll; "still I protest to you that she has never declared any such sentiments to me."

"And after all," said Lahrotte, "you, sir, will look with pleasure on César, as your son-in-law?"

"In all sincerity," said Mr. Ferroll: "let her marry, let me leave her in France, I am contented."

"And madame, she is of the same sentiments?"

"One day she may be."

"I have been thinking," said Lahrotte, "that Mademoiselle Jeannette took great pleasure in her excursions on horseback with the young Englishman, and that if César were to offer her the same amusement, the situation might be one in which an interesting conversation could be well carried on. He shall have my pony, it's very quiet."

"Aye, take care it is quiet," said Mr. Ferroll, "for it would be very awkward to make one's declaration at a gallop, and the gallop against one's will. When will this project come off?"

"I'll arrange it," said the father, pleased at having a scheme to work out, and he returned home to prepare all things for its execution. Janet was surprised next morning to receive an invitation from the doctor to visit the Castle of——, on horseback. He said he had a patient in the neighbourhood, and the ride was one of the prettiest in that part of the country. He omitted to tell her that César was to make one of the party, much less did he say that César was *the* one. Janet looked at her mother; her mother drew up a little, and would have declined; but Mr. Ferroll interposed, "Go if you like, Janet," he said; and Janet did not like, but went. The prudent doctor had determined not to hazard his son alone even on the quiet pony; for he knew that César was much better educated in mind than body, and had some misgivings as to the skill he might evince. The young man, however, was delighted with the project. He was inexperienced enough for a ride to be a treat to him; and in getting himself up for it, it is certain that his mind dwelt more on the excursion than on the project involved. He had no vain fears; on the contrary, he felt himself very much of a man as he talked of what the pony could do, but would not venture to do, if he chose to tighten the rein, and what he and the pony together could do if he chose to let it out. He was busy for half an hour about his straps, sewing on a button, and making a button-hole; he spent some time in tying a string to his cap, and making it fast to his coat, saying, that although it was not probable he should be leaping, or going full gallop, it was better for a horseman to be prepared. He cut himself a switch in the garden, and went down to the stable half an hour before the time of riding, to take precautions about the operation of saddling, though it had been performed there, and on that beast, some thousands of days, and successfully. In fact, he too much neglected pondering on what he was going to say, and gave himself over too devotedly to what he was going to do.

Janet, meantime, unwillingly dressed for riding, and thought of Hugh. She came down stairs step by step, putting on her gloves deliberately; and when she came out upon the door-way, perceived with a little augmentation of disgust that the doctor had smuggled his son into the proposed arrangements. Shy and courteous, however, she greeted him without any manifestation of her feeling, and saw him imagining he assisted her to mount without making him understand that he was much more hindrance than help. For some time they all trotted on together, César bumping along in his saddle, and highly exhilarated with his equestrian exercise. Janet did not know what to say, and M. Lahrotte was intent upon finding an opportunity for leaving her and his son together. But the latter had some latent instinct that he was safest where his pony kept sight of its familiar companion, the horse his father mounted, and defeated the manoeuvre with provoking perversity. "I think," said old Lahrotte, "the plant I was talking of grows on the common there, I'll fetch you a bit;" and was moving away, when to his vexation a horse's feet trotted behind him, and César came up alone, and declared Mademoiselle Ferroll thought he had much better accompany his father.

"Why, what had you said to her?" cried the latter, turning quickly round upon him.

"I said, 'Did not she think you would want me?'"

"Foolish child," cried the father, and rode back to Janet, saying it was hardly worth while to look for the plant just now. Janet assented, and they went on. Presently they came to a nest of cottages clustering on one side of an open heath, which afforded the doctor the pretence, at least, of a patient; and desiring the other two to ride on, he resolutely turned his horse's head in the other direction. But it would not do; five minutes after he heard his name called, and that in no very easy accents, and pulling up abruptly, saw César curbing in his pony with desperate energy, and Janet proceeding by his side at a walk, while the pony irritated by the curb, and anxious to rejoin its companion, evidently gave its rider no small uneasiness. "Mademoiselle thinks," said César, when the doctor turned round and joined them, "that we had better go on to the Castle first altogether; you can call here coming back."

"If you wish it, certainly, my dear lady," said Lahrotte.

"Nay," said Janet, "M. César declared he did not know the way, and asked whether in that case it was not better to wait for you."

"No, *not* wait," said César. "I meant that you. . ."

"Never mind what," said Lahrotte; "let us go together. Awkward!" All together therefore they reached the object of their ride, and dismounting, went under the guidance of the woman who had care of it, to see the whitewashed chateau, and the parlour and entrance room, and polished floors, which made up a respectable dwelling-house, ill described by the English word castle. There was a trellice walk in the garden, however, which was very pretty. The vines hung about it and through it, and at the end was seen a cottage accidentally placed in the vista, which seemed framed by the graceful foliage. Janet, who was hardly at ease, took out a pencil by way of something to do, and in the first page of her pocket-book began a sketch of it. Old Lahrotte walked away humming a tune, as if he were in a reverie—young Lahrotte looked at Janet's progress for a little while, and then went to feed a goat which was tethered in the garden.

"Well, but, César," said his father, "is not this the very moment I have managed for you? is not she alone; have you anything to do but to ask her for your wife?"

"I don't know, father. It is very embarrassing; what can anybody say, except just will you marry me? and that is so short. It does not seem to me she would like it."

"Pshaw! go and sit down by her; get rather too near—perhaps she will say, why do you do that?"

"And what must I answer?"

"What shall you feel?"

"That you told me to do it."

"Is that all?"

"Yes," said César, in a tone as if he had investigated his feelings, and wondered why there should be anything particular there. "Father," said he, resuming the dialogue, "could not you go and do all that? and when she agrees, I shall be ready to keep house, and have a wife, and a servant of our own, and what you like. Indeed, father, I have no objection at all to your plan; but I think it would be better if you settled it."

"I tell you no, César. English girls, I have heard, have no principles like our girls. They are so forward, that they expect before they are married, to be supposed to know the rights of women, much more than they should know; and they are to decide upon questions which, if I had a daughter, should not come into her head, till she was off my hands, and in those of her husband."

"What are those, father?"

"It don't matter. Mr. Ferroll himself can't control that child's choice; and if you are to repay my indulgence, César, if you are to make it worth while to have been allowed this long holiday, if you are to have any hope of an apartment and a servant of your own, you must make up your mind now, or as we ride home, to propose yourself to the young Ferroll as her husband."

"I have no objection, my dear father, I am sure. I should like it—only. . . well, as we ride home—not now," said César, putting off the evil day.

Old Lahrotte gave a sort of sigh, but silently assented, and taking his son's arm, led him away to the house, and there bestowed upon him an overflowing beaker of Bordeaux, putting into his hands a plate of biscuits, and a moderate glass of wine for Janet. The kindly drink did César's heart good, and when they mounted their horses, and began their ride home, his father was cheered to see how gallantly he trotted his pony, and how his tongue seemed loosened to utter observations of various kinds. Janet civilly answered, and even encouraged him, reflecting silently that the ride would soon be over, and that the constraint of conversing with so raw a lad, was repaid by the pleasure it seemed to give his kind old father, so that by degrees they got into a kind of flowing discourse, consisting very much of questions and answers, till old Lahrotte seeing this, gradually fell behind, and whisking suddenly up a lane on one side, was gone before César missed him. Now was César launched on the tide of his destiny; but it was long before he gave himself away to the current. While it was possible he clung as it were to the shore, and indeed resolved in his own mind to say nothing to Janet about his father's project, until the spire of Pontaube should appear over a certain eminence, which he knew well indicated that they were but two miles from home. Meantime, they walked their ponies quietly along; for Janet was waiting for the Doctor, and César was glad to have an honourable release from hard trotting, so that his equestrian feelings were at rest, and he began to say to himself more than once, "It is really very pleasant to talk to her, I think I should like it." At length they arrived at a level piece of ground, where the road ran along an open common, and the soft turf on each side invited them and their horses to turn off upon it.

"I think," said Janet, "it is no use to wait for your father, let us canter on," and putting her horse into quicker motion, she did as she proposed. César was discomposed; the moments were numbered, for the spire rose ever clearer and clearer before them; the subject was delicate, yet he had to rush upon it, when his hands and heart belonged to his pony. Nay, he felt the pony give signs of eagerness to be first, and to take his pleasure along the elastic turf. "Mademoiselle," said he; "mademoiselle, I have something to say to you."

"And that is?" said Janet.

"My father thinks, and I think, that I should make you a husband who would adore you."

"I have not the same idea," said Janet, and impatiently hastened the pace of her horse, which she had been restraining to keep back with César. Then César's pony showed his own will. César felt that fatal feeling too well known to timid and inexpert riders, as if the hinder part of his horse were getting first, and the next moment he was mastered, and away went the pony full gallop. Janet laughed; she was much better mounted, and overtook her lover in a couple of minutes. Adroitly bending down, she seized his rein, and soon pulled up both horses; but she kept his in her hand, and led him along the road. "I will prevent him from running away again," said she, "and we'll talk of something else."

In a few days after this César returned to school, and all the projects of the town of Pontaube concerning the Ferroll family came to an end, for they set off on their way to England.

VI

It was in November that the Ferroll family again took possession of the Tower; not a genial time to move from sunny southern climates to the short days of England. It was on a dank morning of the month, that Mr. Ferroll, leaving his wife and Janet re-arranging their life in the house, walked down to a cottage a little way outside his garden, and inquired for one Martha Franks. There came out a little stout woman some sixty years of age, whom when he saw he drove as it were inside the cottage, and came and sate down opposite to her by the fire. "You could not rest then, on the other side of the Atlantic?" said he.

"No, indeed, sir; I hope your honour won't be angry for not following your advice, but I had such a longing to come over, that one day when I found I had money enough I set off, as it were, all of a sudden, as if a wind out of the desert had driven me."

"I'm not angry; it is all alike to me—but I know you would have been better there."

"Ah, sir, as long as Richard lived he always said the same—he would not come back to a country where he and I was once pointed at as murderers, he said. But it's such a long time ago now, sir; and when Richard was gone, it was so very lonely."

"Why did you write to me for advice, if you were resolved beforehand what to do?"

"No, sir, no, not that; but I wanted your honour's consent to my coming."

"And you did not get it."

"But I thought if your honour was to hear all the reasons from myself—and I can speak much better than writing, I am such a poor scholar."

"Yes, you made up your mind to see England again, and you do see it. Good luck to you with it. It is no kind of matter to me."

"I fear your honour's angry with me."

"Not I—poor wretch! But what made you think of me after fifteen years of silence? It was that day fifteen years since I sent you some money, that I had your letter last year."

"Oh, sir, we was always thinking of you. It was you who was never out of Richard's head; he could think of nothing but the poor lady and you."

"Who?"

"My poor lady—to think anybody could harm her. He often said just those words, and he would tell it all over and over again, and talk of you all at the same time. Who *could* it be, sir, did it? Who *could* it be? For my part, I would not have harmed her, no more than if she had been my child."

"Who said you could?" asked Mr. Ferroll.

"Nobody, nobody, Lord, sir, nobody; but I was only saying it was a thing quite unpossible."

"Then what's the use of saying it at all?"

"Well, I don't know, sir; except that coming back fresh, it all turns again in one's mind just as if it were new again."

"Pshaw! you must remember that all of us have been living here ever since, and that it is not quite so new to us as to you."

"But your honour has been away these fourteen months as I heard, and it was you being away, as I was told in a letter from Mabel, as made me think more to come; for I was not sure if I should be a pleasant object to you—only across the sea I should be out of your sight."

"I had business in England which brought me suddenly back— that does not matter. For your own sake you would have been better where you were, and I told you so. See your friends, settle your affairs, and go back again, I advise you—put the sea between us if you will. I agree with you, that it is not the pleasantest thing in the world to see the person who was connected with that—with my first wife's murder."

"Lord, sir, you do frighten me with such words—and connected with it? you know, sir, I fainted dead away when we was all examined."

"Other people will remember that, too," said Mr. Ferroll.

"Remember what, sir? they can remember nothing against me except that my husband was said by the judge to be an innocent man."

"And you?"

"God forbid I should ever be said anything to, sir, by judge or jury."

"Amen, you poor old soul!" said Mr. Ferroll. "But what's the matter?" for the old creature for a minute past had been standing up, and now trembled violently, and caught at the table for support.

"Oh, sir," said she, "I enjoy a very bad state of health. It's a way I have about the heart," and she fell down into a chair, panting violently.

Mr. Ferroll pushed open the door, and gave her his snuff-box open. The pungent weed revived her. "Are you often ill like that?" said he.

"Not very often, sir; but it's very bad when it comes. The doctor in New Southampton said it would be the death of me," and she leaned her head on the table, exhausted with the attack.

"I'll send your neighbour to you," said Mr. Ferroll, rising; "you'd be better in bed, I dare say," and opening a door, which led to a cottage under the same roof, he called the woman of the house by name and walked away.

"Die, die!" he said, and went hastily on, buried in thought.

The Tower had a flight of steps before the door, with a large spreading balustrade on each side. The entrance hall was octagon, and just opposite the door was a great fire-place, with noble logs burning on it. The room was furnished with rich-coloured carpets and table covers; chairs of dark wood and light velvet; pictures in four sides of the octagon, in carved frames, and various other objects of luxury. The possessor was plainly a man who commanded the pleasures bought by money, and whose tastes and education placed him among the upper half of mankind. The possessor entered this pleasant room—this room rich in enjoyment; but the scene in the cottage still left an impression on his face—not for long, however—not longer than while no one else was present. In the adjoining drawing-room he heard his wife's voice, and that of some other person, and whatever emotion had surged up, and made itself visible, was thrust back, and pent within his heart. It was Lady Lucy Bartlett who had come zealously to the Tower to welcome her neighbour; her daughters were gone off with Janet into some other room, and all were busy in telling and hearing what had passed.

"It is better of you than we hoped, Mr. Ferroll," said the lady, "coming back at this time of year—just in time for Christmas. We had no hope you would return till the bad weather was over."

"I had business in England," said Mr. Ferroll. "To be sure I might have left Elinor and Janet behind, but what should I have done without them?"

"Or I? left behind alone," said Mrs. Ferroll.

"At all events I'm very glad you are come; only Mrs. Ferroll must take care of herself, she looks delicate."

"Does she?" said her husband looking earnestly at her; "so Janet said."

"So don't I say," Mrs. Ferroll answered gaily, and rising lightly from her chair, the delicate colour flushing over her face. "See, Lady Lucy, here's a little present we brought for you from Paris. You like china still, I hope?"

Lady Lucy was delighted. "We shall have everything pretty and new again, now you are come home," said she; "and my dear Hugh also sent me the prettiest chains from Venice. It's so unlucky, this journey of his to Egypt. Do you know, my cousin Ewyas wants to bring him forward for the county?"

"Ah, indeed; is there a vacancy there?"

"Quite sure to be one; for Mr. Aldry cannot live another week, and then it would be the best opportunity."

"Indeed it would; and where is Hugh?"

"Gone to Egypt, I am sorry to say."

"That's unlucky; and he is too young to be put in nomination during his absence. Nobody knows anything about him, except his name."

"No, nothing; though everybody likes him I assure you."

"And who is there to stand if Aldry dies, and Hugh is absent?"

"I don't know at all. Lord Ewyas said they were all in perplexity. I dare say you will hear everything about it when they know you are come back."

"Oh, somebody will apply for my vote no doubt."

"Yes, yes; we shall have the trouble of a contest. Lord Ewyas is coming to me the day after to-morrow. You *will both* dine with me, won't you, and Janet too, who is grown so beautiful, I am astonished at her."

"Oh no, no; that's been settled long ago."

Lady Lucy looked disappointed. "I thought," she began, "when you returned you would have changed old habits?"

"Why so? You forget that we have been living on day by day, though to you we seem to have skipped a year."

"Well, I'm glad you've come back at all events," said Lady Lucy, rising to go.

Mr. Ferroll went with her into the hall; there she looked wistfully at him, while prolonging the putting on of her clogs, and at last began hesitatingly: "Do you know what a very strange thing has happened in the village, do you know who is come back?"

"Oh, the old woman Martha Franks, you mean."

"My housekeeper, who is new since *then*, you know, came to me and said one Martha Franks asked to be put on the broth list. I said no, on no account; but I did not say why."

"She must have been astonished at your prompt uncharitableness."

"But Mrs. Ferroll knows nothing about it, does she?"

"Certainly it is not a subject upon which any judicious person would wish to entertain her."

"I am sure I shall not," said Lady Lucy; "and the girls know nothing."

"About the trial of her husband, I suppose you mean; and his acquittal, and this woman's freedom from suspicion, trial, and acquittal?"

"Yes, I believe so; but it is a very unpleasant thing, for a poor woman like that to come from America, and bring up all the old story again with her."

"Most uncommonly so; and I dare say I shall be spared it after the first moment of interest."

"Certainly; but I could not help speaking of it once you know."

"Certainly, to be sure. Janet, Lady Lucy is waiting;" and so with good byes and kind words, they parted. Janet was very happy to see her friends again, and indulge in girls' talk with companions of her own age. She also heard of Hugh; and as the young Bartletts were very unsuspicious, literal young ladies, they had not formed any such definite idea as that of their brother becoming the husband of their childhood's companion, but only vague notions of Hugh sending her messages, and thinking her prettier than he thought them; and thus the better-instructed Janet could talk freely to them about him, and learn a great deal more about him than they knew themselves.

Mrs. Ferroll also was glad to be at home. She was not ill, but her strength was reduced from the old standard, before any attack on her nerves had shaken it. She was open to impressions of evil, and resembled the blossoms of a peach-tree, whose life depends upon no frost coming. There was a feeling of shelter and of rest in being at the end of travel; in being among all that was her own; in the many luxuries of home; though frost, and snow, and cold, bleak winds prevailed outside, the warm hearth, the low, luxurious chair, the curtains amply draped over the windows, hothouse flowers on the tables, seemed a more genial climate than that of a stranger's country. She expressed this feeling to her husband, as they sate together that evening. "I am happy, Paul. I have a feeling of good about me, a kind of light of serene days. I am anxious about nothing."

"My bosom's lord sits lightly on its throne," said he.

"I don't like you to say that. Romeo's was a false presentiment. Mine shall be true. Have not I everything I love within arm's length—you, and Janet?" she added, stretching her hand towards the door, out of which Janet had lately gone.

"Yes, yes; let it be so. This actual moment is as still and calm, as if there had never been, could never be storms. This is a good moment; let us enjoy it."

"Storms there have been indeed," said Mrs. Ferroll. "When I think of the danger you have been in, and how I might have been here alone—oh, my dearest husband, I don't know how to be glad enough."

"Yet the things we are sorriest for, are in fact the great good sometimes," said Mr. Ferroll; "only not seeing them to be such, prevents us from acknowledging it. Who knows but what, if the Providence over you had taken me away—if the angel of your destiny had stooped and completed the sacrifice—who can tell, Elinor—who can tell, my Elinor, what future pains might have been spared you? Nay, dearest, I say who can tell—*who* is an unknown person—Mr. Who; Sir Thomas Who; Who of Who Hall. He knows; but I don't."

"If he knows anything, he knows I should die with you."

"No, no; you would not—you *should* not. Life is a fair open sea for you still—for us both—your child was born before you were twenty, and now she is but just seventeen. You are young, you are beautiful, you are in the perfection of your feelings and intellect. I am older than you."

"Just eight years older than I. I was a child when you loved me first."

"What would my soul give if that first could come again! We hold our fortunes in our hand at one time of our life, and I threw mine away. Aye, what would I give if we could be as we were, when your sweet girlish face looked at me in that innocent way! Between that time and the moment when we stood together at the church's altar, what moments of torment, of madness; what darkness, what despair! And this weak little flame, this beautiful painted bark, what a marvel that it came safely through such a tempest."

"Well, well, it is all the same now. Whatever the bark went through, here it is in its safe haven," she said, resting her head on his shoulder.

He clasped her to his heart; but at the same moment cast a look upward, which never crossed his face when her eye rested upon it. "Your will was always an omnipotent will," she said, "whether to harm yourself or obtain good."

"That's true, Elinor; yet sometimes I have willed to be guided by such poor mean agents."

"You have willed strongly, to be governed by a weak cause."

"Aye indeed; it is the fate I have made for myself."

"What do you mean?" she said, smiling; "am I that weak cause?"

"Aye, my Elinor—that's my good destiny. Do you not guide me with a thread?"

"Yes; when you have a mind to go my way."

"THERE'S A POOR OLD CREATURE, mamma, of the name of Franks, come to the Broom cottages," said Janet, returning from a walk. "She lodges with the waggoner's wife. They want broth for her."

"Is she ill?" said her father.

Janet was surprised at the question, for it was very seldom that her father took an interest in the lesser concerns of his neighbours.

"Very ill."

"Going to die, Jeannie?"

"Oh no, papa, I hope not."

"But the waggoner's wife thinks so?"

"Those people always think or say so, when any one is sick."

"Give her what she wants. Let her be taken care of. You must not neglect her," said Mr. Ferroll.

Janet was again surprised, when in the course of the day she went to see her father's injunction carried out, to find he had been there himself, and had taken excessive pains that the best medical advice, and all kinds of necessary remedies, should be provided for the old woman. After all, however, she had grown up in the habit of carrying comforts and remedies to the cottages with her governess; and there was nothing unnatural in anyone else doing it, only her father generally was too busy with other things.

The villagers themselves were surprised at the care taken of the old woman. "To be sure they are unaccountable kind to you, Martha, at the Tower. You've everything like Mr. Aldry himself. Dr. Swine came to you by the Squire's order, before he went to Squire Aldry."

"Aye, to be sure; and a courageous dose he gave me. It did great execution."

"And you know," said the other gossip, "Mrs. Poole told me herself, in the room at the Tower, that the Squire is quite in a fidget-like to have strong broth for you. I was taking up the eggs, and she was counting 'em out, and paying me 1s. 2d. a dozen, and she said to the kitchen-maid, Lord, Lucy, see the broth is good for that old 'oman."

"Though I am none older than I ought to be," said Martha Franks; "no more than she herself."

"And it *is* good," said the other old woman, supping of it. "Do look up, Martha, and take a cup."

Martha obeyed, and with a handkerchief tied round her head, and hanging down in two long comers, imbibed the good things provided for her from the Tower. "I never knew the Squire take so much care before," said the gossip. "Miss Janet often is among the poor; though when I was in the fever, she refused me wine, that's sure, at the same time old Dick had enough, and to spare; but the Squire never do take the least notice till now. You was about the first madam, was not you, Martha—that's it, I suppose."

"I suppose I was," said Martha.

"And you was acquaint perhaps with things in the family?"

"I don't speak of what I have known," said Martha—"though people did set store by me perhaps, as you may have some judgment now."

"Aye, the greatest people find out sometimes they have need of the little," said the gossip.

Old Martha nodded her head affirmatively.

"But then why did the master send you and your husband over sea? We all thought he wanted you away."

"If he did, I wanted to come back," said Martha—"and here I am, and you see, if he ben't enamoured to see me again."

"He's desperate good to you, that's true; but he's a very strange gentleman, and takes whims sometimes."

Neither Martha nor Mr. Aldry fulfilled the expectations of their friends by dying at this moment. The potent demon of physic can often charm the departing spirit, and bind it for awhile to the bleak, barren edges of life. And so it was with the rich member of Parliament, whose station in life commanded for him whatever the luxuries of illness, such as they are, consist of; and with the poor cottager, whose life a caprice of her rich neighbour sought to defend by every possible act and resource which could prevent its forfeiture. Still, as it seemed, both made little by little an advance towards "this silent shore," and after every wrestle with death, from which their ally the doctor drove him discomfitted, the observing eye might see that even in defeat death had gained some minute footing towards the fortress which he was ultimately to take. At least with Mr. Aldry this was becoming apparent; and the consequence was, not what the newspapers announced respecting the extreme regret at losing the respected member, but a great anxiety to know who was to succeed him.

The eyes of the party had been cast more than once towards Mr. Ferroll. His political opinions were well known, and he was a man of notoriously independent habits, upon any and every family in the county. He was an active member of all public business, a man of high intellectual reputation, of a fortune sufficient for the position; and subscriptions for the expenses of election had been already offered. The great doubt whether he would accept the offer, added perhaps to the interest with which his name was canvassed. The party was in great want of a representative, and several of the influential men, who failed to agree about other names, had no reasons to quarrel over this. Mr. Ferroll himself was not without suspicions of their intentions; gossip had already brought the report to the Tower, Lady Lucy Bartlett having delivered it with much eagerness to Mrs. Ferroll; but she, from her previous experience of her husband's dogged rejection of all advances tending to bring him into association with his fellow-countymen, had rejected the idea, and given assurance that it was out of the question. When we know people best, and think that upon a particular point we can answer for their conduct with certainty, sometimes they exactly act, or will to act, in the contrary direction.

One morning Mr. Ferroll's servant answered his hasty question, which was less gracious in form than in substance, "Is that old woman better?" with the news that the nurse had been up to say she thought she was dying.

Mr. Ferroll's face was impassable to those with whom he talked; his actions, however, implied much interest in the news, for he said at once, "Send for Dr. Swine. Let him see the old woman directly. Poole is to go down to see if anything can be done for her. O, omnipotent death," he murmured to himself, as the servant went out; "end, end this."

That morning, before early dawn, Mr. Aldry had died. Breakfast was not yet ready at the Tower when a messenger came there, from Lord Ewyas, being the request of the party to Mr. Ferroll to stand for the county. "We are to have a private meeting," it went on, "at two o'clock to-day, and by that time make up your mind if it be possible, my dear sir, to do us this service. I send to you the very first moment in order to give time for that deliberation which I hope will end in a favourable answer to your party, and I trust so honourable a call, and at a time of such peculiar necessity, will not be unattended to, when we know how highly qualified you are to render us this important service &c." Mr. Ferroll held this letter in his hand long considering, and his face was animated, his eyes looked freely forward as though the thoughts worked healthily in his brain. Once more the door opened and he turned hastily round.

"If you please, sir, Mr. Swine will attend immediately," said the servant.

"Humph," said Mr. Ferroll, with anything but a delighted voice; and it was some moments before he resumed his more agreeable reflection.

When he went to breakfast, we held out the letter to his wife, and said, "See what they ask of me."

Mrs. Ferroll smiled. "Ah, well, they little know how vainly they ask."

"You think it would not do?"

"Nay, if you *think*. . . but have you any idea? . . . you are by far the best man for the thing—but you always. . ."

"Always may end sometimes. Should you like to see me proud of the honour, bearing in my breast the proud thought of representing such an unparalleled county?"

"Ah, you are laughing at them now, Paul."

"No, I am not, really—look at the letter. It is very well put, is not it? and I *could* do it well."

"That I am sure you could, and I should be happy if I could see you known as you ought to be known—oh, Paul, do agree to it."

"I must think a little bit longer, I must have some further facts to go upon, and then you shall know. Some tea now, Jeannie. Have you been out this morning?"

"No, papa."

"Oh, I thought perhaps you had been down to the Broom. I have known you take such fits of charity."

"I will, directly after breakfast, if you like," said Janet; "the old nurse was here this morning for wine, and said she could not live through the day."

"Don't disturb her then; what could he done for the old creature has been done. It is no fault of mine that she dies, is it?"

"No, indeed—no, indeed; they all say she must have died weeks ago, if you had not helped her so."

"Would she?" said Mr. Ferroll.

Mr. Ferroll took no one into his counsel; no one knew whether or not there was any agitation within his breast respecting the proposal made to him. He was out of doors and in action, but whoever had to speak to him, found him as usual, clear, determined, sure of what he himself willed. What he did seemed very foreign to what he had to determine; it seemed a most unlikely thing for a man to do who had but an hour more to resolve upon a purely personal question, and that one which must influence all his future views. Instead of attending to the request of the county, he went down to the old woman's cottage. Here at the gate he saw Dr. Swine's horse tied—it had trodden the soil into furrows, seeming to have been long waiting there in the cold.

Mr. Ferroll passed it, crossed the narrow garden and pushed open the door. The women were kneeling by the bed, the doctor bending over it. He looked up when the door opened—"The crisis is over," he said, "she will live—I came just in time; but now plainly she is in a better way to recover than she has been at all."

Mr. Ferroll said no word that was intelligible—something he uttered which was enough for a sick room in a critical state, and going out again, softly shut the door. Then by a way over the garden terrace which was in fact no way, only a mere strong scramble, he rushed back to the house, snatched a sheet of paper and wrote a few words of decided strong refusal. He commissioned a servant to take it—and when he was alone again, leaned his head on his arms, which were flung along the table. He lifted it again to wipe off the cold sweat which had burst out over his forehead.

So because an old woman recovered from her illness a clever man refused to represent his county in Parliament.

VII

M r. Ferroll went out of his house, half an hour after the messenger was gone—it was a miserable winter day; excessively cold, and the air was saturated with moisture, which clung to every object, and drowned all the country in a dim gray haze. Something had taken place in his mind in consequence of the circumstances of the day, however insufficient they seemed to produce such an effect, which agitated and bent his spirit, like the forest tree in a tempest. He walked on, entering the Bartlett park by an obscure path, and pursued his way through leafless damp woods till he had forced through them to a large piece of water, which was kept quiet for the sake of wild fowl, and which no human creature at this time was likely to approach. Here he sat down on the trunk of a small tree which had been torn up by the wind, and which lay partly in the water, partly on land, fronting the desolate scene. The mind at times is so oppressed by its own burthen that it seems unable to take thought for its companion the body; it rather gives itself up to the mechanical impressions of the body, and like two whom fate has joined and inclination severed, they abide together, but neither does its office friendly, to the other. Thus he sat, certain that he was unseen; and released, therefore, from all necessity of acting a part— the dark spirit communing with itself, the listless body abandoning itself to all the painful impressions of cold and desolation. No word escaped his lips; his eyes gazed unmoved on the black water; his folded hands lay listlessly on his knee; hours passed which he did not mark; the moon, seen early in the winter evening, began to struggle faintly through the fog. Then the chain of thought snapped; or the spirit having had this tormented sleep, woke again to a new feverish life; he rose, and like a man able to cast off one half of his burthen, and girding himself to carry the other, moved again, strengthened himself, summoned his spirits. He went home hastily—passed at once into the room where he heard the voice of his wife and Janet. All was bright, warm, and prepared for enjoyment.

"Where have you been this cold, dark day?" said Mrs. Ferroll. "Janet and I have been enjoying life by the fire, but not thoroughly till now:" and she made way for him in the warmest hearth-nook.

"Not till I came," he said, smiling.

"No, certainly; when I hear your foot in the hall, things go well; then I am happy—not till then."

"Yet you have heard it nearly twenty years."

"But even less glad to hear it at first than now."

"Now? this very now? do you know what it is? do you know it is the last day of the year?"

"To be sure I do: here is a silk chain which Janet is finishing for you to-morrow, on account of the beginning of the new year."

Janet blushed deeply: she had been thinking whether her father, who was generally a great neglector of days and seasons, would scarcely accept it; whether he would deride her present.

"Give it to me to-night, Janet, why wait for to-morrow? it is finished, I see, a little minute atom of a clasp put on, all very delicate and neat; to-day is our own, but not to-morrow. I will have it this minute."

He took it from his daughter's hand as he spoke, and kissed her forehead. She hesitated before she said, "And a happy new year to you, papa."

"A happy old one, at all events," said he, "as much as remains. Come, come, life is delightful here. I'll pile the fire till it is as warm as June; I would burn cedar logs if I had them. At this moment I think I would set my Cellini's carved Apollo on fire, if I wanted a match to light a candle."

Mrs. Ferroll laughed. "The dismal day gives you spirits," she said.

"Oh, no, not the dismal day, but the last day, as you call it; the bright room, the bright flowers, the pretty wife, especially after all the darkness of the fog and storm. Elinor, you should light this lamp to-night; do you remember when I gave it you?"

"Paul, I can't forget that."

Janet looked as if she longed to know, but did not ask. It was a beautiful alabaster vase, wrought in great perfection, and preserved by assiduous care in the same beauty which it had at first; it had a lamp inside.

Mr. Ferroll took up a flask of perfumed oil which stood in a jar on the table, and poured it into the lamp. A little floating light was ready at hand, he set it on fire and the light spread, looking like rising moonbeams over the space around. "That's right," he said; "now go and make yourself exquisite for dinner. You have a gown of sober velvet, Elinor, put it on, will you? and don't think about the cold. Women ought to adorn themselves, and look beautiful; people don't suffer when they are doing right."

He sent them to dress: and he desired his butler to bring some wine for dinner which had been sent him from the best cellars of Burgundy, as a costly return for the pleasure a book of his had given there. He himself had forgotten it till now; the butler had thought too much of it ever to find an occasion illustrious enough to produce it. To-day brought the potent and high-pedigreed spirit to light. He asked for more wax lights in the room; he went into his green-house, and gathered a heap of camellias, which he put into a Dresden bowl, and set it on the table.

When they sat down his soul flowed freely as the wine; and Janet herself—the watchful, shy Janet—laughed out beyond control, at the witty nonsense he talked. "So that hour is gone, too," he said, as they rose to go to the drawing-room. "Stay one moment, I will finish my friend's Burgundy; why should profaner lips touch it?"

He poured a full measure, and then taking a spoon from the table, filled it, and poured it into a glass before his wife, and was laying down the spoon, but an involuntary movement of her lips was perceived by him, and he took it up again, and did the same for Janet. "No healths, no healths—don't drink my health, Janet."

"I was not going to do it, papa," she said, colouring violently, and her eyes illuminated by moisture, for it did not come to tears.

"I'll *do* it though for thee," he said, smiling. "The little bark is towed along, Elinor, in our wake, and gets hid in the waves sometimes, but it has its own affairs, has not it?" Mrs. Ferroll pressed Janet tenderly to her side. Janet was embarrassed: she took up some water to pour into the basin of camellias.

"You had better not," said Mr. Ferroll, "they will grow yellow at the edges, and lose all the beauty of their first moments. Let them be beautiful, and die—die on the scullion's heap of ashes, though they have lived in a poet's parlour." So saying, and without looking again at the flowers, he walked by his wife's side into the drawing-room, where the alabaster lamp burned softly. Here they sat before the glowing logs of wood, which crackled and flamed cheerfully.

They had a habit of reading each a favourite book after dinner for an hour or so, till they were ready for tea; though Janet would often at that time be employed by her father to copy a Ms., or make a plan; or, on her own account, would work at some pretty collar or cuff, an employment which pleased her father's eye, owing to the grace of the employment which became her feminine and exquisite beauty. To-night he brought her a few verses to put into her neatest handwriting, which was rather a slow operation, but which she executed in a manner that gave the copy an independent merit of its own. These verses were to go to London by the post to-morrow.

"Mr.—— wants something of mine, and I found these in my desk, and he shall have them. I'll tell you where they rose, Elinor; at Gaëta, years ago, when we came across the bay from Mola, and landed by Cicero's villa. Do you remember as we went up the steep path to the inn, seeing an Englishwoman sitting just in the angle of one of the turns? The gardener's wife who was sewing on the seat at the top, said the lady was lame, and she did not know how she had managed to get down there; but she had been sitting quite still on the same spot for an hour and a-half, while her friends were in a boat on the bay."

"I recollect; the woman said she had three or four times peeped over the rock, but the lady always seemed contentissima, come se stesse in Paradise."

"That's the exact expression that struck me; it came into verse the other day. Read it, Janet—no, give them me."

I

"Gaëta's orange groves were there,
Half circling round the sun-kiss'd sea;
And all were gone, and left the fair
Rich garden-solitude to me.

II

My feeble foot refused to tread
The rugged pathway to the bay;
Down the steep rock I saw them thread,
And gain the boat and glide away.

III

And then the thirst grew strong in me
To taste yet farther scenes so bright—
To do like those who wander'd free,
And share their exquisite delight.

IV

With careful trouble then, and pain,
I pass'd a little down the hill,
Each step obtain'd was hard-earned gain,
Each step before seem'd distant still.

V

But when I reach'd at last the trees
Which see that lovely scene complete,
I sat there all at peace and ease
A monarch of the mossy seat.

VI

Above me hung the golden glow
Of fruit which is at one with flowers;
Below me gleam'd the ocean flow
Like sapphires in the mid-day hours.

VII

A passing-by there was of wings;
The silent, flower-like butterflies;
The sudden beetle as it springs
Full of the life of southern skies.

VIII

A sound there was of words afloat
Of sailors, and of children blent
At work and play beside a boat;
Sounds which the distance mix'd and spent.

IX

A brooding silence too was there
Of mid-day, and a wide-stretch'd bound;

And I sat still, with open ear,
That drank the silence and the sound.

X

It was an hour, of bliss to die;
But not to sleep; for ever came
The warm, thin air, and passing by
Fann'd Sense and Soul, and Heart to flame.

XI

The sight I saw that noontide, grew
A portion of my mem'ry's pride;
And oh, how often I renew
The beauty of the steep hill-side.

XII

It comes, when by the northern fire
I sit and shiver in its heat;
While with vain longing I aspire,
To rest upon my rocky seat.

XIII

A longing, such, thou gracious land,
As thou must ever leave on those
Who bask on thy enchanted strand,
And see thy heavenly shapes and hues.

XIV

And if, methinks, to roam and climb,
At my free will, to me were giv'n
O'er such a land, in such a clime,
It would be, what will be, in heaven."

"They are very pretty," said Elinor; "you have put yourself into the situation as if it had been your own."

"That's a compliment; but that's the quality which is wanted for an artist, and you are the woman to appreciate it. You know that a poet conceives—does not describe."

"To be sure; Shakspeare and Scott were not Juliet and Dirk Hatterick."

"Aye, Scott never killed a Kennedy, though he conceived a Dirk Hatterick seeing him wriggle on the strand; but as far as that goes, I could draw Kennedy from experience, could not I? do you recollect my telling you that this hand killed James Skenfrith?"

"Oh, my dearest, don't talk of that. I don't mind most things, but I can't bear that."

"Can't you, Elinor? can't you bear me for having blood on my hand?"

"But you have not; what you did was in self-defence, in defence of others—that makes the whole difference."

"Then all depends upon. . ."

"But you have not."

"To please me, however, suppose I had. I want to know what you would think of me under all circumstances—that circumstance among others. . ." He was going on when he felt his arm touched by Janet's fearful hand; he turned, and saw her look appealingly at her mother, and sign him to be silent. "What is it, Jenny? what are you making mouths at?"

Janet even trembled at having her silence thus put into words, but being discovered, she spoke out. "It does mamma harm," she said.

Mr. Ferroll laughed. "Does it? then I won't do it, little defender. Come, come, all this is nonsense. Let me hear some music this holiday; I want some music." It was Mrs. Ferroll who made the music, Janet never played or sang to her father, for he had not patience for an inferior talent, when a superior one was present. Mrs. Ferroll pleased his taste and feeling beyond all others, and a few songs he liked to have over and over again, a few passages on the pianoforte; seeming to hear in their meaning a voice which none else heard. "This is a heavenly pleasure," he said, as she repeated one of these bewitching pieces of music. "Again, my darling, again." Janet, the defender, looked beseechingly. "Oh no, she is not tired; people don't get tired by doing what they do so well. It is a very bad compliment to say 'I am afraid you will tire yourself.' People never like music much who think the performer is tired;" and so Mrs. Ferroll sang and played till past eleven.

"I am tired now, however," she said, rising, "and I will shut up the pianoforte. The old year is very nearly gone, the fire is low, the lamp—no, my alabaster lamp beams brightly still."

"Oh, yes, I will put more logs on the fire, and the lamp has abundance of oil. It is only violence that could put out its light. We burned it the first evening we were married, did not we, Elinor?"

"Certainly, most certainly; and not very often since. I could reckon every time. I wonder what made you light it to-night?"

Mr. Ferroll made no answer. The dry wood had speedily burned up, and the room was brightly illuminated by it. "Let us look out," he said. "Let us see the old year's departure among the stars." He opened the window, and they stood together looking out on the night. The wind had risen, and blew wildly among the trees; the clouds chased along the sky, and the moon seemed swiftly walking among them. The heavy curtains were swayed by the breeze. At a little distance rose the tower of the church, and a light was seen through the narrow windows.

"They toll out the age of a person who dies," said Mr. Ferroll; "are they going to toll? Aye, does not that sound like it?" he added, as the clock began to repeat the quarters, and then with a deeper note, the number twelve of the hour. The twelfth stroke of the clock was struck; a few seconds after the bells of the church broke out with all their might a jolly peal.

"Pshaw!" said Mr. Ferroll; "perhaps the clock is wrong; other clocks are not so fast." At that moment they heard in the room a slight crash; the alabaster lamp had slipped from its pedestal, and lay broken on the floor.

"What's that? oh, my lamp!" cried Mrs. Ferroll; "my dear lamp!"

"How could it be?" said Janet; "was it the wind?"

"The lamp is broken—the oil run to waste—the year ended—the clock was right," said Mr. Ferroll.

"Mamma, it is only in two pieces. With isinglass cement we might mend it, perhaps."

"No, Jeannie, better leave it," said her father; "piece it as you will, it will always have been broken."

THE NEW YEAR BEGAN TO wear on its course day by day, which so soon brings one far away from the close of the old, and commencement of the new. Mr. Ferroll was busy with an important pamphlet, and in the occupation it presented, recurred no more to the unusual excitement of the 31st of December. He bore patiently his wife's and Janet's experiments on the alabaster vase, which with great delicacy of finger they put together, but as he had said, no mending could restore the first beauty. Neither would he replace it with another, though at this time he was more than usually profuse in luxuries, and seemed intent upon enjoying life in all the points it could be made to present.

One morning while he was lingering after breakfast in the octagon hall, where they were talking and looking at engravings, the sound of the bell announced a visitor, and the servant who answered it, came back to say Mr. Monkton, an attorney of the neighbouring town, wished to speak to Mr. Ferroll.

"So there's an end of pleasure," said Mr. Ferroll, laying down the print; "but I'm glad I delayed here so long. I ought to have been in my room twenty minutes ago working, and I have given them to myself for play up here. I am glad I gained that twenty minutes of play."

"Is this man going to stay all day then?"

"Nay, I don't know; he may keep me a long while." And he went to his own room, where Mr. Monkton awaited him.

After the common greeting, Mr. Monkton began his errand with some embarrassment. "I'm extremely sorry to trouble you, sir, upon a painful subject. What I have to say, will bring very disagreeable impressions before you. You will excuse me."

"Say whatever you please—what is it, Mr. Monkton?"

"It relates, sir," said the attorney with great hesitation, "to the. . . to Mrs. . . to the late Mrs. Ferroll, sir."

"Exactly, sir." Mr. Ferroll said nothing more, and Mr. Monkton had to recommence the errand. He did not do so till he had fumbled in his pocket and brought out a small parcel which he opened. It contained a gold locket, the outside ornamented with a device in enamel, the reverse containing hair.

"This ornament, sir—do you recollect it as belonging to her?"

"No, I don't."

"The old woman Franks had the folly, it might make one smile, to wear it at a neighbour's tea-drinking. She it is who was in your house at the time of Mrs. Ferroll's death, I think—the first Mrs. Ferroll; and the woman who brought it to me, said it was one among many which are secreted in her drawer."

"Yes, and what next?"

"The suspicion is that she stole them."

"Not unlikely; but I made a parcel of all the ornaments I knew of, and sent them to her brother."

"Together with a list of her effects?"

"I think so; a little book containing a list which I found."

"Yes, sir, which I have seen; and this ornament appears to be specified among them. By the kindness of Mr. Gordon, I have examined the list."

"Then it probably is as you suppose."

"But, sir, in that case, suspicion falls upon her of. . ."

"Of the murder—do you think so?"

"Don't you, sir?"

"No; I don't. The husband was tried and acquitted."

"But not the wife."

"Well, sir, do as you please."

"I am very sorry, Mr. Ferroll."

"For what, sir?"

"I am aware it is most annoying to you."

"Annoying perhaps is not the word; but it does not matter what the thing signifies to me. You will of course do exactly as you think right."

"It is almost a pity, sir, the woman did not die when she was so ill. It would have been a happy thing," continued Mr. Monkton seeing he was not answered, "if the subject could have been at rest for ever, You have been most kind to her, sir, otherwise. . ."

"Yes, I have kept her alive," said Mr. Ferroll. "She was so serious an annoyance, as you call it, that I could heartily have desired her death, and for that reason took extravagant pains to keep her alive; there she is now to explain how these objects got into her possession."

"Her neighbours have had their attention excited not only by the trinkets they have discovered, but by expressions used by her—in fact I consider there is evidence enough to issue a warrant for her apprehension."

"Be it so," said Mr. Ferroll, rising. "You don't ask me to be active in this business I suppose. At all events, I absolutely decline any share whatever."

Mr. Monkton rose also. "In that case, sir, I will go to Mr.——. Perhaps we shall find it necessary to beg you to identify the trinkets."

"What you please. As to the one you showed me, I have no recollection of it whatever, but that proves nothing. It is many years since those things have been absent from my memory."

Mr. Monkton took leave, and Mr. Ferroll turned his attention strongly to the work he was finishing, and wrote with an excited mind and a free flow of ideas for several hours. At the end of that time his wife came into the room with her cloak and bonnet. "Writing, Paul," she said, "I thought you had been detained by Mr. Monkton—but you are only writing. You were to have walked with me to Esco. You have forgotten me."

"No, I did not forget, but it is necessary to finish this thing; and I found my wits work freely this morning."

"Do you want to send it by post time?"

"Not so soon as that; no, I have more time than that, but I don't know how much. Never mind; I'll put all by now, and go with you— here put your arm under mine, and once more, once more—poor pretty Elinor. . ."

"Why poor?"

"Well, leave out poor—say pretty, and come on." They went out together—and alone—it was very seldom that Janet accompanied them—and walked quietly along, enjoying the soft winter day. There was a clear sun; and among the woods it shed a glory on the brown leaves which hung on the oak and beech, and which now showed a beauty equal, though unlike that which adorns them in summer. The deep sense of beauty animated both of them; and in great enjoyment of the scene, they stood together in the silent wood admiring it. But they were soon at the end of the pleasure—a sound broke the great winter silence; the branches rustled, and a servant came forward with a letter which Mr. Ferroll read. "There," he said, "there—our walk is at an end, Elinor, you must go home alone; I thought so—you must be alone—nay, I have only to go to Mr.—— who is examining the old woman, old Franks."

"Who do you mean? not the old sick woman of course."

"Yes, indeed it is. The business, is remarkably unpleasant—never mind it—don't listen to it or think of it, till I come back—I shall surely come back. . . by dinner time."

"Nay, tell me more; what is it to you? what is it you mean?"

"Oh, a terrible past story—the woman who was once your enemy, Elinor, that poor soul, somebody fancies they have discovered something about her end." Mrs. Ferroll's colour rose vehemently. She comprehended, and was very grave at once, but said not a word—only drew away her arm, and was ready to go.

"Nay, I'll come with you to the corner of the walk," said he, snatching her arm again, and holding it under his. Neither, however, spoke any more, and at the walk they parted; a look grave and affectionate, bidding him good-bye.

At Mr.——'s he found, as he expected, the old woman Franks in an agony of fear and grief, surrounded by the persons who had to attest the facts upon which she was accused of the almost forgotten murder. Various trinkets lay on the table, among which Mr. Ferroll recognized at a first glance more than one which had belonged to the wife whose end had been so terrible. The old woman was even beforehand with her accusers in proclaiming her guilt respecting them. She sat in a chair, which they had allowed her, wringing her hands, and rocking to and fro, and to every question, addressed to her or any one else, crying aloud, "Oh, it's true, all true; I did rob her, poor thing; it's come out—it's come out—oh, my conscience is as heavy as lead—but I did no worse—oh no, no, no."

And when Mr. Ferroll came in, and she heard the questions asked him about the identity of the ornament, "What's the use of asking him?" she cried. "It is the very chain she went and bought one day for him herself and would put it about his neck, and he took it off, and laid it aside, and she laid it on her table, and she left it about, and I did take it—I did—but never did I harm the poor creature; oh, I would not have taken the life of a fly."

"She criminates herself by these excuses," said Mr.——, in a low voice, to Mr. Ferroll.

"Not necessarily—there is no art in her declarations, she is frightened."

"What are ye saying, gentlemen?" interposed the trembling woman. "I tell you all, I am making my conscience clean. It's inside out before you like a sick stomach. I was seduced of Satan with the chains and rings, but as to her precious life. . ."

"Nobody is accusing you of that," said the attorney, "mind that what you say now may go in evidence against you."

"And how can it be against me when I say I never touched her—why I could not bear so much as to see her—looking so pit'ous there. Lord, Lord, I can't bear it now." And the poor wretch turned fearfully pale and sank down in one of the fits which came upon her under any excitement.

The occupants of the room looked one at the other, and whispered their suspicions—all but Mr. Ferroll, who had scarcely spoken a word from the time he came in, and whose eyes were fixed on the accused woman with an expression which was readily to be explained by the strangeness and uneasiness of his situation.

A woman of the household was called, and took Martha Franks under her charge to apply the necessary remedies; and then followed a consultation what to do respecting her committal. "She is undoubtedly guilty of robbery," said Mr. Ferroll, when they required his opinion. "Is it not enough to accuse her of that—you cannot prove the murder against her."

"These are the words you said respecting her husband eighteen years ago," said Mr.——, "you were right then."

"Did I," said Mr. Ferroll, "the time is come round I suppose—however, now let me go—I don't want to influence your decision in any way—I am not the person to judge this case; the poor foolish soul must abide the consequence of her antique vanity." So saying, he left the room, and the matter ended in the committal for trial of the old woman, on suspicion of being concerned as necessary to the murder of Anne Ferroll.

VIII

There was still some time to elapse before the assizes, and though the county eagerly took up the subject, which made some impression also upon the general press, nothing could be done about it, and it was one which certainly never was mentioned in the Ferroll family. Mr. Ferroll was restless, though not pre-occupied; he was as much, or more than ever, awake to all the pleasures and occupations of his life, and if possible more than ever averse to mixing in any degree with his neighbours. Lady Lucy had news at this time that her son had turned homeward; and it occasioned a sensation at the Park which absorbed almost the whole of what otherwise would have been created by the affair of the Tower. She was intent upon a welcome for him, but could not get the attention of Mr. Ferroll for a moment. It was Mrs. Ferroll and Janet only who minded her, and it could not escape the mother's attention that Janet had silent feelings on the subject, which were the stronger perhaps for being unspoken. She mentioned it to her husband. "Hugh is coming home," she said, "and you don't know how evident I thought his attachment was while you were ill at Pontaube. I am sure also she likes him. If she is forced to mention his name, the colour flushes into her face, and she uses any circumlocution to avoid it."

"And can't you put your pretty white hand on the matter, and crush it?"

"After all, why should I if I could? which I don't think possible. Speak seriously."

"Why? That never occurred to me before. Why can't time run backward, and fetch me yesterday, out of the treasures of God? I never thought of that before."

"My dear husband!" said Mrs. Ferroll, shocked at his expression. "But since you think thus, we must do something; I must take her. . ."

"You shall not leave me," he exclaimed; "not now;" and then changing the expression of his voice, he added more lightly, "You never left me but once, and that was when Janet had some fever or measles; and do you recollect, how I very nearly died of it? Nothing should make you leave me now."

"Why now especially?"

"Nay, I have just told you. Don't you recollect that time?"

"Oh, that I do—and it was her illness only which could have induced me to leave you."

"Yes, yes, I know; but she is not ill now. Pshaw! a young girl in love; what is that to a husband who loves you?"

"But I was once a young girl in love."

"True; bless you, my dearest, for that pretty word; and now you are a loving wife, whom I will listen to, wish what you will. Come, Elinor, will this do? I am going to London with my Ms. for a couple of days. I will take Janet with me. My kindness will so astonish her, that she will forget her own for Hugh."

"Going to London?"

"Yes, I must, and to-night. I had a letter this morning. I was going to tell you when we walked—for you must walk with me to-day, though it is very cold, and very likely to rain, and you have got a cold, and all that. We will go directly, for I have finished what I had to do."

Elinor had nothing to say in opposition; but she did delay her outdoor toilette for a few minutes, to tell Janet she must be ready that evening for the journey, a piece of news which Janet could hardly credit she heard rightly with her ears. However, it was an order given; and she set about her preparations without further inquiry, though with some perturbation and expectation in her own mind.

London was new to Janet; and it was with eager eyes that the next day she walked with her father along the streets, cheerful and brilliant with a fine February morning. The sun was warm in St. James's Street. The ugly old place smiled in its own way, the light coming under the arch, and the clock glittering above. A few brilliant uniforms reflected the light in the street—the sound of the band changing guard was heard in the yard; the great plate-glass windows of the clubs and shops showed gaily in the extremity of polish and brightness.

"This way to the right goes across the Park, Jeannie," said Mr. Ferroll; "and to the left along Pall Mall; which way shall we go, it's the same thing to me?"

"Oh, not the Park, papa."

"Oh, you don't want to see trees and country; well so the left then. A handsome street, is not it? but nothing like Paris."

"But it is very beautiful," said the admiring Janet. Now it must be remembered, that of all beautiful objects that day in Pall Mall, including every occupant of every carriage, which during the whole twenty-four hours rolled along it, Janet herself was the most so. Just developed, with the colour of the peach blossoms on her cheek, with delicately lined eyebrows on the noblest and whitest forehead, auburn hair, features modelled to an exquisite fineness, and the sweet, earnest, good expression of a fine mind and disposition—with round, light figure, filled by health and youth with graceful activity, and over all, the shy, unconscious modesty of a girl unacquainted with admiration, she came to the great capital in the very season of her perfection, and was in every way qualified to make part of its best brilliancy. There was no one, not already preoccupied, but turned to look at her. Yet neither she nor her father observed it. He was thinking of other things, and so was she; but the objects of their thoughts were very different. The past, future, absent, filled his mind. The present was all in all to her; the things without, the new world.

But at last Mr. Ferroll was roused by a voice addressing him. It came from a brougham which was standing by the United Service Club, and from which Lord Ewyas jumped, and held out his hand. "So I see you at last," said he, (for they had not met since the Ferroll family came from the continent); "I am glad you are returned—you are all well?" and at the same time his eye rested on Janet, who had forgotten him, and made no sign of recognition. Greetings passed; and then he went on, "But Miss Ferroll does not remember me. I must call myself to her recollection, for one can't afford to be forgotten by such a lady." And with the fatherly gallantry of an elderly man to a very young girl, he took both her hands to welcome her. Janet coloured, and looked prettier than ever, and in her wish to remember him, did not catch the name her father said. "Ah, well," said Lord Ewyas, "we must get better acquainted. It will be but a very short time before there is no one in London who will not envy me my right to make myself known."

Mr. Ferroll turned to look at his daughter, and smiled. "Oh no, no, my lord, I am going home two days hence. I brought my daughter merely for a glance at London, which she does not know."

"Going away in two days? Impossible. You must not allow that, Miss Ferroll."

Janet looked at her father with a shy glance, as much as to say the idea that she should allow anything was absolutely ridiculous. The look said so, and was very pretty. Lord Ewyas was enchanted. "Tell me where you are at least, and Lady Ew. . . and my wife must try her power of persuasion."

"Nay, I assure you I am obliged to go home. I am at Mivart's; but I go home on Thursday. Good day, my lord; many thanks." And taking Janet's hand under his arm, they walked on. "It's of no use, you know, Janet, to call and be called upon, when one remains in a place only a couple of days."

"No, it's of no use," said Janet; but in her heart she thought she should have liked to see the inside of one of the great palaces of London.

It was in the evening of that same day when the dusk had well set in, that Janet was alone in the hotel, her father having left her there, when he had had walking enough with her. It was the hour when gentlemen so privileged either by years, or by permission, or otherwise, delight in making their morning visits, and Lord Ewyas chose this time to come to Mivart's, and desired to be shown to Mr. Ferroll's apartment. Ladies are apt at that hour to trim their fires, and place their chair comfortably, but Janet was not so occupied. She had the window open, and was out on the balcony with a water-jug brought with some difficulty from her dressing-room, from which she was pouring as skilfully as she could, a slender stream upon two half withered aucubas, which were there in pots. She turned as the waiter announced her visitor, and had to rest her great jug upon her knee for a moment, while the flame of the gaslight illuminated her and her employment, and showed her in a pretty and unexpected attitude to Lord Ewyas. It was only for a moment that she stood thus. With a little embarrassment she set down the water and re-entered the room, closing the window, a task which the waiter took from her, and looked superciliously upon her, whatever Lord Ewyas might do.

He addressed her, so as to set her at ease, and Janet told him she had waited till the sun was gone in order to water the plants, which it was a pity should die, and which she thought no one had attended to for a long time. Lord Ewyas could not but smile, and began a playful attack upon her for her cares, which Janet answered timidly at first, and then with an awakened spirit of lively self-defence, which proved her no mere inanimate beauty. Her companion was delighted, as might easily be the case when so lovely a creature talked at all, and before conversation flagged, went on to the main subject of his visit. First he apologised for Lady Ewyas, who had not called because she had a violent headache; a complaint great ladies are very subject to, when their husbands ask them to call on country neighbours; and next, he said he was the bearer of a card and a message, begging Janet's presence

CAROLINE CLIVE

with her father at Harold House, the next evening, which was to be the occasion of a great ball given in honour of Lady Ewyas's birthday.

Janet looked on that ball as she had often looked at the moon, longing to be there, but without hope. She said at once she knew it was impossible; and then, in answer to Lord Ewyas's well-put questions, told him she had never been to one, that she loved dancing, that a London ball must be the most beautiful thing in the world; but, finally, again, that it was quite impossible; and seemed so contented to resign what she so ardently desired, that his admiration of her good training rose as high as that of her person and manner. He stayed on, stayed on, resolving to see Mr. Ferroll, if he found he could wait so long without any languor in conversation, and so skilful was he in it, that before Janet had perceived a pause, her father came in. At first he was as cold and abrupt in his refusal as ever, but after a time some change came over him, and he said, "It's your own doing, my lord, Janet shall. . . I will bring Janet."

"Certainly, I ask no better than that it should be my own doing," said Lord Ewyas, laughing; and to Janet's infinite surprise, nay, almost terror, now her wish was granted, she found herself engaged to a London ball for the next evening. The persons mainly engaged in this affair being men, did not perceive the importance of the question of dress, which might have justified Janet's assertion of impossibility; and as for her, though the idea glanced through her mind at once, she thought the white muslin which had been sent with her to London, would do very well for her. After dinner she was bringing sugar for an orange from the table to a little stand beside the fire, and said, "I must not let a grain fall on my gown though," and then it occurred to Mr. Ferroll what was passing in her head.

"That's your ball-dress, is it, Janet? how well you will look in a London assembly; a heroine in book-muslin, with a simple blue ribbon." Janet was ashamed, and lost all pleasure for that night. Nay, next morning when she woke, her first thought was a heroine in book-muslin; and when she saw her father, she dreaded the very name of the ball on account of the book-muslin. But though careless of giving her uneasiness, it was not his intention that she should appear without the advantages which would do her justice. Breakfast was no sooner over, and the newspaper read, than he bade her take her bonnet and come with him. His wife's fashion-merchant was the person to whom he meant to go at once, and proceeding with Janet along Grafton Street to Dover Street, No. 16, he brought her into an abode of satin, flowers, and mantles, such as she had no idea of.

"This young lady is going to-night to Lady Ewyas's ball."

"Oh, exactly, sir, we are sending home a dozen dresses for it."

"There must be a thirteenth, Mrs. Johnstone. I must depend upon you to supply her with everything that is necessary; she must do you credit, remember that."

"A dress, sir—an entire dress? you are very kind; however, whether it is possible? it's absolutely eleven o'clock."

"Very true; the difficulties may be prodigious, but the success is the more glorious. You see I throw her upon your mercy. Mrs. Ferroll has so high an opinion of you, that I feel I can't do better."

"Mrs. Ferroll is most kind" (and, indeed, the bills incurred, and the promptitude of payments were such as to inspire any milliner with love). "Anything possible I will do. Here's a most beautiful thing; a satin petticoat made up as you see, sir; the body might be covered with this Brussels. I think this is exactly Mrs. Paul Ferroll's style."

"Very well, if that's the right thing for a girl."

"Well, indeed, I cannot say it is the right thing, sir, as you observe. Here's a most delicate moirée; but, no, no," said Mrs. Johnstone, too generous to deceive a man and a girl who plainly knew no better, "that is not a ball-dress neither. I really—but now I come to think a little, there *is* a dress, if you had no objection, which was made for a lady—I won't deceive you, it was made for another lady, but I'm sure it might be altered for Miss Ferroll."

"What lady? what's the story? she did not like it, I suppose? that will never do."

"Nay, sir, she did like it extremely. I recollect her very words—'That's delicious, Mrs. Johnstone,' she said."

"Why did not she wear it then?"

"It was poor Miss Emsey," said Mrs. Johnstone, lowering her voice.

"Who died broken-hearted after her lover was arrested?" said Mr. Ferroll.

"That's it, sir; and the family got me to take back a few of the best things. But, perhaps you would not like. . ."

"I think it will suit her very well," said Mr. Ferroll, scarcely casting a glance at the dress which an assistant was holding up in her two hands. It was gay and youthful, the delicate gauzy texture, the trimmings of downy feathers, the ribbons and fine lace, and exquisite fabric of the soft shining petticoat beneath, all suited a young and lovely form like her's; and Janet's heart beat as she put it on, and as the skilful needlewoman undertook that it should fit her perfectly. The head-dress, and all necessary concomitants, were examined; and with an air of the most perfect simplicity, the dress contrived to combine every quality which made it best and most expensive. Janet's belief would have been too severely taxed had she known the total of the bill lying by her father's request at the bottom of the deal box which punctually brought home her gown that night. Janet was accustomed to be well dressed, and was not herself aware of the manner in which this one showed her beautiful person to advantage; but Mr. Ferroll felt it the moment she came into the room ready for the ball, with flowers in her auburn hair, and with the perfection of toilette tracing the outlines of her form.

"I'm not too late, am I, papa?" said Janet, looking a little fearful, as she saw him dressed, and standing at the table.

"No, no; besides you are worth waiting for." Janet coloured at her father's praise, and looked at herself shily in the glass. It reflected her father's face and figure also—the face and figure upon which her own were modelled—the noble, intellectual expression, the finely-wrought features, the just proportions; and his age no more than five-and-forty, when though the beauty of youth is passed, the man is in the perfection of mind and body. A pair most admirable were the father and daughter, as they stood ready for the assembly, Janet putting on her cloak lightly over her pretty dress to go down to the carriage.

Some servants were standing about to see the ladles go to their carriages that night, as several had invitations for the ball. A stately dowager had just swept down the stairs, well shawled, and the odour of eau-de-Portugal still lingered where she had passed, when a gentleman who had taken her down reascended, and looking up, as he perceived figures meeting him on the stairs, Mr. Ferroll saw it was their old friend Lahrotte. He knew Mr. Ferroll also at once, and with his cheerful French tone of voice, and friendly hands both clasping the one hand and arm of Mr. Ferroll, joyfully greeted him, but Janet he did not immediately recognise. "Is it possible, not mademoiselle? not Miss Jeanette:"? and no doubt César came into his mind—raw César, whom he had proposed for the husband of this splendid young English lady. Janet's pretty voice gladly greeted him, and there was more of respect than he had thought it possible to feel towards the helpful, ready young girl, in the way he took the hand she offered him.

"And what brings you to London?" said Mr. Ferroll. "You must not be in England without coming to us at the Tower."

"I intend it; I'm glad a chance has brought me," said Lahrotte—"a droll chance. You saw that lady going down." And he told how a very great English woman had fallen ill, rather ill, at Bordeaux, and how he accidentally had been called in, and had pleased her so well with his treatment, that she had not rested till he had promised to accompany her on her journey, and remain with her till her health should be quite re-established in England. "I think she heard my name through you, or some one who knows you—a milord: and, indeed, you are a credit to me," he added, laughing, but gazing on Mr. Ferroll with the admiration and interest which a surgeon takes in the patient he has repaired.

"That's possible," said Mr. Ferroll; "but, at all events, I'm obliged to her for bringing you here. We are busy for an hour, going to a ball which a country neighbour is giving; but I shall see you again to-night, for if I take Janet I don't intend to be long there. And remember, we must arrange a visit to the Tower—promise."

Lahrotte again went down stairs, giving his hand to Janet as she got into the carriage, the old man wondering more and more at the impression she made upon him in her full dress. But Janet's heart was in the ball-room; she mounted the grand staircase, and entered the reception rooms in silent delight. She had never seen a splendid house thoroughly awake from its trance of chair-covers and silence before, but now she beheld one not only awake, but adorned like herself in gala attire. Lights sparkling, flowers wreathing, splendid colours on all sides—figures, faces, voices, all keeping holiday; and what a new light of jewels flashing around her. It was the splendour of the older ladies which seized most upon Janet's imagination—ladies whose front bore stars, whose gowns were looped and laced with diamonds, whose arms carried manacles of diamonds, who flashed the colours of some unearthly stone-rainbow as they moved. There were still more slender forms in clouds of muslin and lace, but on those Janet looked as young girls like herself; it was the jewelled elders who had all her admiration.

With gradual progress they advanced through the rooms, where the master of the feast met them with expressions of cordial welcome brought out by the contribution of beauty and novelty which the daughter bestowed on his ball, and by the pride of having a literary lion like the father, who had scarcely ever been seen before in the circles of London. And taking Janet's arm under his, he led her through the crowd to present her to Lady Ewyas. All eyes turned on the group, and not one satisfactory answer could he given to the universal question of who she was, until from the crowd, with whom Lord Ewyas exchanged greetings and words as he led Janet along, pressed out a young man, and was the only one, as it seemed, who had the privilege from former acquaintance of speaking to the beauty of the night.

"Oh, Hugh," cried Janet, stopping and drawing away her hand to give it heartily to the young man, "you here? When did you come back?" Then she turned to look for her father, and authorize her greeting, by first making Hugh's presence known to him. Mr. Ferroll saluted him more ceremoniously, without pleasure and without surprise; but Hugh had neither eyes nor ears to dwell on any reception except that given by Janet, nor to take notice of any presence except that of Janet, shining in a loveliness such as he had never seen before. Lord Ewyas was not surprised at the good fortune of his young kinsman in being thus received by his beautiful guest, but all around, he became an object of the envy of those who looked on Janet for the first time. Janet's spirits were fluttering gaily, and her heart all open, not sentimentally, however, but according to the scene around her. She was very glad to see an old friend to share her pleasure, and to be her safeguard among all these strangers.

"Hugh," she said, after he had told her that he was just landed, etc., "I am so glad you are here; now I shall be sure of a partner."

"Oh, Janet, I am afraid. . ." said Hugh, and stopped.

"What?" said she, fearful of having advanced too boldly; "oh, I dare say you are engaged all night, Hugh. I did not mean. . ."

"Nay, nay, what *I* mean is, that I am afraid you'll have far too many partners to remember me." And at this moment Lord Ewyas, who did not want her to engage herself to an obscure country neighbour, called away her attention, and almost directly made his way with her to his wife.

Lady Ewyas was surprised and charmed. Her ball brought out the girl who plainly was to be the beauty of the season, and her own patronage would be rewarded with having first claims on the beauty to adorn all her great doings. She rose graciously, said right things to Mr. Ferroll, and, regretting Mrs. Ferroll's absence, added, that she herself must insist on replacing her for the evening in the care of Janet.

"It will enable my little girl to prolong her pleasure," said Mr. Ferroll; "for I am obliged to see a friend, and must have taken her away early."

Lady Ewyas would hear of no such thing: Mr. Ferroll told his daughter he would return for her.

"And if you claim her too soon," said the lady, "my sister is staying in your hotel, and will bring back your daughter, I am sure—won't you, Annie?" she added, addressing a stately matron near her, who bowed all her jewels, and said, "Yes," Janet's heart quailing at the thought of depending on such magnificence. "Sit down," said Lady Ewyas, making room on her own sofa. "Are you engaged to dance yet?"

"Oh, no," said Janet.

Lady Ewyas smiled. "I think here's an applicant then," said she, looking towards a young man who had his eyes fixed on Janet after a glance from the lady. "It's Lord Trevil, my son; you don't how him?"

"No, I only know. . ."

"Who?"

"Nobody," said Janet, "except. . ."

"Except whom?" said Lady Ewyas.

But Janet had no mind to pronounce Hugh's name, though conscience forbade her to declare her ignorance absolute; and the son of the house now came up, and was introduced by his mother, of whom he had desired the introduction by a look.

"And, Trevil," said Lady Ewyas, as they were moving away, "mind you are to bring her back to me when the quadrille is over, I'm her chaperon. Remember that, Miss Ferroll." Under these auspices did Janet dance the first dance of her first ball, and was puzzled at the close of it to find how many more dances she might immediately engage in if such was her pleasure. Hugh, however, claimed her while others were obliged to be seeking introductions, and she had a delightful feeling of security and ease while he was her partner. "How good-natured people are, Hugh," she said; "though nobody knows me, there are three who have already asked to be introduced to me to dance, and it is not for want of partners, for there are plenty."

"Not plenty like you," said Hugh; "you can't think that, and look in one of those great mirrors."

Janet looked and was pleased with herself. "Oh, I am all very well," she said; "but certainly no better, nor nearly so well as a great many."

"Lord Trevil seems to think you are; for you are going to dance again with him, are you not?"

"Oh, yes; but then he is obliged to be civil to his mother's guests—particularly as she is so very kind to me."

"Obliged to be civil! It is very well you don't depend for dancing on that, Janet."

"But come, Hugh, there is an exquisite waltz. How beautiful it is—how it is played. Let us begin," said Janet, making a step or two, as if she had been alone at home.

"Enchanting!" said a voice at her side. She looked hastily, and saw a man of middle age, with a glass hung round his neck, but he was near enough to see her without its help. His gaze was fixed on her. He was smiling as she looked up, and made the half of a bow, from which, however, her eyes sank, and resuming her good behaviour hastily, she walked away with her partner.

"That's Sir Henry Cronet," said Hugh. "His approbation is thought more of than anybody's. How he admires you."

"Laughs at me, I think," said Janet; "but I did not know anybody was looking at me." Too humble, however, to resent being laughed at, she soon engaged with full enjoyment in the waltz, and whirled round on Hugh's arm, as happy as when they were facing some steep hill together, and exercise called up their health and spirits. They paused at length for a few minutes, and then this same Sir Henry came up with Lord Ewyas, whom he had engaged to present him to Janet.

"This is your first ball, Miss Ferroll? though I need not ask that, as it is the first time I hear your name."

"It is the first, and I am afraid the last," said Janet. "We are going home to-morrow."

"Oh, of course you return for the season. I know you will. I am an old prophet, and assure you that we shall meet in at least six ball-rooms every week during the months of May and June."

"I *might* get tired of quite so many," said Janet, doubtfully.

"Do you think so already?"

"Oh, no. It does not seem to me as if there were anything so delightful."

"You are not like the peasant at Pisa. I asked a very young girl—very young indeed, what she thought of a luminara, which had made the most *blasé* of us exclaim with pleasure. 'Non c'è male,' said she, composedly."

"I could not say that, when I think it is the most lovely thing, and the pleasantest, I ever saw in my life," said Janet.

"Your life cannot have had time yet for many such things," said Sir Henry.

"Oh, yes, I am old enough; but I have had no such opportunity—have I?" she said, appealing to Hugh, who had stood by silent.

"No, indeed."

"Then take my advice—take an old man's advice, as they say in play books—make the most of the feast while your appetite lasts—you will be tired of it before the shows have ceased to court you; or if that face *could* fade—you would find the shows cease to care for you, before you were tired of them."

Janet paused before she answered, looking at him with the words on her lips, but not quite sure if she should venture them or not. "That will be all fair, if I cease to be pretty," said she at last, half afraid that he would think her silly or flippant; but the *mot* from such a beautiful mouth, especially accompanied by that shy, appealing look for mercy, had vast success.

Sir Henry applauded, and went away to tell it. "Such an exquisite creature; and such a mind too! But who is that Mr. Bartlett?" However, Hugh did indeed get little opportunity to enjoy his superior intimacy with the beauty. Lord Trevil, the son of the house, was deeply enamoured of her for that evening; and so many at last had been presented and engaged her hand, that Janet was bewildered, and forgot them all. People saw how it was; that she was totally inexperienced, and that what little she knew of the *rules* of society, was technical, and leaned merely by rote, while in all its *principles*, she was a proficient, because they belonged to her habitual intercourse and good sense—her mistakes, therefore, were delightful, and all about her delightful.

"Perfectly dressed too—is she rich?"

"I don't know."

"I don't know of what family she is."

"She's Paul Ferroll's daughter, the author."

"Oh, really; people say he is very rich. The man who will never go out anywhere?"

"Yes; that's he. He lives in—shire."

"Oh, yes; he never got over his first wife's death, did not he?"

"Well, I've heard something about it. Is this her girl? Who was she?"

"I don't think she was anybody."

"Oh, but you know she was murdered."

"Nonsense."

"Was that what made him recluse? What was it? Did they think he murdered her?"

"Pshaw! what nonsense you do talk."

"I did not know. Is he here?"

"Yes; somebody said so."

"No; somebody said he was gone."

"And left his daughter! How very odd."

"He is very odd."

"Is he? What is it? Is he mad?"

"Pho! There's another accusation on the poor man."

"Oh, I don't accuse him. I know nothing in the world about him. There's the duchess; and there is the Prince of Piedmont—royalty."

Lady Ewyas, even in receiving royalty, did not forget Janet. She called to her sister to receive her charge from the hand of Lord Trevil, with whom Janet had last danced; and the other great lady took hold of her arm, as if she had been her daughter, and walked about with her.

"Your mother is in town, my dear?" said she.

"No; mamma is at home. Mamma is not very strong."

"Ah, that's the reason you are here alone. It is rather a trying position, my dear; but you must be the more prudent. I have some experience. You see that lady with sapphires, and white velvet; she's pretty, is not she?"

"Most lovely," said Janet, earnestly, as she caught sight of the person in question—a lady in the full blaze of a young matron's dress.

"She's my daughter. Now I always said to her—you are pretty, and people will tell you so; but they will say a great deal more than they mean, and you must believe a great deal less than they say. And so it will be even with you; trust me when I tell you so."

"With me?" said Janet. "Oh, that lady is very different from me."

"Different she is. You are far handsomer—are you not?" said Lady—, perceiving that Janet most honestly believed in her own inferiority.

"Oh!" said Janet, blushing deeply, "papa told me to-night I looked well; but I believe it was only this new dress."

Lady—laughed. "Did nobody else say the same?"

"Except my old play-fellow; but I have known him all my life."

"And these young men with whom you have been dancing."

"They could not say that, as they know me so little; but they were all very good-natured and lively."

"My pretty little thing," said Lady—, "unless your old playfellow, whom you have known all your life, has an interest in that heart of yours, you are in some danger here."

"What danger?" said Janet, quickly.

"Well, well, I'll take some care of you."

"Miss Ferroll," said Hugh, "are you engaged?"

"Yes, Mr. Bartlett," said Janet, smiling gaily, for she thought her old friend was thus formal, merely for raillery's sake.

Hugh looked very grave, and retreated, making her a low bow. "What can he mean?" said Janet, "he looks angry—may I go for an instant?" and gently but swiftly withdrawing her arm, she went a few steps and half-beckoned, half went to meet Hugh. "I spoke as *you* spoke, Hugh—of course I did not mean it."

Hugh's face cleared like a summer's sky—he knew better than she did, the value of her advance, and how it would be envied him by others. "Then, Janet, will you dance with me?"

"I can't this time; nor the next, but as soon as I can."

"And when will that be?"

"I really don't know, but don't go far, Hugh, and me when nobody else wants me—I must go back to Lady—"

"Who's that, my dear?"

"His name is Hugh Bartlett."

"Not your brother, not your married cousin. Is he the playfellow you've known all your life?"

"Yes."

"You are going to be married to him." Janet coloured deeper than ever, so that the tears came into her eyes.

"Oh, certainly not."

"Well, I think your mother might be of use to your prospects in life—why, child, you might marry anybody."

Janet seemed to think this had very little to do with the ball, or with her, and made no reply. She had great interest in hearing the names of people of whom she had hitherto only read, and whom she now saw with her eyes, and amused her chaperon by her astonishment that such a one could be the prime minister, and another the Secretary for Foreign Affairs. "It is very foolish," said Janet, "but it seems to me quite odd to see the Prime Minister, with his spoon eating ice—and see he is bringing a chair for that lady."

"That man, by the fire, is—," said Lady—.

"Really; and in his book he is all over dirt, and eats a fish's entrails."

"And the one coming in, do you hear that name?"

"Oh, yes—let me see *him*; how does he look when nobody would so much as fire one pistol at him."

"What an odd idea."

"Now they are going to dance again."

"Miss Ferroll, allow me to claim you," said the partner who was happy enough to have engaged her. And Janet danced on delighted. It was very late, when her father not appearing, Lady—proposed to take her to the hotel. Janet was ready, though still engaged.

"Let me take you down to the carriage," said Lord Trevil, giving his arm, and next assisting in the cloaking—a most unexampled attention on his part to any young lady. "The ball is over now, Miss Ferroll," he said, "I shall go to bed."

"Is it," said Janet, "then that's the best thing you can do."

"Nay, you pretend to misunderstand me," said he; "you know that there is no more pleasure in it now you are gone."

"That would be a very great pity," said Janet, "for I shall never be at another, I am afraid."

"Are you afraid—are you sorry?"

"With all my heart," said Janet, "and thank you for making it so pleasant."

"Thank me! have *I* made it pleasant?"

"To be sure. I mean to say. . ." The noise at the door drowned her voice; at least Lord Trevil did not catch her words.

"What did you mean to say?" he asked, stooping, and rather impeding her progress.

"I mean, I wish. . ." but Lady—cried to her to get in quickly, and with a "good night," she sprang into the carriage, and the gay scene faded behind her.

"I mean, I wish. . ." said he to himself, laughing, and he went up stairs to tell his giddy friends that the beautiful Miss Ferroll's last words to him were "I wish. . ."

"I wish you good night, I suppose," said Sir Henry. "Certainly she is a most exquisite creature; and so simple."

Mr. Ferroll was in the sitting room, alone, when she came in, writing at the table. He was kind in inquiring into her pleasure, and told her that next day he would stay in London till the evening, so that she might sleep as long as she pleased; and be in no hurry to join him in the morning. Janet was not aware of it, but she was tired; and whatever were her resolutions when she went to bed, her slumbers remained unbroken far into the next day.

Not so young Bartlett's—he had seen the object of his faithful devotion become the point of attraction to the most practised and fastidious circle, and however great his own admiration of her had been, he found it had not been great enough, when judged by the opinion of the world and of the most refined observers. Jenny, Jeannie, Janet, his old playfellow was the beauty of a great London circle—the courted and admired of all; and could he bear the prospect of losing that first place in her favour to which he had always looked as the object of his wishes, but of which he had felt secure till to-night. But for Mr. Ferroll's strange opposition she would have been already his promised wife, but now with such homage surrounding her, could he bear to lose a minute's turning this *might be*, into it *is*? He slept scarcely an hour, and waking, too impatient to bear the attitude of repose, started up and dressed, and took his impetuous way to Mr. Ferroll's hotel, where his inquiries were answered by finding Mr. Ferroll alone, his solitary breakfast concluded, and the table relaid for Janet.

"Good morning, Hugh, you are a very early visitor," said Mr. Ferroll, formally shaking hands with him.

"Unwelcome too," said Hugh, "perhaps; but whether I am so or not, I am come to speak to you, Mr. Ferroll, on the one subject which fills my heart and mind. You have prevented me hitherto, but to-day I must speak."

"If you are aware that I have prevented you, you are aware that I have only an unfavourable answer to give."

"No, I am not, I will not be aware of it," said Hugh, "there is no reason why it should be unfavourable. You know, Mr. Ferroll, that I love Janet, I have loved her all my life."

"And has Janet said the same to you, and sent you to me?"

"No, she has not—she feels your influence and dares not—what do I say? forgive me, but at last I must speak out. I believe, yes, I do believe Janet could love me, if you allowed her—and why not allow her; why come between a man and all the happiness of life—a man to whom her happiness would be his—what is there in me, Mr. Ferroll, to cast me away as you do? I tell you truly I love her with all my heart, and I do entreat you give her to me—why should you not?"

Mr. Ferroll was silent for a few moments, but the defences he had raised had all been swept away by the impetuous straightforwardness of the lover. "Why should I not? Hugh, at least you know that all your life I have been withholding you from that question—have I not?"

"Yes; but now I *will* ask it," said Hugh.

"You are brave—you are manly—you are good, Hugh," said Mr. Ferroll. "I have acted for your good—though I don't claim that as a merit, for it was not of that I thought—but you have set yourself above me, you have taken the part you had a right to take. Hugh, I have something to ask of you. Everything about me assures me there is a crisis coming in the great malady of life. I have a struggle going on at this moment which no one can know or share. Do me a kindness, a favour, Hugh—forbear your suit for a month longer. Let me be so long, the same opposer of it that I have hitherto been. After that let us talk of it again if you will." Mr. Ferroll took his hand and pressed it, but instantly let it go. Hugh was quieted, overpowered by the manner of a man whom he had hitherto seen asserting such superiority to him. He had not thought when he entered the house that anything could have caused him to leave it again without having extorted permission to advance his just suit to Janet, yet the new light in which Mr. Ferroll placed himself, altered his feeling, and he acquiesced with an emotion of almost awe. "What can he mean?" was a natural question to himself—but there was hardly a temptation to ask it of Mr. Ferroll, and none to repeat the conversation to anyone else.

That evening the father and daughter returned to the Tower, and Janet was talkative almost for the first time, in telling her mother about the ball. The attention she had received amused her excessively; she repeated the most silly and the most witty of the pretty speeches made to her, as if she had been telling them out of a book. She would have heartily enjoyed more of the same pleasure, and there was such simplicity and such *finesse* in her enjoyment, that both parents felt for the first time, how in scenes congenial to her youth and qualities, she would open to the sun, like the freshest rosebud that ever unfolded in a May morning.

Mrs. Ferroll said something when alone with her husband, about the expediency of letting her see the world, but Mr. Ferroll gently told her, that she, his wife, was his only, and must think of no one else. "We might have been one earlier in our lives. We lost years which we might have enjoyed; we have been together but eighteen years: and if one die before the other, we shall want the remembrance of having enjoyed all days we could. No, Nelly, you chose me; you are *my* partner, not Janet's. Look at me, think of me. Be with me. . . while we can."

Mrs. Ferroll said no more, wished no more, but had a vague purpose of doing something for Janet when the weather should be fine.

Mr. Ferroll saw her pondering, and said, "But there's a thing I forgot to tell you, which really comes on purpose to realize your wish to give Janet a little dissipation. Here it is ready to your hand. Some one is coming to see you."

"That's strange enough just as I was wishing for it."

"But, alas! it is not a man for the silver dishes. Guess."

"I can't."

"Well, it is no other than old Lahrotte; we met him in London. A sick lady has engaged him to accompany her to England, and he means to pay us a visit before his return. Janet," he said, calling to her, "remember that your old friend Lahrotte is coming to see you."

The colour flushed into her face, for at the unusual circumstance of any appeal made to her by her father, she fancied he referred to César, and to the suit he had once favoured; and she looked at him half frightened.

Mr. Ferroll laughed. "You have not forgotten César then?"

"No, papa," she said shily, but venturing to speak because he laughed, "nor yet how I caught his pony when it ran away."

"And threw his suit, if not him," said her father, smiling. "Well, well, it is only my kindly old surgeon, Nelly, who is coming."

"When?"

"Oh, in a few days, I believe. Did not he say so, Janet?"

MEANTIME, WHILE JANET HAD BEEN enjoying her pleasant glimpse of London, and while they then talked of domestic arrangements, poor old Martha had been passing her time in the terrors of prison, her trial hanging over her head. It promised to be a trial of great interest and excitement, and all the county people who had an appetite for mental food of a strong taste and nourishing quality were to be present. To the Ferroll family it was of course a painful subject, and one which never was talked of even among themselves; so that Janet was scarcely aware any such existed, and Mrs. Ferroll avoided it as an ungainly, unnecessary pain, in the midst of prosperity. There was an understanding between her and her husband that such a painful circumstance existed, but it was one which, like other personal sufferings, the modesty of nature would naturally avoid bringing under discussion, and into notice.

Mr. Ferroll usually took his part in the county business, and was present at the periodical meetings: but from this one he abstained in his magisterial character, and was not summoned on the trial of old Martha in that of a witness. The attorneys on both sides had questioned him, but his impression was so decided of the innocence of the accused, and yet his recollection so exact of circumstances which were evidence against her, that neither party ventured to call him. At the Tower it was, therefore, as if no such event were going on as that which made the conversation of the other drawing-rooms of the county.

It was one evening at this moment, not long before the time for dressing for dinner, that Mr. Ferroll came into the room where his wife and Janet were arranging flowers, and told the former he was suddenly summoned to the county town, and they must dine without him.

"I'm so sorry, Paul; it is dark already—it's raining; we have been putting fresh flowers ready for you. Must you go?"

"Good bye, Elinor," he said, not seeming to hear what she said.

"But you'll come back to-night?"

"Yes, yes, come back! . . ."

"Ah, you mean no."

"I am going, dearest; I came to say good bye." He took her by the hands, and kissed her; and seeing her look inquiringly at him, said, with a sudden laugh, "Are you going to have one of your panics? Do you think I can't find my way in the dark? Nay, nay, there may be moonlight for aught I know. As your cousin Rose said, one never can tell when there may be a moon." And holding and pressing her hand a moment, he went away. In a minute more he came back, and stood looking into the room.

"Have you lost something? Do you want anything?"

"No, I had forgotten how that picture hung; I should have been tormented if it had not been clear to my mind's eye. Farewell."

Janet, to whom he had said nothing, had been a close spectator, and was frightened at what she observed in his manner. She followed him into the hall, and saw him leaning on the table like a man trying to draw breath which would not come. When he saw her, he started upright. "Janet, what are you doing here?" he said, severely.

"Papa!"

"Well, I want nothing—what's the matter?"

"Are you well?"

"Did *she* send you?" said Mr. Ferroll.

"No, mamma did not send me. I was afraid you. . ."

"*Be* afraid, Janet, and say nothing. Take care of your mother—be tender, be officious to her; now I am going."

He went towards the door; Janet still followed, but he took no notice of her. She laid her hand on his arm, but did not dare detain him; and as if unconscious that she was there, he descended the steps, and she saw him mount his horse, and ride swiftly away alone, and quickly disappear in the darkness. He galloped on while he was in sight of his own house, then relaxed his speed, and collected his thoughts, which had been absorbed by one object—in quitting his wife. But now again the ideas which had governed him, and fashioned his conduct for years, resumed their full influence; he was about to act in the presence of men, and gentle feelings were no longer suffered to affect his mind or his conduct. It was late when he arrived at Bewdy. The business of the day was over, and the persons engaged in it were eating and drinking, and resting from its excitement. The sheriff for this year was Sir Amyas Rufford, one of those gentlemen who had been most eager in his offers of service when Mr. Ferroll had been accused of the death of the rioter. He was at the judges' dinner; and to their lodgings Mr. Ferroll proceeded, and requested to speak to Sir Amyas in a private room. The request excited some surprise, for he kept so entirely aloof from the county, that no one could recollect an instance in which he had sought an interview with any of them. Sir Amyas went to him at once, and after slight greetings, Mr. Ferroll began—"I heard an hour ago, Sir Amyas, that a verdict had been given against Martha Franks for the murder of my first wife."

"Aye," thought Sir Amyas to himself, "of course, that's his business. How came we not to think of that?" and said aloud, "It's very true, the evidence satisfied the jury."

"But they are wrong."

"What's your reason for thinking so? have you any proof sufficient to demand a new trial for her?"

"I am the murderer!" said Mr. Ferroll. Sir Amyas heard, what his mind could not receive; the words were there, but not the meaning. Mr. Ferroll spoke again. "Another person must not suffer for my deed." The next and the nearest supposition of Sir Amyas, when he said this, was that his reason was gone; he sought involuntarily to justify this suspicion.

"You are agitated," he said; "this horrible business has been brought distressingly before you. . ."

Mr. Ferroll smiled. "I don't think you can say I am agitated. I tell you the truth in the most simple form. I declare myself guilty; but I should not have done so if the sentence had not fallen on another person. Had that woman's innocence been pronounced, suspicion could have attached to no one, and I should have continued to keep my secret. In order to assure any other person from the consequences of suspicion, should I have been dead, or by any means prevented from presenting myself, I deposited in writing an account of the deed, together with the instrument of it, in the coffin of that woman. Search, and find it if you will."

Sir Amyas sprang up in horror, retreating a pace or two hastily, and his face contracting with the expression of detestation and pain. "And you have lived amongst us. . ."

"Yes, but not with you. No one can say I have been his guest—no one can say I have received any good office at his hand; I have been churlish to prevent all from crossing my threshold; I have been of use to some of you, but I have been the companion of none. My wife. . ."

"And she too—oh, horrible!"

"She! don't speak so. I tell you she is pure as angels are pure. She believes me, still she believes me a fit object of her pride and love. It is coming upon her, but no matter. Have not I kept even her the secluded property of these hands, which you so detest? My daughter I have prevented from matching with any of you. . ."

"Ah! God—poor, poor things!"

"True; but it is of myself only I came to speak. I come to die for the deed I have done."

"Hardened, impenitent!" said Sir Amyas, flushing with horror and indignation.

"It is not the first time I have contemplated this extremity, Sir Amyas. I am not here to justify, nor to condemn myself, nor, in fact, to do any but the simple thing of putting myself into the hands of justice. The forms of a trial must be gone through, but I shall take no steps except those which will assist the court in satisfying itself of the truth. You must commit me, and I wish it might be done without delay."

Sir Amyas muttered something about consulting, and moved towards the door; then looked back perplexed, the ideas of a felon and of escape being entangled in his mind. "Don't fear to leave me alone," said Mr. Ferroll, smiling. "I had no thought of avoiding justice when I came to deliver myself up to you to-night."

The high sheriff went out, stunned with what he had heard, and hardly yet believing the evidence of his senses. He went to tell the story, and to concert what to do, bidding instinctively a servant watch at the door, and allow no one to come out. Mr. Ferroll was alone, and he did not remain a moment absorbed in the past interview, but at once turned to the table, where there were writing materials, and sat down to profit by the few minutes he should probably pass before the return of Sir Amyas.

My Elinor

We have parted for the last time. I committed a crime to win you eighteen years ago, and I must die for it. Scarcely an hour during that time has the moment which is now come been absent from my mind. I have acted over this scene a million times in my imagination, but never in all those times parted from you with a jest as I did in reality just now. Wife, mistress, darling, my joy, my life, you cannot hate me, though all else already do so. You cannot; when you read this, you and I alone in the world shall love one another, for I am a murderer, but you are my wife. This scene has been so long present to my imagination, that I can hardly feel it is new to you; and I cannot write at leisure to bring you gently to it. One word must make you believe it by violence. Elinor, I swear it is true. My darling, you know I have told you to apply to Harrowby if ever trouble came upon you, and I should be away: and also, dearest, for my sake, in all your misery, open and examine the iron drawer, of which I hung the pretty golden key round your dear neck, and told you to wear it for my sake. There have been many words between us, Elinor, which you will understand better now than when they were spoken. And now, and here, end eighteen happy years.

"I am, for two perhaps three days yet,

Your living, loving husband,

Paul Ferroll

He folded and sealed the letter, and stood holding it in his hand until footsteps were heard approaching, and the door re-opened to admit Sir Amyas and two other gentlemen. No trace of emotion appeared on his face; and those to whom this was a sudden and new horror could not

CAROLINE CLIVE

reconcile their emotion about it, and the calm of the man whose pride in the first place ruled his conduct, and from whose mind it had not been absent, as he wrote to Elinor, for an hour. He repeated what he had said before, and then silently let them exhaust the wonder, dread, and abhorrence, which he excited, waiting till they should proceed to the forms by which he was consigned to the felon's apartment in the county gaol. The judges, whose business had been concluded, delayed their departure the next day for this unexpected call upon them; the courts were reopened, the lawyers all eager to share in so interesting a cause; but Mr. Ferroll summoned no one, and passed the long night in solitary communings with himself. Whatever he might feel, it was easy for a man with such habits of self-command, perfectly to conceal it for the few minutes during which the officials of the gaol came into his room. He had asked and obtained a messenger for his letter to the Tower; indeed, the man of business whom he usually employed, had, in kind feeling to the yet unconscious wife, taken possession of it, and carried it to the Tower himself. He was not aware, however, how perfectly ignorant of what had happened Mrs. Ferroll was; and he placed the letter in her hand with no other preparation for his dismal news than his grave and sorrowful face.

Janet's heart died within her when she saw him. She had said nothing, but she had been filled with terror by her father's manner and words, and had waited ever since, listening for bad tidings and expecting them. But how far short of the reality had her imagination fallen in its worst conjectures! How little could she interpret her mother's face, which she watched reading the fatal letter! The furthest suspicion of the truth had never crept on her mother's mind; and yet in the course of eighteen years' devotion to and from her husband, materials had accumulated there unknown to herself, like the growth of fire in the gradually-heated homestead which breaks out in universal flame at last, consuming the beloved home at once. She could understand enough to believe all; the broad flame spread a dreadful light which flashed on her brain and her heart; she sank on the floor like one withered by the stroke, life ebbing from all its strongholds. Janet's arms caught her, but she, too, could only fall beside her.

"But he is not dead," said Janet, "for he writes." Death was as yet the bitterest calamity her imagination could conceive. Her mother neither heard nor answered. She clung to her child instinctively; but except the gasping of her breath, no sound was heard from her. "Tell me what it is!"

cried Janet, looking up distracted to Mr. Monkton's face. "Where is my father?" He shook his head—the tears overflowing his eyes. "Where?" cried Janet, rising as far as she could out of her mother's unconscious hold.

"I can't, I can't," sobbed the kind-hearted man. "Read that; perhaps he tells all."

Janet took the letter from his hand, for he had picked it up from the floor, and in vain read it eagerly through. "They are going to kill him!" she said, bewildered. "Mamma, mamma, speak to me. Save him!" She rose up vehemently; and Mrs. Ferroll, almost like one who had already lain in the grave, struggled to rise. Mr. Monkton helped her, and the servants whom he had already summoned, ran in; but when she recovered consciousness enough to stretch her hand for the letter, the touch of it seemed to pierce her again with a vital wound, and groaning deeply, she sank into a swoon. They carried her to her bed, and a groom rode off impetuously for the useless help of the doctor, Janet vainly attempting to arouse the veiled faculties, and to renew the vital action of the mother, to whose arms she would fain have fled for shelter.

Mr. Monkton could not bear it. He took the oldest of the servants aside, the wife of that Capel who had been with them at Pontaube, and made her understand the real nature and full extent of the misery, and promising to return, and do anything—if, indeed, there were any possible thing to be done—rode away, leaving the burthen of explanation to her. He returned in haste to the town, where every mouth was full of one only subject—the trial of to-morrow; and, indeed, the morrow was very near its dawn before discussion of what it would bring forth was over.

Again a prisoner in the same court, and for the same offence, but in how changed a position! His answer now to the question of the challenger was at once "Guilty."

"You have evidence against me there?" he said, pointing to a heap which had been covered with a black cloth by one of the attendants of the court, and which was placed on a table. The cloth upon this was removed, and a discoloured box, bound with iron, appeared below, of small dimensions, out-side which was fastened a key.

The clergyman of the parish where the Tower stood was examined as a witness. "What do you know respecting this box?"

"I received a request from the judge last night, at a late hour, to permit and attend the opening of the vault and coffin where the late Mrs. Ferroll was buried. By daybreak this morning it was done."

"What did you find there?"

"I found among the remains of the body, and of the grave-clothes, the box which you see."

"Was there any appearance that the coffin or vault had been opened since the interment?"

"None; the vault was closed with masonry."

"Enough, sir. Open the box."

It was done; and expectation held all in such silence, that the grating of the key was heard throughout the court. The contents were lifted out; Mr. Ferroll's eyes fixed upon them with the resolution of a man wound up to give no sign of emotion. All others, according to the force or weakness of their nerves, were awaiting the impression about to be made. There was a cloth largely and darkly stained—the red hue in most places had deepened into brown. As it was opened, the emotion of the man who unfolded it, caused him to drop the object it contained, and it fell on the table with a clanging sound. He took it up, and showed it. It was a pointed knife with a long handle; and on the handle was something written, not engraved, but plainly worked in with common ink. "Read it," said the judge.

"It's a name, my lord."

"What name?"

"Paul Ferroll."

Another piece of discoloured cambric was next taken out. It was a woman's handkerchief, and in the handkerchief was wrapped a watch. There was besides a bit of parchment, safely secured between two leaves of iron, and on it, when taken from between them, was still easily to be read, "I, Paul Ferroll, did this deed."

As the disclosure of these things ended, the murmur of popular indignation broke out. There was the stir of human feeling through the court. It was checked by the authorities; and then Mr. Ferroll requesting to be heard, stood statelily before them all, and spoke—"It is not the sight of those objects, nor the position in which I stand which gives me any new feelings respecting the deed of which I have declared my guilt. I have been aware, from the moment of its commission, that this time might come, and have constantly acted with a view to it. I took measures which effectually concealed my crime; and also I took measures by which I might declare it should any other person be in danger of suffering innocently for it. The vanity of the poor old creature who was yesterday found guilty, has brought about the catastrophe. She is the only person to whom suspicion could attach. Had she escaped, or died, I should have been free to conceal this deed to the end; and I intended to do so. I am not going to speak of what I feel or what I think, respecting my crime. I resolved, when I was eighteen years younger, to commit, and also to conceal it. I have lived with the consciousness of it; and you are just in condemning me. Beware, however, of involving another in my guilt. Believe that my deed was a thing unsuspected by the wife who. . . by my wife. I could as soon have made her person the object of public scorn, as I could have opened to her innocent mind the guilt by which I bought her. She thinks of me as one high in public opinion; as a man above the reproach of the world; as proud, as standing alone. Believe me in this thing—you believe when I come to confess I have done a deed for which I must die."

He said all this with a clear voice, which only once gave a sign of faltering; and opinion, which is so easily moved, began to sway towards him; but justice had no relentings, nor could have. There was nothing more to be proved; nothing to be disputed. The great apparatus of the law was reduced to-day to small compass. The prisoner had pleaded guilty, therefore there was no question for the jury to decide. The judge in few words expressed the horror of the deed, and the danger of forgetting in sight of the prisoner's composure, that the reason for his calmness was the familiarity which his mind had obtained with the subject; and then proceeded to pronounce the last doom of the law—the doom of Death.

Mr. Ferroll heard it quite unmoved. He had too much the habit of self-control, to appear to feel a thing so entirely expected. When all was over, and he was to leave the court, he looked round the assemblage, searching for some one. He was looking for Hugh, and his keen eye detected him in a shadowy part of the court. There was such deep misery on his face, that Mr. Ferroll, who meant to look but for a moment, kept his eyes fixed on him. Hugh half rose, observing his look; an almost imperceptible, sad, motion of the head, expressed that to which Hugh knew he alluded. The month was not yet gone which Hugh had engaged to wait; but how ruinously was all over. "Poor, poor Janet!" he said to himself, tears swelling into his eyes; and to avoid all comment on the scene just passed, he forced his way through the crowd; and as Mr. Ferroll was led out to the prison, passed hastily away at the principal entrance. Among those who suffered this day, Hugh had feelings as much torn, and prospects as utterly destroyed, as any.

　　　　　　　　　　　　　　　　　CAROLINE CLIVE

He had cherished a wish all his life; latterly it had become a hope, and he had given way with all the impetuosity of his youth to the passion which he had so long nurtured. Now the whole glittering fabric had vanished. The innocent and beautiful girl remained unchanged; but the guilt of which she was so guiltless, separated her from him, as if it had been her shroud. He heard on all sides talk about the trial. He ascertained that the whole of to-morrow would pass before the law was executed; and then leaving the town, and avoiding speech with anyone, he returned to his home, long lingering when he came in sight of the Tower, within which such misery was going forward. His sister met him at the door of his own house as he came in. She had been weeping, and when she saw him, tears broke out again. "There's more bad news," she said; "poor Mrs. Ferroll. . ."

"What of her? poor—poor thing!"

"She's dead, Hugh."

And they were both too young and prosperous to look upon death as the gentlest doom that fate could bestow upon her.

"My mother must go to Janet," said Hugh, "or you."

"I would if I could be of any use; but they said, for Miss Harden and I went to the house the back way, that Janet was not able to speak to anybody. She was in the room with her mother; she died only this morning. Mr.—— was there about the funeral."

"But my mother could be of use—won't she go?"

"She said Janet should come here as soon as the trial is over and Mr. Ferroll comes back—only. . ."

"Comes back! nay, it is all too true."

"Mamma cannot believe that; but still she says, it is so very unusual for a man to be tried for murder twice, that she thinks there must be something very odd about him."

"Oh, Carry, it is beyond all words sad—and my poor Janet, can nothing be done for her?"

"I don't think there can to-day. Miss Harden said we would go again to-morrow, and the housekeeper said that would be best, for she told us, that when she asked Janet what she could do for her, Janet said, Will you please to let me be alone with mamma?"

Hugh turned away, and hid his face. Deep, indeed, was the gloom spread over his house, and sadly passed the few hours remaining of the early spring day. They went through the form of dinner, for it was little more, and when his mother and sisters had left him, Hugh took his hat, and in the now darkened evening, wandered out he did not precisely determine whither. But his steps could take but one path, and that was to the Tower. The gray building was shrouding itself in the dusk; and calm in the silence of approaching night the garden with early spring flowers, lay in its accustomed well ordered condition; and in the meadows Hugh observed by the small lake which they enclosed, the swans which had been an ornament and an object of interest. The excited mind catches the impressions of small things when it is on the stretch with greater. The petted animals who were sharing in the downfall of human beings, and who wondered, according to their power, at the absence of habitual care, struck him among other dismal emotions. He went silently round to the other side of the garden where it lay beneath Mrs. Ferroll's rooms. This side of the house had belonged to her, and four of the windows were those of her bedroom and boudoir. One of the latter was cut low to steps which went down to the garden; and which were her habitual mode of access and egress. The two windows of the bedroom at this time were half open and a narrow gleam of light proceeded from them—the watch-lamp, doubtless, of the death chamber. Hugh stood by the lower step and strained his ear to catch any sound that might give him intelligence of the deathly house. But there was no step nor voice nor rustle—heavy curtains closed over the open windows, and nothing moved without or within—oppression and dread were on Hugh's heart; pity for Janet that almost broke it swelled within him; and the feeling grew, that without seeing her, and at least saying how he mourned with her, it would be impossible to return to his own serene home. He softly and slowly mounted the steps one by one, pushed up the window and entered. The open door to the bedroom admitted a faint beam which lighted him, but before he could advance, a step rushed strongly forth to meet him, and Janet stood before him. "You must not go there," she said, in a hoarse whisper, and pointing to the door of the bedroom.

"Janet, it is I," said Hugh, who saw she did not know him. She stopped and gazed a moment. "Hugh! I heard a step and thought it was robbers," then her head sank on her bosom, her hands clasped themselves over her face and she murmured, "I am too bold to speak to you so."

Hugh beheld her with mute agony.

"He had not seen her, since in Rod'rick's court.
A radiant vision in her joy she mov'd:"

CAROLINE CLIVE

and now, pale and colourless as one wounded to death, a black cloak or mantle wrapping her in its folds, shame on her brow and in her attitude, she stood, and guiltless and lovely as she was, bowed to the very dust by that which another had done. Hugh caught her hands and gently drew them from her face, bringing a chair near her and inducing her to sit down in it while speechless himself—there was no comfort for Janet, he could but hold her folded hands in his, and caress them with his own, trying involuntarily to convey his pity and sympathy by that mute language. At last, "Janet," said he, "is no one near you—are you here all alone?"

"Oh, yes, but they were very kind to me—they wished to watch, but I begged them not. They could go to sleep, and you know I could not."

"But how cold you are; the night wind blows upon you—don't you feel it very cold?"

"No, indeed, I did not know it was cold; but don't stay here; there is too much misery in this house."

"And are you to bear it all alone?—oh, no, no, only let me be of a little use to you."

"How good you are to think so kindly of me still."

"Why, wherein have you done the shadow of wrong, Janet?"

"Oh, but he—he," said Janet, shuddering through all her frame.

"Yet can it fall on your most innocent head?"

"Oh, but tell me. . . can it be possible. . . tell me what horrible dream it is that has come upon us."

"Janet, it is all true."

"But they kill those who. . ."

"Oh, God, my dear Janet; oh, my poor, miserable Janet."

"Kill him!" repeated Janet, "where is he now? I have never seen him since the moment he went from the door—oh, he is dead already," she cried, starting up, "and I meant to go to him, Hugh."

"He is alive yet," said Hugh.

"How long?"

"The day after to-morrow."

"One day! oh, sir," cried Janet, sinking on the ground before him, "save him. I beseech you have pity upon us. Think what a death—you are come here when all else despised and shunned us—you can be an angel to us—save him."

"Do you believe I can, and that I do not?" said Hugh.

"You are the only one," said Janet, "you are free—you loved us once—you can save him—oh, don't lift me up; the very earth is the best place for me." Hugh kneeled beside her—lifted her head on his shoulder; warmed her hands—she was silent for a long time, but at last, with an old caressing gesture which he remembered in her early childhood, she laid her hand upon his arm, and looking in his face, said, "Will you save him?"

"You break my heart, Janet," he cried, striking his forehead vehemently; "you shall be obeyed. I will die sooner than not try—but till this moment I should have said it was a sheer impossibility; and now—now, I say to you, hope nothing—believe me I will try, yet *must* fail."

"Only not to die so," said Janet.

"But your poor mother," said Hugh, trying to quit this worst of subjects.

"She is very happy to have died," said Janet. "I am glad; she could not but die—but, indeed, *I* did not understand all till it had killed her—now, however, she looks at peace." They both together moved into the next room while Janet spoke; and went up to the bed, where in the profound calm of death, the beloved and beautiful woman lay. Janet spoke and felt calmly concerning her, but when she came and stood there with a companion, gazing on that inanimate clay, her bosom heaved, her eyes began to overflow, and sinking down she sobbed in a smothered voice, "Oh, poor mamma, dear mamma!"

Hugh stood by in inexpressible compassion. His sympathy was the only thing that could touch her, and broken words of pity, not comfort, reached her ear. The agitation of her grief did not last long, for, indeed, she was exhausted with suffering, and it was only when roused by some new circumstance that her tired nature broke out into fresh expression. "Janet," he said at last, when he saw her again rise, and grow calm, "there must be things that ought to be done—were no directions left you, nothing to do?"

"I don't know," said Janet. "See, he wrote; the letter is there, he told her to open a drawer, and because he said 'for his sake,' she tried to do it—oh, she was dying then."

"And you found?"

"Nothing but money," said Janet.

"That was to provide *her* against all emergencies."

"No doubt," said Janet; "come and look into it." She drew open the drawer, and there they found two packets, one of them seemed directed with ink, not long since, fresh. It was labelled 'to pay bills.' Hugh opened it and found it to contain money for the wages of the servants, and to defray up to the present time current expenses, all of which were detailed on a written paper. The other packet enfolded money to a great amount. There were gold and notes for several thousand pounds.

"I will take this, Janet," said Hugh. "I will do something for you with this, if it is possible. What else is there to do?" Unopened letters lay on the table, which had arrived this very day. Hugh opened them. Many were receipts for bills, which seemed to have been just paid. There was one letter for Mrs. Ferroll from Mr. Harrowby, briefly saying that the time was come to which he had been long desired to look forward by her husband, when she might be in want of assistance; he had to tell her that for many years an income had been secured for her in the United States, and that in the course of a few days he would come and put her into a way for speedily reaching it. There was another letter in a foreign hand—this too he opened. It came from old Lahrotte, who fixed the day for his visit; the conveyance by which he was to travel would reach the county town early this very next morning. Janet wrung her hands, thinking of a time when they were happy. Hugh took possession of the letter, and said it might be of use. "And now, dear, dear Janet," he said, "cannot you sleep an hour or two? You are worn out, and ill. Do but lie on this sofa, wrap your cloak round you. I will do it."

"I will try," said Janet meekly. "Thank you. You were always good to me; but now, I did not think anybody could be kind again." Bitter tears of shame stole through her fingers, with which she covered her eyes to hide them. Hugh's voice was choked. He knelt down beside her, the instinctive suggestion of nature to do her reverence in her deep abasement; and laying hold of her cloak, kissed it. Janet caught his hand, and pressed it in both hers. He rose, and fervently kissing those cold trembling hands, said, "God bless you, Janet;" and gently departed. Poor Janet lay there a few minutes with wide open eyes, and a heart throbbing with the misery which oppressed her; but she could not bear the position of repose. Before long she started up, and with noiseless foot, as though the dead could be disturbed, walked through and through the apartment. Then she came near the unchanging bed of death, and longed that she likewise might flee away, and be at rest. She knelt down, and sent her thoughts to Heaven; but how could she pray? The objects of her fond heart were, one beyond the sphere of prayer— and one, who had been her pride, her reverence, oh! where was he? but the unworded appeal perhaps was heard and answered—for while she kneeled, sleep came down upon her troubled spirit, and with her head bowed on the bed of death, she slumbered. Hugh returned home, only to order his horses, and to tell his mother, who was sitting up in her room awaiting his return, that there was some business to be done in Bewdy for the Ferroll family, and that he thought it better to go there at once. Accordingly he did so, carrying with him the money found at the Tower.

ABOUT ELEVEN O'CLOCK THE NEXT morning, a note was brought to Janet, from Mr. Monkton (their man of business), begging to see her for a moment, and when she went down to him, he told her that he had been commissioned by Mr. Bartlett, to bring an old friend, a medical man, to the Tower, and to inform her that he had obtained permission for her admission to the prison, and that the gentleman alluded to would accompany her. He himself was to remain at the Tower to make some payments, which Hugh had pointed out, and which it was thought better should be immediately accomplished, and other arrangements. Old Lahrotte upon this came in. Janet had covered her face with a bonnet and veil. She felt that Hugh must have some purpose in sending him; and shrouding herself in her concealment, she received him, with a word of welcome.

"You will go?" said Lahrotte.

"Oh, surely, surely I will go."

"And how? Mr. Bartlett would have you quick. He said your little pony carriage would be ready soonest. I shall order it."

"What you please," said Janet, not questioning anything appointed for her to do. Mr. Monkton made no observation whatever. He felt that the presence of any human being, in such a moment, must be torture to Janet, and withdrew without a word, to do what he came for. The little carriage was quickly at the door; and Lahrotte, though the day was mild, wrapped himself closely in his cloak, while Janet, shrouding and hiding herself as much as possible from observation, took her place by his side, and they drove rapidly away towards Bewdy. Neither of them said a word during the drive. Every fresh object so struck on Janet's heart, that at last she covered her eyes with her thick cloak, and ventured not to look up again. She felt it was an awful interview that was approaching; to-day was almost more than she could bear; and beyond to-day, she dared not for a moment carry her thoughts. But the patience and modesty of her nature buried all expression of this inward tempest, lower than could be penetrated by human eye. At last she felt the rattle of the paved streets, and heard the sound of passers to and fro. Almost more than before, she shrank under the cover of her thick cloak; but at the most crowded part of the town, and at a moment when they were compelled to move slowly by the crowd, Lahrotte for the first time spoke to her, and asked her a question, which seemed strange at such a moment, "Whether she could see to tell him by the market clock what was the hour of the day?" Janet always meek, was now broken, and did as he bade her. She uncovered her face and looked up, and was then aware that several persons were looking at and saw her— their eyes seemed burning flames to her, and cowering down again, she did not remark that M. Lahrotte failed to inquire the result of her examination. At last they stopped at the terrible gate of the prison. The porter examined their permission, and put down their names; and the gaoler, Captain Rede, came forward to receive them.

"Very well, sir, the time will suit exactly," he said to Lahrotte; but Janet heard and heeded not. The reality seemed to grow as she heard bolts and chains behind her, and saw the long passage strongly framed within by walls and vaults. At last the door opened, which held within such a fearful scene for Janet. She stood just within the cell, trembling, and making no step in advance. Her father was writing, but finding that whoever it was that had entered, did not address him, he turned at last to see who was there, and the shining sunlight fell upon his child.

"Janet, is it possible you come to see me? Where is your mother?"

"Mamma is dead," said Janet, her voice sinking like cold snow at the word.

"Dead!" he repeated. Father and child said no more. He stood as the man wounded to death stands, about to fall. Janet crept towards him step by step—she was afraid of him; the total pallor of his face, his white lips, the dew gathering on his forehead, and his absolute silence, struck her as if death were again present. She laid her hand on him; she gently, then more strongly pulled his arm from its position; she took her handkerchief, and wiped his forehead, now beginning to cling about him, and calling upon his name. "My poor child," he said at last, rousing suddenly; "do you cling to me? Have you no safer shelter?"

"Oh, let me stay here," she said, as he put her gently away.

"This is no place for you. Don't you know what is to be to-morrow?"

"No, no," cried Janet, burying her head in his breast, and folding her arms about him. "Don't talk so—oh, my father."

"Will you still call me father? Alas, poor darling, what have you not yet to go through." It was very rarely that Janet had heard those kindly words—the presence, the voice of the being whom she had always so worshipped, put out of remembrance all that had darkened over him the last two days. "Take me with you wherever you go. Don't leave me alone in the world."

"Have patience. You will be better without me. I am. . ."

"No, no," cried Janet, stopping her ears. "You are my father."

"But for one short day. Ruin, ruin, indeed. All dark at home; all darker here. I had thought to have borne all. I forgot all my blessed one and you, my child, had to bear. What will become of you to-morrow?"

"We will save you," said Janet, speaking low. "Hugh hopes."

"No one could wish, much less hope that," said Ferroll. "There was but one in the world to whom I could now be dear, and she has died for loving me."

"Oh, yes, one more; *I* love you," said Janet.

"Then you don't know all. In pity to you, they have hidden it from you."

"All, all," said Janet, shuddering; and her arms dropped from his neck.

"No," he said calmly: "nor did I expect. . ." But for the first time in her life she interrupted him.

"Oh, believe me, I love you. I have but you. I never had any but you and mamma. *She* said, though it was in delirium, 'Save him—die for him.' I would if I could, for love of both. Father, call me child."

"*She* said so," he repeated slowly. "Elinor, wife!" He bowed his head; and Janet's tears burst forth. At this moment the door was unlocked, and Captain Rede knocking first, entered. Mr. Ferroll became calm by a mighty effort; and Janet covering her head with her bonnet and veil, concealed her emotion. "Sir," said Captain Rede, "has the young lady mentioned to you? Does she know. . ."

"Know what?"

"That you are free if you choose—that is, you have a good chance for freedom. I have resolved to accept the young gentleman's proposal, and having resolved, I am eager—yes, sir, eager, to carry it through."

"I do not in the least understand you."

"Well I dare say you may not; but a young gentleman came to me last night—names are nothing—this morning rather; but I was not up; and attacked me in a point where I'm tender. I have several reasons for wishing myself in the United States with £2,000 in my pocket. It has been the idea before me for a long time; and in my office in this prison, I can live, it is true; but I can't save. Now that sum he puts into my hands to-day, if I open the door for you. It's wrong, I know; nay, it is a great crime."

"Don't commit it then," said Mr. Ferroll.

But Janet sank at his feet. "Save yourself, father—save me."

"Aye, for the young lady's sake, who is a tender bird in a rough storm. No soul to take her home, innocent though she be."

"I came here knowing all that."

"Nay; not quite. You did not know the poor lady at home would die of it; and what you came to do, sir, is done; the other life is safe; the old woman was brought into court to-day, to be tried for the robbery, but clear of all suspicion of the other affair. It was a strange sight. I'll warrant your getting off if you'll undertake it. It's I propose it, sir, though it goes against my integrity."

"I remember, sir," said Mr. Ferroll, with a smile, "when you were a candidate for the gaolership, I objected to you on account of a trust betrayed, which was said to be the first, and should be the last."

"It's strange enough to cast that in my teeth," said Captain Rede. "I little expected the prisoner to object, if I did not."

"Oh, yes, listen to me," cried Janet, eagerly flinging herself before him. "For God's sake, for all that is pitying, set us free."

"You are reasonable, madam," he answered. "There is not many a man would prefer dying a dog's death, when another offers to carry him through, and bear the blame into the bargain."

"And what is your plan?" said Mr. Ferroll, in whom the doom of to-morrow was the fixed idea to which his mind was made up, and admitted none of escape.

"The plan is good enough," said the Captain, "if the actors are willing. It is now near one o'clock, when the workmen go to dinner, and the streets are fullest, so that nobody looks much at anyone in particular. Your little chaise is at the door; that was a notion of the French gentleman, to *unlook*, as he said, like an escape. And he tells me, he made it be observed as he came in, that it was Miss Ferroll, and so the carriage will be taken no notice of when she goes out; but all that is a *finesse*, as he calls it, which I think does neither good nor harm. Then I have his cloak here for you which he kept well about his face, and under his hat so, and jabbered a little French at coming in, which he says you have the trick of, as well as himself. You will go out with the young lady and me, as if you were the French gentleman, and get into the chaise, and drive away—homewards, I advise, and hide in or near home, where they will be least likely to seek you, till you can get on board a ship, and away."

"But what becomes of M. Lahrotte?" said Mr. Ferroll; "and of you?"

"He will wait in my room as long as possible, and at last ring to ask where I am, and say I told him I must go out, but should be back in half-an-hour. Then I suppose it will come out. Inquiry will prove that I went out two hours ago with the French gentleman; but the French gentleman is still there. With whom then did I go? and so on, sir. You should see him acting the scene which is then to take place, sir. I am only afraid he will overact it."

"And if he does?"

"Suspicion might fall on him; but I think it is very unlikely. He bade me tell you, he should not regret it, and that even if he were detained for a time, his young friend had provided that his age should profit by his *leetle succor*."

"And you, sir?" said Mr. Ferroll, in whom the first revival of the idea of life wrought, though slowly.

"I shall walk down the street deliberately as you drive off; but the by-lanes of the town are not far, and once there, I will change and rechange my dress, so that a person very unlike myself will speedily be on the way to America."

"There is another person, yet," said Mr. Ferroll. "The young gentleman whom you mentioned?"

"I protest he is safe," said Captain Rede. "We had better not talk about him."

"Without more assurance of that, I cannot move," said Mr. Ferroll.

"Pshaw, sir, I give you my word of honour. How can you delay for a notion of that kind, when I tell you he is perfectly safe?"

"Because it is of far more consequence that he should be safe in name and reputation than that I should live," and he turned away.

"Father," cried Janet, appealingly. Captain Rede touched her arm, but she thought of her father only, and pressed up to him.

"Well," said Captain Rede, "I must betray secrets then; here, madam, is a letter the gentleman gave me for you, but I fancied it was to have been between you two in private."

"Oh, how impossible," cried Janet, opening it, and holding it to Mr. Ferroll to read with her. It was this:—

"The money in the iron drawer is sufficient for everything; I inclose to you what remains. I served you to the best of my power, for you were my one treasure on earth; and fear nothing for me; I am safe. You think for everybody; that I know, and will use the means of safety the more readily, because I tell you I am safe. May God bless you, brave, good, dearest Janet."

Mr. Ferroll read it, and a sigh that was a groan, burst from his lips.

"Well, sir?" said Captain Rede.

"Sir, let us attempt it," he answered. He took up the letter, and would have folded it, then seemed to recollect himself, and gave it to Janet. "Alas, poor child, it is all that remains to you of earthly happiness," he said, and Janet, who would have taken it tearlessly but for that word, sobbed uncontrollably behind her veil, and pressed the paper once and again to her lips. But she mastered the emotion and stood silently by while Captain Rede adjusted the cloak about her father. Before undertaking the escape of his prisoner, the gaoler went out to see that no one was near to observe the apparent French gentleman coming from the chamber which he was known not to have entered; and when they had passed Captain Rede's own door, he considered them safe, as it was natural to suppose that at that point the French gentleman had joined Janet, and was now to accompany her home again.

Accordingly they proceeded unseen beyond the point of danger, and then Captain Rede breathed freely, as if all difficulty were passed. He had Janet's arm under his, and was amazed that it should be so thin; even when they met a servant of the prison, which they did more than once, it never quailed. It was only at last when the porter had to unlock the door, and they stood to have their names put down, that he felt her fingers grasp his arm. He shook them roughly, and spoke out, "Peters, I am obliged to go out for half-an-hour. If any one calls, say I am with my Lord Ewyas, and shall be back as soon as I can get away. Miss Ferroll's carriage," he cried, as the door closed behind them; and the groom aroused from his colloquy with a dozen persons round him, hastily drew up. "Poor young lady, poor thing; out of the way, fellows," he said, "how can you stare so? There, ma'am, there—now, mounsieur. Ah! a terrible, terrible business. Good bye, sir—bonn jour—adew!" and he saw them drive off. He acted his part perfectly, looked after them for a few moments, then without any appearance of too much or too little concern, walked deliberately towards the judges' lodgings, where the Lord-Lieutenant had an apartment, and disappeared from the eyes of the spectators, who, indeed, had other things to do than to think of him.

"Everything depends on speed, Janet," said Mr. Ferroll, speaking to her in French. "We have two hours' advantage, and must hazard all to profit by it. Tell the groom to go to the Harold's Spear, and order a chaise to go instantly to the Tower by the Lorton road, for a gentleman going to Uptruck. We must wait here."

Janet gave the directions required, and in the transport of her eagerness for his return, forgot how indifferent to all existing things she would have been and would have appeared, had her father been in the prison where he was supposed to be. Several persons saw her white face, as she strained her eyes to see the servant returning, but she observed nothing, till one of these in passing, raised his hat to her as he went by. Instantly she shrank into herself, cowering behind her veil, with such a throb at her heart as gives one vital blow to the fine human frame which at last is to perish under the various influences of decay; but the groom came back, and they again proceeded. Once again in motion, the crowded state of the streets prevented, as Captain Rede had foretold, attention from being directed towards them; and threading their way as fleetly as possible, so as not to obstruct that of any one else, they reached in safety the outskirts of the town, and went on at the fastest trot of the ponies towards the Tower. All familiar objects rose and sank before them as they pursued their way, but neither spoke; neither in that excited moment was sensible of the full impression the last time of seeing all this was calculated to excite. It was not till they were at the summit of the hill, whence the Tower on its knoll surmounting the narrow valley appeared, that the anguish of the time forced itself into words. "And she is there, all alone. Oh! wife, wife." Such was the exclamation in a low tone which forced itself from Mr. Ferroll's lips as he looked down on the gray house; and at the same time there floated up the solemn swing of the church bell, which once in every minute gave out mourning for their dead. The interval, during which sound quite died away, and then returned with a loud deep clang, heard from the distance, very far over the silent landscape, smote on the hearts of each with renewed torture every time. Janet wept abundantly; Mr. Ferroll bore the torture silently, yet felt it harder to await the repetition of the measured tone, because another was dreading and suffering from it beside him. The good-hearted groom shed tears also; he, as well as his young mistress, and her French companion, as he deemed him, knew for whom the bell was tolling.

They had now entered the road where the carriage from the inn was to turn towards the Tower, and where, by taking an opposite direction, they would get into the road for London; and they could only move slowly on, until their much longed-for means of escape should appear in sight. Janet's ear first distinguished the sound of wheels. "It's coming, father," she said, and in a minute more the vehicle appeared passing over the ridge of the hill, and making towards them. Mr. Ferroll got out of the pony-chaise and helped down Janet.

"Lawrence must know me," he said, and giving the reins to the groom, in his usual tone he said, "Is that the carriage you ordered?" The man, little accustomed to meet any emergencies except on horseback, stared at him with the most alarmed countenance, the most incomprehensive; and when his master repeated the question, nothing suggested itself to him to say or do, except to touch his hat and answer, "Yes, sir."

"Listen to me, then. I am going away; you thought you brought an old French gentleman back with Miss Ferroll, did you not?"

"I thought so, sir," said the groom, looking round.

"Well, then, merely avoid saying you did, or did not. Go home, and say nothing till you are asked. When you are asked, say your young mistress and the old French gentleman went on the south road in a post carriage. Can you do this?" said Mr. Ferroll, putting into his hand a bank note of £10. This sight and sum opened his eyes to what was the real state of the case, more than the actual sight of his master had done, but at the same time operated upon him as a sudden tie and bond, faster for the moment than death.

"I'll do it; I'll do anything, sir," he said.

"Go home, then; mind, it is the only thing you can do," and walking a few yards to meet the chaise, so as to prevent the groom from communicating with the postilion, Mr. Ferroll opened the carriage before the postilion had time to dismount, and following Janet in, bade him, imitating a foreign accent, but without any explanation or comment, drive to Uptruck, the first stage on the London road. The man might think it all strange if he would, but he had no reason to dispute the order; and in a time when the Ferroll family was known to be in such a depth of distress, it did not seem unaccountable that the daughter should be removed from the scene of their tragedy. This, indeed, was the version which he gave at the next stage, and which, if Mr. Ferroll had known it, would have made him less scrupulous in enjoining speed on the next driver, an injunction he was afraid at first to press, lest he should awaken any suspicion of the true state of the case, and so overthrow the enterprise in its commencement. However, as he got further from home, he believed the mode in which he and his companion first began their journey, must have lost itself in the transmission from mouth to mouth, and now ventured to quit his disguised pronunciation, and to urge speed by every possible inducement, leaving it to the imagination of the innkeepers and drivers to assign such motive as they pleased for his haste, and perhaps enabling the pursuers, who must by this time be on his track, to follow it up more directly, but still the advantage of flying quickly before them far more than compensated the power he might give them to pursue.

In fact, M. Lahrotte had been obliged to betray himself sooner than he intended, and thereby to hasten the time, which he had been anxious to postpone, of pursuit. He had established himself as much in the attitude of a waiting and expecting man as he could; had half written a letter as if to kill time; had opened a book; had rumpled the newspaper, and was intending to wait at least half an hour longer, when a sharp knock came at the door of his room, and the servant of the gaol opened it, announcing that Lord Ewyas and Mr.—— were below waiting to speak to Captain Rede.

"And me also, I desire the same thing myself," said Lahrotte; "why he comes not?"

"Thought he was here, sir, beg pardon," said the man, going out again.

"Here's the moment," said Lahrotte to himself, but he resumed as well as he could the air and attitude of a man weary with waiting; and in a very short time another messenger came running, and begging to know whether the gentleman could tell where the Captain went.

"I shall not tell you," said M. Lahrotte; "what he telled me is, he goes to one milord Ooiase?" This answer being reported by the somewhat puzzled messenger, brought Lord Ewyas in person, who in his own language gained from M. Lahrotte all he chose to tell, and caused the porter at the door to give the information that the Captain went out after seeing Miss Ferroll and the French gentleman into the carriage. Suspicion, investigation, and conviction of the truth now followed so quickly, that there was little time for Lahrotte to act the scene upon which he had so set his imagination; and indeed most of the details into which it had been his purpose to enter, were lost in the rapidity with which the impromptu actors performed their real parts, and with which looking upon him as an instrument in the hands of others, they hastily consigned him to temporary detention, and organized a pursuit both for the gaoler and the prisoner. The traces of the latter were very easy to follow—the thin French disguise was penetrated at once, and the postilion who had gone as far as Uptruck, set them at once on the right road. A carriage was ordered, and four horses; "he is not a couple of hours before us, having gone round by the Lorton road and all." Very true, but two horses draw an unloaded post chaise as swiftly as four, and a couple of hours in advance remains therefore a couple of hours. Yet everywhere they were no more than that a-head. Everywhere, it was perfectly easy to ascertain their course, any accident, the want of horses, the loss of a wheel, an upset, going at the pace they were described to go, would bring them within the grasp of the pursuers—even the very last stage the pursuers were lucky, for they met the post boy not a mile out of London returning to Barnet, who said he had deposited them at Steven's Hotel in Clifford Street, thus guiding the chase at once, even amid the maze of the capital. A pang of suspicion struck the pursuers that it was too great luck to think of finding them where they had been an hour ago, yet the chase was so exciting, and the chance so far possible of lighting upon them that they urged on like hounds upon a very hot scent. Out ran the waiter to the four clattering horses, the landlord himself among the number.

"Sir," said one of the pursuers, commanding his emotion, "is a gentleman here, perhaps may have been here an hour or more, with a young lady in black? Came on the north road."

"Yes, sir, came just at two o'clock, sir, and it's now half-past three."

"Can I speak to them?"

"Certainly, sir; will you please to walk up to their room. They've walked out at present, but will soon be back."

"Oh," groaned Mr.——.

Meantime where were Mr. Ferroll and Janet? In no better nor worse place than a lodging in Baker Street. Mr. Ferroll had thought, and perhaps justly, that no wilderness could be so great as the unvaried uniformity of houses in Baker Street. He thought they would be nearly the last places suspected, and newly the hardest to individualize— therefore, when they left Stevens's hotel, they turned into Bond Street and walked steadily forward, until Mr. Ferroll, whose eyes were carefully alive to everything, observed a hackney carriage with drooping horses come slowly along the street; and conjecturing, but forbearing to inquire, that the jaded animals were probably from a distant stand, and would, after conveying himself and Janet, go out of the way of inquirers, beckoned to it, and ordered the driver to Baker Street, giving him the address of a shop which he happened to recollect. Here they alighted, and were rejoiced to hear the driver ask for a tip, on the plea of being from the City, and having come out of the way to accommodate the gentleman. Mr. Ferroll added a slight gratuity, made a trifling purchase in the shop, and again they walked on. The patient, silent Janet proceeded at his side, but too many emotions, too much fatigue were wearing down her frame. She had been in London but once before, and that so lately—and the peace, the cherished safety, the health and spirit, and enjoyment of that time seemed to her now like burning sunlight to outwearied eyes. All that was left behind at the home she was never to see again, all the agitation of the prison and the journey, the bodily fatigue, and the misery of the present moment nearly exceeded the power of even the finely organized frame, and mind, which endured it; still she was silent; and her father, buried in his own thoughts, failed to observe his patient child. And before she quite gave way, they reached a door where lodgings were set forth, and inside the shelter of whose entrance, father and child were glad to find themselves. It was easy to say they had arrived that day and had walked out in search of an apartment, and would send for their baggage if they liked this one, and in a short time the bargain was made and money paid in advance, Janet still standing by her father's side. But the indifferent eye of the stranger, when set upon small courtesies, often sees what the careless eye of the nearer kindred overlooks—and the woman of the house compassionately set a chair for Janet, and pitied the young lady for looking so tired. Then her father noticed her, and was struck with the change in her appearance. It flashed through his mind how she had looked when she entered his sitting room before Lady Ewyas's ball, all bright with pleasure and expectation. "Yes, you're tired," said he, "the journey was fatiguing—rest on the sofa, till I come back; I will return to the office, for what we have left, and be here again before dark."

"Oh, are you going out?" cried Janet, starting up. "Let me go with you, pray?" The woman of the house smiled. "Nay, miss, don't be afraid to stay with me; your papa won't be long, I'll be bound."

Janet did more than smile, she laughed at this address; and Mr. Ferroll measured her exhaustion more justly by that unnatural expression than by any other symptom. He dismissed the woman on some trifling errand, and then sat down, and spoke calmly to Janet, placing her in an easy chair, and laying his hand on her arm.

"We have prospered—thanks to you, Janet—so far. There now remains the difficulty of getting on board some vessel, no matter where bound—*that* must be done to-night, for no doubt the pursuit has already reached London; therefore, I must hazard something. I will put myself into a cab, and get down to the river; if we can't get on board to-night, we be safer here than anywhere else. Wait for me. On no consideration, nor under any emergency, leave this house till you see me, or have undoubted news of me. Wait—rest—eat; you will serve me better so, than in any other manner."

Janet's heart died within her; to lose sight of him seemed to her to lose him for ever. Remonstrance rose to her lips, half uttered itself, but he would hear nothing, and her passive habits in the family prevented her from speaking. Yet, when he was gone from the room, and she heard him descending the stairs, the anguish was too much for her; she sprang up, and running to the landing-place, saw him still there, muffling his throat and face in a concealing neckerchief, tried to speak, then paused, for he was in her sight; then, as he laid his hand on the door, uttered his name, but he did not hear; and as the door turned on its hinges, louder and more resolutely—"Papa!" but he was gone. "Gone! oh, shall I ever see him again?"

And now Janet was left to the worst anguish of suspense. To have seen her no one could have conjectured the fever that was raging in her bosom. Whenever the woman of the house came in, she found her lying in the chair which she herself had put near the fire, and back in which Janet quickly threw herself on the opening of the door, or apparently engaged in partaking of the tea which the good woman had prepared for her, or reading a book which had lain on the table, and which she mechanically held in her hand; but of its contents she in vain tried to possess herself, even while the time was yet passing during which it was impossible to expect his return. She had calculated, as far as she was able, how long he would be in going, how long in returning, how long there; and had even added half an hour to the calculation, that she might be sure not to expect him too soon; and during that time had resolved to allow of no fear if she could help it. But when the limit of that time drew near, she began to dread that the ample space thus allowed should end and not bring him; for how should she after that account to her imagination for a yet longer time. And when it passed—when a quarter and half-an-hour passed—and still he came not, the idea began to grow fixed that he never could return; the unworded notion arose that if it were possible he should return she should be happy, but that it was a hope gone by. But this notwithstanding, she waited, and expected, and heard every sound, and feared to hope it was the right one; detected at once it was the wrong, and yet hoped again it might prove right. Then silence came again; the step she had heard on the stairs mounted and passed her door; the street-door was open to a knock more than once, but the person entering spoke in a strange voice; several times the house-bell was rung, and then for five, nay, for ten minutes after, Janet stood waiting with gnawing impatience for a note or a messenger. If the mistress of the house entered within that time, Janet's eyes devoured her, her hands wrung each other under her black shawl, but her gentle voice still controlled itself to answer the indifferent remark, or the still more torturing question which came at last, "Do you think, miss, your papa will come to-night?" When it came to this length of time, her impatience for the sight or sound of him became incontrollable. It was like the frenzy of hunger—the ear ached, the heart bounded rather than beat, her head burned, and for the twentieth time she flung open the window, and stretched herself into the night air. The steady roll of carriages at intervals passed along the street, foot passengers went and came, the bright lamps showed the whole stretch of the uniform houses. A man walking opposite stopped and looked up at the house; it seemed he only stopped to light his cigar, yet he came across the street, and she heard a very low yet distinct voice, pronounce "Jeannette!" She stooped out, a pang of hope shooting through her heart.

"C'est moi," she answered.

"La poursuite est des plus acharnées. Descends."

Now Janet was nerved again; she ceased to tremble, ceased to suffer. The only difficulty was to get out of the house unseen; but her lightest foot passed along like mere snow falling, her dexterous hand unbarred the door almost like satin, and she was out in the street, and with trembling hand grasping his arm. It was, indeed, her father, and without a moment's pause he moved on with her quickly, told her that as was natural the ships in the port were objects of search, and he was aware of having more than once met persons in pursuit of himself; but that down the river he had met with a small Spanish vessel just ready to sail, which had agreed to delay an hour while he came back for Janet; that he had satisfied the captain of the certainty of great reward if he landed them in safety on the coast of Spain or Portugal, and had so engaged him that it was his own interest to take them. Therefore, though the hour must be exceeded before they could get back, he had good hopes of being waited for.

He had left a hackney carriage just in Oxford Street, and springing into it with his daughter, the driver set off at his best speed back to the City.

"Without me you would have been already in safety," said Janet.

"Without you safety would have been little worth having," said her father.

Neither spoke again. Mr. Ferroll was passive, wrapped up in a cloak in one corner; Janet was keenly alive to the stoppages, the hills they came to, the slow pace occasionally necessitated by some great dray before them; but she hardly knew where they were going. She confused the present with the past journey, when she had been in haste to get home to the Tower to tell her mother of the ball, and she fancied something had gone wrong with her pretty dress. Then she roused herself, and thought her father had been in some great peril; yet, no, how foolish, there he was safe: yet, why did she feel as if he were not the same father whom Lord Ewyas had been so proud to get to his house? She refrained from speaking, however, though she had great inclination to talk, and she fancied there was something dreadful behind from which they ought to fly quicker. At last her father's voice stopping the carriage roused her. "Janet, can you walk a little way, though I'm afraid you are tired: further on, the ship's boat will be waiting for us, if they have had patience."

"Oh, yes, I'll try," said Janet, and quickly followed him.

He paid the driver, and taking her arm under his went on over the wharves, and among great packages and cables. Janet tried to keep up, but her head was so giddy she did not know where she went, except by clinging to his arm. Next she seemed to lose her footing, and ceasing to feel the earth, to be borne irresistibly through the air. She uttered one cry, suppressed so as to be a low though a shrill one, "Save me!" and the last thing she remembered was feeling herself falling down what seemed to her an endless precipice, and caught in her father's arms. Janet knew no more: friend or foe, pursuit or safety, the boat found or gone, sea or land, all was long a blank to Janet. Her brain was fired by the miseries and excitement of the last few days, and ceased to be conscious of impressions from without. At last there seemed to grow over her a long unknown feeling of ease and rest—a something to which she was sensible, and which might be the feeling of a summer leaf long tormented by the winds, till driven at last to the base of some sheltering rock. She seemed to herself to lie at peace, and that consciousness was enough, and not to be disturbed by any effort on her part. Even of that she became soon unaware, and knew no more; and then after a long interval roused to stronger perception, unclosed her eyes, stretched out her hand, and was conscious that life again heaved in her bosom. She did not know the place where she was. The air was warm and perfumed, the windows shaded, the room quite a stranger to her. An elderly woman, with a black silk mantle on her head and over her shoulders, spoke to her. She did not understand the meaning, but she knew the words were Spanish. Then the tide of recollection rolled back, and the black cold night came full before her, which was the last thing she recollected.

"My father!" she said, rising as well as she could.

The woman had gone to the window, and beckoned, and in another minute Mr. Ferroll stood by her bedside.

"Can you still love me, Janet?" said he.

"Love you? Oh, yes—my father!"

Concluding Notice

M r. Ferroll and Janet, as soon as the latter recovered strength, took ship, and crossed the Atlantic to Boston, in which city he had by degrees accumulated a very considerable sum of money, as Mr. Harrowby had written word to poor Elinor. This money was in Elinor's name and in Janet's; he had nothing to do with it, for however fixed his eye had been upon the future, he had never contemplated more than two possibilities for himself: either that he should be led by circumstances to declare his crime and die for it; or that circumstances should remove the only person liable to be falsely suspected, and leave the secret for the future impenetrable. But that *he* should live and Elinor be dead, had not entered into any speculation of his. Fate is stronger than the strongest man, and had dislocated his conclusions. He had not, therefore, a shilling, and was glad of it.

Janet was put into possession of the whole sum under her father's christian name of Paul, in which it had been secured, and by which they now went; and telling her it was his will that she should entirely dispose of it, she did so, with admirable simplicity, asking his advice and following it as if she had still free choice; although advice from him was to her immutable law.

Except that one word, "Janet, can you still love me?" nothing ever passed between them respecting his situation. Conversation might even come upon the very crime which had been his ruin, and cause no embarrassment; for Fate and Necessity were not stronger than seemed the impossibility of applying to him that crime which both were so darkly conscious that he had committed. It was as if he were two men: one with regard to a deed which had been told and could not be forgotten; and one in his outward deportment and to Janet, in all but her inner, unworded consciousness. In one sense, he had done that, which in the other was like a thing which did not exist.

Neither did he ever mention that name which used to be ever on his lips.—"Your mother," never escaped him. His silence on both subjects was equal, but the character of the silence was different. It seemed as if respecting himself he were unapproachable; but respecting her, he were a wounded man, multiplying coverings that his naked wound might avoid the touch. He had no memorial of her, for had they not escaped with bare life? Neither did either ever wear black for her; but Janet, who observed everything, saw that her father never again gathered a flower, nor, if one were casually offered him, kept it in his hand or on his person; he never murmured the notes of an air, or walked in the calm moonshine or still morning with his old deliberate pace; on the contrary, he would close his eyes sometimes on the more exquisite shapes and hues of Nature, as if his spirit were unable to endure them, especially when they came unexpectedly upon him. Still he suffered in silence; and Janet, who would fain have relieved her heart at times by speaking, suffered too.

Mr. Ferroll (or Mr. Paul, as he was called in Boston) easily found literary work to do, which supplied him with what money he wanted for personal expenses, and which he silently prevented Janet from daring to offer him; and he was brought into connexion with various persons by this means, who perceived his merit, and were desirous of his acquaintance. But these claims he scarcely admitted—nor, indeed, could he have rewarded them as in England; for his powers of conversation were either gone, or else he had no longer the spring within, to call them into action. Janet could judge only by circumstances what it was that occupied his thoughts, for his talk to her was of books or business, while *his* heart and *her's* were far away.

For instance, she had a little housewife which her mother had made, and which, from long use, she had ceased to connect habitually with her mother. She had often used it, still working silently in the evening; but not now at pretty ornaments of life, but neatly and plainly sewing at a seam, or hemming the edge of a collar. It occurred to her one day, that the sight of this book might pain her father; and blaming herself for thoughtlessness, she laid it carefully aside, and employed some other box or bag instead.

The second evening that she did so, her father, breaking a silence, said to her, quickly and suddenly, "Janet, have you such a thing? I want a silk thread."

Janet looked up, colouring, trying to know what the words meant, beyond what they said. The next moment she gave him exactly what he asked for, and said nothing at the time; but next morning she took the little book out of its foldings of silver paper in which she had laid it by, kissed it, and then put it in their common room, near her father's letters, which she knew he would come in a few minutes to seek. She herself moved silently and swiftly away, and taking up her great straw hat in the entrance, went out to the garden, and thence along Summer Street, for a couple of hours, under the chestnut trees.

Her father was writing when she returned. She put down her hat, and stood for a moment looking for a book, neither of them speaking; then he rose, and drawing her towards him, passionately kissed her hair, and pressed her against himself, but said nothing—even avoided her eyes— and resumed his seat, trying to write again; but Janet perceived that his pen stopped, and that his hand was thrust into his bosom, where probably the little embroidered book unconsciously was moved by the throbbings of his heart.

The winter of that sad year came on; the severe yet brilliant winter, which acted on Janet's youthful frame with healthy influence, and seemed to brace the hidden spring of hope, whose elasticity had been so slackened by trouble. Her father had sought and found for her a companion—an Englishwoman who had married in Boston, and whose husband had died after a few years of unruffled, but unmarked, married life. She was a ladylike, common-place sort of person of good sense, and useful to Janet, as a sensible woman is to a young girl. They took exercise together, and at Mr. Ferroll's request, Mrs. Fowler found errands to do here and there, which required the exhilarating conveyance of a sledge. Janet's health grew firm again, but she could not be allured into any long absence from her father, especially when she perceived, as she did almost as soon as any outer symptom appeared, that whereas *her* strength was reviving, *his* was giving way. He had always been abstemious, with keen appetite for the little he ate; but now she saw that the food on his plate was often sent away nearly untouched. He suffered from the cold, and impatiently wrapped himself in fur, and raised the temperature of the close, stove-heated rooms. She heard him going late to rest, and sometimes he would appear late in the morning; sometimes rise early, and ask for cold water even in those freezing days. Mrs. Fowler thought there was nothing the matter, because he said nothing. Janet was willing to believe her, but was too intensely interested to be deceived. Still, whatever inquiry she ventured to make of him, was silenced kindly but decidedly, and his habitual reserve and self-control, concealed from her for a long time the fierceness of the fever which was preying on his life.

One night he allowed that his head ached, and disliking the light of the lamp, he would go to bed, where he should be most at ease. Mrs. Fowler was not present—she scarce ever was when Mr. Ferroll was in the room. Janet observed that he seemed to feel for his candle rather than take it at once, and, very much alarmed, took it up and carried it for him; a service he did not resist, but even laid his hand on her shoulder as he went up stairs, to steady himself. His burning hand felt burning through her dress, and she ventured to say, "Indeed, you are very ill."

"I think so, Jeannie," said he. "To-morrow—what is it? somebody says, 'To-morrow ends thy earthly ills.' Thank you—good night."

Janet went down and sent for a physician, and when she had told him all she knew of the illness, he said, such a degree of fever must produce delirium, and the room ought not to be left without a watcher. She shuddered, and he bade her be comforted, for the danger need not therefore be imminent; but it was not the *danger* she had thought of; it was the *words* which might be uttered in delirium. She took on herself the office of watcher, and went to his door and listened; but hearing nothing, she opened it, and perceived he was in a troubled slumber—a heavy, stupified sleep; and the thought came across her of that sleep which she had beheld, holding her mother's hand, when she was ten years old. The physician followed her, and sat down by her side awaiting his awaking. Nothing could be read on the doctor's face, though he looked long at her father, and had made up his own mind as to the result.

The hours went on, and the physician slumbered; but Janet's senses were awake to the slightest sound, and it was about midnight when she heard him faintly murmuring as he turned on his restless pillow. Far, far were his thoughts from the present scene; far from the images which had held such undisputed dominion over him. He talked of his parents whom Janet had scarce ever heard him mention: he said, "Lift my head, mother;" and when his trembling child raised him on his pillow, smiled and said, "Dear mother." Then he forgot her, and the most trifling concerns came across him, vexing and perplexing him: he could not get dressed in time for some engagement—he got to the engagement, and was without the papers he was to bring there.

Janet called the physician; he came, felt the pulse, renewed the scrutiny, and said, "Have you any friends?"

"Only this one," said Janet, looking at her father.

"I meant any others," said the physician. "Alas! he is dying."

"And will he never know me again?" said Janet, kneeling down, with her arm under his head, and her other hand grasping his restless fingers.

"Yes, he may, just at last. But don't stay here, dear young lady. You shall be called if he asks for you."

"Oh, sir!" said Janet; and then her voice was choked, and she bowed her head quite down to her father's face.

"They are gone," said her father. "Why did she go away. . . not you, not you"—and then wandering away from that thought, he said his horse had broken its bridle, he could not force it out of the water. This agitated delirium went on hour after hour; the dawn of the winter morning began, with its chill, more chilly than all the night before— the room was become cold.

Suddenly, while Janet's eyes were fixed upon his, she saw their unsettled motion cease, and reason looking out at the last close, he again was aware that she was near him. "Janet," he said, breathing once deeply "it is death—I remember—I perceive—I know everything. All is clear as mid-day." Then looking round and seeing the physician standing near, and Mrs. Fowler who had crept in, he said in the lowest voice, "What have I been saying?"

He motioned her to stoop close; she did so, and whispered in hardly the faintest tone, "Nothing, my father."

"Right—then stay alone with me, these few minutes."

"Go, sir, go," said Janet; "shut the door—we are father and child— leave us;" and he did so, drawing away Mrs. Fowler, and closing the door on the solemn parting.

"Janet," said her father, "best child in the world, farewell. My crime explains my conduct to you. . . Your mother was so deep in my heart, that she has torn it in two. . . You are alone. I have thought you would perhaps return to Europe, and I looked for a quiet, safe companion for you. . . Some men, Janet, will say I can be forgiven—some will say I cannot. I have thought much. . . There is a God, and *He* knows. Farewell, dear and pretty Janet."

His lips tried to smile, but he had nearly lost power over his muscles— only his eyes were fixed on her fond, weeping face. They remained fixed—looked still, when their meaning faded—then began to glaze, and Janet approaching her face closer and closer to his, perceived the slower breathing come at intervals, till the last made itself just felt over her lips, and he was gone.

The End

A Note About the Author

Caroline Clive (1801–1873) was an English poet and novelist. Born in London, Clive was the daughter of Edmund Meysey-Wigley, Esq., M.P. for Worcester, and Anna Maria Meysey. From the age of three onward, Clive suffered from physical disabilities brought on by a sudden illness. In 1840, she published *IX Poems* to critical acclaim and popular success, albeit under the pseudonym "V." That same year, Clive married Reverend Archer Clive, with whom she raised a son and a daughter. Over the next decade, she published four more collections of poetry, including *The Queen's Ball* (1847) and *Valley of the Rea* (1851). In 1853, Clive published a sensational novel, *Paul Ferroll* (1855), an immediate commercial success. A pioneering work of detective fiction published years before the work of Wilkie Collins, *Paul Ferroll* marked the apotheosis of Clive's literary career. A sequel, *Why Paul Ferroll Killed his Wife* (1860), and another novel, *John Grewold* (1864), would follow.

A Note from the Publisher

Discover more of your favorite classics with Bookfinity™.

- Track your reading with custom book lists.
- Get great book recommendations for your personalized Reader Type.
- Add reviews for your favorite books.
- AND MUCH MORE!

Visit **bookfinity.com** and take the fun Reader Type quiz to get started.

Enjoy our classic and modern companion pairings!

9 781513 278407